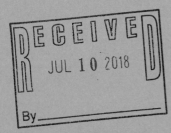

Praise for EDEN

"Among the many reasons to read the fierce and wonderful *Eden* are its sly structure, its delicious pacing, its humor, its meditation on the strange, indelible phenomenon of being a sister, and its abiding interest in the ways tragedy defines us and the ways it doesn't. What I love most is the way these elements conspire to deliver a fresh and moving portrait of an artist. A spirit sister to Patti Smith's *Just Kids, Eden* tells the bounteous, searching, sorrowful, invigorating story of what it is to make a life out of making art."

— MAUD CASEY, author of *The Man Who Walked Away*

"Andrea Kleine's gripping, intelligent novel is a work of great honesty. We meet Hope as she sorts through her strained life having survived abduction as a child, and journey with her as she accumulates strength in a search for her half sister, Eden. I was engrossed by this story through its final pages."

— ALICE ELLIOTT DARK, author of *In the Gloaming*

"*Eden* is totally consuming and hard to put down. Andrea Kleine writes with wit and heart in this devastating and beautiful novel about sisterhood, violence, and how a single event can shape a life."

— SWAN HUNTLEY, author of *The Goddesses* and *We Could Be Beautiful*

EDEN

ALSO BY ANDREA KLEINE

Calf

EDEN

a novel

Andrea Kleine

Houghton Mifflin Harcourt
BOSTON   NEW YORK
2018

For information about permission to reproduce selections
from this book, write to trade.permissions@hmhco.com or to
Permissions, Houghton Mifflin Harcourt Publishing Company,
3 Park Avenue, 19th Floor, New York, New York 10016.

hmhco.com

Library of Congress Cataloging-in-Publication Data
Names: Kleine, Andrea, 1970- author.
Title: Eden / Andrea Kleine.
Description: Boston : Houghton Mifflin Harcourt, 2018.
Identifiers: LCCN 2017045484 (print) | LCCN 2017051671 (ebook) |
ISBN 9781328884541 (ebook) | ISBN 9781328884084 (hardcover)
Subjects: LCSH: Life change events—Fiction. | Sisters—Fiction. |
BISAC: FICTION / Literary. | FICTION / Family Life. |
FICTION / Suspense. |FAMILY & RELATIONSHIPS / Siblings.
Classification: LCC PS3611.L454 (ebook) |
LCC PS3611.L454 E34 2018 (print) |DDC 813/.6—dc23
LC record available at https://lccn.loc.gov/2017045484

Book design by Kelly Dubeau Smydra

Printed in the United States of America
DOC 10 9 8 7 6 5 4 3 2 1

for my friends

1

It was embarrassing to take the bus, but it was doubly embarrassing to hand the driver a coupon that had been cut out of the back of a Cheerios box. My father ate Cheerios for breakfast every day except Sundays, and then he ate eggs. When my parents divorced, back when I was ten, my father moved from Charlottesville out to the country, sort of toward DC but sort of toward the mountains, and fixed up an old house. My sister, Eden, and I took the Greyhound bus to visit him every other weekend because neither our father nor my mother was willing to make the ninety-minute drive each way. My mother insisted it was our father's responsibility. Our father thought he was paying my mother more than enough for child support, considering she had a decent job and he never had to pay Eden's mom, Suriya, anything. He tried to bargain with my mother to drop us off at a shopping mall halfway, but she refused. He drove us the first year and a half until he spotted the bus coupons on the back of the Cheerios box, and then he never picked us up or drove us home again.

Eden always let me give the tickets to the bus driver. I was excited at first that she let me do it, since she was two years older, but when I realized I had been duped into having the uncool job, she said, "No givebacks." I had to go on the bus first and hand over the tickets, and Eden could wait and lag behind, distancing herself from me and the embarrassing Cheerios coupon. Her preferred seating arrangement was to have her own two seats and she would sit wherever she wanted, forcing me to move closer to her if she sat too far away. If I tried to sit down next to her, she would say, "Hope *not*," which was her way of politely saying "Fuck off," since my name is Hope.

The bus station was next to a dentist's office in a small strip mall of only four shops and a Jack in the Box that had been closed since our dad moved to his small town. If our dad wasn't there to pick us up, Eden and I would wait inside the station on the single row of connected plastic chairs and read or do homework until he showed up in his old VW bus, which we called The Camper. When my parents divorced, my mom got the car and our dad got The Camper.

One Friday, when I was in my first semester of high school, our dad was late. I got tired of trying to do my Algebra homework. Eden put on her headphones and popped a mixtape in her Walkman and ignored me when I asked for help, even though she was taking Trig and was good at it. We stared at the television bolted to the ceiling and watched as the programs segued from news to game shows to a really dumb movie to news again. The parking lot had grown dark and we couldn't see anything out of the windows except our own muddy reflection. We were the only ones in the station and other buses had already come and gone. The guy behind the counter asked, "You girls need to call someone?" and Eden quickly replied, "No." The ticket agent sighed, like he was just trying to be a nice person and why did Eden have to be so unfriendly in return. He hit a button on his cash register and printed out the long receipt of the day. A few minutes later he said he had to close up the station for the night. "You girls are going to have to wait outside," he said, obviously somewhat uncomfortable with the situation but not wanting to get involved with us any further. "There's a pay phone over there if you need to call someone," he said, pointing to a post at the opposite end of the strip mall. Eden and I sat on the curb outside the station and watched him drive away.

Eden lit up a clove cigarette. I liked the way they smelled, so I didn't pester her that she shouldn't smoke.

"Why didn't you want to call?" I asked.

"Because I didn't," Eden said. She dug her Walkman out of the pocket of her trench coat and flipped over the cassette.

"If we had called, Dad would've been here by now," I said.

"No, he wouldn't have answered because he's either on his way or his car broke down."

"What are we supposed to do if his car broke down?"

"I don't fucking know," she said.

"Maybe he got the weekends mixed up and he doesn't know to come and get us."

"Then he's really fucked up." She put on her headphones and pressed PLAY and I was cut out. She was done with me.

Finally, headlights turned into the parking lot and swept over us. Eden half hid her cigarette behind her hip and pulled off her headphones. A pickup truck drove up next to the bus station and a skinny guy in jeans got out. "Hey," he said. "Sorry you girls had to wait so long. I'm Larry. I'm a friend of your dad's. He had some serious car trouble so he asked me to come get you."

The whole thing played out like the script they read you in school about how you shouldn't get into a stranger's car, even if he offers you ice cream, even if he says he's a friend of your dad's. Larry probably sensed this, because he said, "I met you before, but you were really little. You probably don't remember. It was at a birthday party for you"—he pointed at Eden—"when you were three or four maybe. You were just a baby," he said to me.

We stared at him, unsure of what to say. Eden was usually the one to take charge in these situations, but she was silent. Eden thought that once you were over sixteen you were basically an adult, and she didn't like being reminded that she had ever been a little girl. She flicked away her cigarette and crossed her arms over her chest. Larry leaned back against the truck. "Or, do you want to wait out here another hour while your dad finds someone else to come get you? 'Cause I do want to eat dinner at some point before breakfast."

Eden picked up her backpack. "Let's go," she said.

Larry walked around to the driver's side. "You want to squeeze up front, or you want to sit in the back?" he asked.

"The back," Eden said.

"Wait," I said.

"What? The back is better," Eden said. She lowered her voice. "I don't want to sit next to him."

"I don't want to go," I said, slightly above a whisper.

"Why not?"

"I don't know."

Eden rolled her eyes. "Lots of people ride in backs of trucks," she said.

"I don't like him."

"Well, too bad. He's friends with Dad."

"How do you know?"

Eden rolled her eyes again. "Do you have to have proof of everything?" she asked.

"Dad would've given him a note or something."

Eden sighed a loud sigh. "Look, I remember him from my birthday party."

I was shocked that she did because I couldn't remember my fourth birthday party at all. "You do?"

"Yes," she said. "It was in the backyard and we had little individual containers of ice cream. I dropped mine on the ground and we didn't have any extras and that's why I'm crying in all the pictures." She flung her hair over her shoulder, exposing the multiple ear piercings I wasn't allowed to get until I turned fifteen in the spring. "Now, can we go?"

Larry honked his horn a short beep and Eden pulled on my backpack strap and tugged me to the rear of the truck. "Just climb on in and sit down," Larry said.

Eden climbed in first and helped me up. The truck bed had lots of junk in it, tools and wooden crates and sacks of stuff. We sat down with our backs against the cab, and the bus station got smaller and smaller as we drove out of the parking lot. Eden would later say it was like watching the end of a movie. She would also later say that she didn't remember her fourth birthday party, but she had heard the story so many times she felt like she did.

2

When I was thirty-five, my mother was dying of cancer. She had a cough she ignored for weeks, months maybe, she said, maybe a year, and when she went to the doctor he didn't have great news. She told me it wasn't a big deal. I didn't need to come out, she said. Her friend would drive her to her treatments. "They ask you to bring a friend to drive you home because you can be groggy afterward. It's the same thing they tell you when you get an abortion," she said. My mother had volunteered at a women's health clinic for years. When she had given me and Eden the obligatory teenage birth control talk, she confessed that she had had an abortion. "I was too young," she said. "I couldn't be pregnant at that time. It was barely legal. I had to drive to a different state." Eden and I didn't have much of a reaction to her abortion story and I think it disappointed her. When she told me she had cancer, she bypassed me having a reaction. "Don't worry," she said. "People get this kind of thing every day."

I flew out to see her in October. Since she moved to the West Coast I rarely visited because the plane ticket was out of my poor, starving playwright price range. She was sicker than I thought. For a moment I didn't recognize her. She was thin and gray and slow-moving. Her skin was translucent in places. It was hard for her to breathe. She had an oxygen tank on wheels that she trolleyed around like a small dog. She looked at me when I first arrived and I couldn't tell if her eyes were watery because she was crying or if she was happy to see me or if it was some side effect of her treatment. I was dressed in jeans, a T-shirt, and a leather jacket, and my mother said, "You're cold." She went to a closet and pulled out a fleece sweatshirt and insisted I put it on, which I did, even though it was two sizes too big and a shade of purple I would never wear. She nodded at me approvingly and then said, "You need better socks. This is the Northwest." She started rummaging through the closet again and I said, "You don't have to do that." And she said, "I've got some extra wool socks in here." I said, "Mom, it's really okay." I said, "I packed other socks. I'm pretty good at dressing and taking care of myself." Her oxygen machine started beeping and she said, "Oh, be quiet," to it, and when it wouldn't shut up, she bent down and tapped it and whispered, "Please, please, please." Then she got a little lightheaded and teetered backwards into the closet, her extra clothes and blankets cushioning her fall, her oxygen tubing getting tangled up in the buckle of a winter coat and sliding up her cheek. She waved me away when I tried to help her up. "Happens all the time," she said.

My mother's friend Gail came by with cannabis oil and instructed me to rub it into my mother's chest. Gail had basically moved in. "It's not good," Gail said. "It's spread to her lungs. There's not much more they can do for her unless she can get on a clinical trial." I wasn't sure how I reacted to Gail; I tried not to show any reaction. I didn't know Gail. My mother had mentioned her a few times, but I didn't keep track of my mother's friends. Gail told me that everything was in order, my mother's papers and things. Her estate. "There really isn't anything there of substance," Gail said. "She didn't have good insurance and had to spend down her assets, what she had of them. It's probably all just going to break even. She said you weren't expecting anything monetary like that anyway." Gail said, "You won't have to worry about the paperwork. She didn't want to bother you with it. She knows you're busy with your career."

Gail didn't guilt me on any of that, on being the absent daughter, or being the daughter who didn't rush to take care of her mother. She knew my mother didn't operate that way. My mother was all business, no fuss. She had delegated her health to Gail, who sent me periodic updates via email.

I started calling my mother once a week. She thought it was odd. "Anything wrong?" she asked after the third time I called and it appeared it was going to be a regular thing. "I'm not dying," she said. I asked her how she was feeling, and she snapped, "I'm not going to talk about my fucking cancer! I'm fucking sick of it! There's more to me than this fucking disease!" She was quiet for a second, huffing as best she could on her oxygen machine. I had never heard my mother so angry, not even when she was in the middle of divorcing my dad. I meekly said I was sorry. She strained to catch a decent breath. "We're not going to do this," she said. "Do what?" I asked. "We're not going to have some heart-to-heart, mother-daughter moment where I officially say goodbye to you. Life is for the living," she said. "Go live your life."

Gail was the one who called me. "I don't know how to get in touch with your sister," she said. I was silent, in disbelief that this was how it was happening. Your mother dies and you get a call on your cell phone when you are at a temp job and out on a break, walking aimlessly around midtown Manhattan to avoid going back inside a soul-sucking cube farm, dressed in a faux corporate costume you would like to burn, so obviously an alien among all the other passersby on the street who seem to have no problem with normal life. You are the freak standing on the curb, not walking when the WALK sign says walk, frustrating people shoving past you with their salad-bar lunches. You are exposed as the impostor you always were.

I told Gail I didn't know where Eden was and I doubted my dad did either. Gail asked if I wanted her to call him. "I have his numbers," she said. I said no, I would do it. She asked when I would come out for the service, and that's when I started crying. It was near Christmas and flights would be astronomical. I embarrassingly blubbered something about that. The thing you wish you didn't say the moment you learned your mother just died. How expensive it was going to be.

3

I spent two weeks in Oregon, cleaning up my mother's death. Or cleaning up her existence. I didn't do much but sign papers Gail put in front of me and nod when she said she could store my mother's belongings in her son's garage until I needed them. I wandered around a house I didn't know very well, staring at my mother's things and random objects that had survived my childhood before Gail wrapped them in newspaper and tucked them in a box. Then, to avoid going home, I changed my ticket and went to my father's house in Virginia, where his new girlfriend attempted to conquer my grief with good Christmas cheer. I had no gifts for anyone and she assured me it was okay. My father acknowledged the situation with only an extra hug when he picked me up at the airport. I slouched on their sofa and catatonically flipped through cable TV channels for a week and the three of us did a good job of ignoring each other.

When I got back to New York, a pile of mail was neatly assembled outside my apartment door. The locks on my build-ing's mailboxes had ceased to work for most of the apart-ments a long time ago. This pissed off the postman because it took him twice as long to sort our mail. If you were gone for more than a few days, he dropped your mail on the floor and left footprints on it on his way out. Every now and then, in a display of neighborly concern or holiday spirit, some-one would collect and sort the fallen mail and distribute it throughout the building.

I had inherited this apartment from my old professor, Cort-land, who had unofficially moved to France. It was an ille-gal sublet and I paid his girlfriend in cash every month. We would meet at a café, and somehow part of the deal was that I had to pay for her giant latte and sometimes a cookie. If I suggested swinging by her office, she would say, "No, that's okay. I can totally meet for coffee."

The top letter on my stack of mail was from the landlord, and it was addressed to Cortland. It didn't have a stamp. It was the landlord who had clearly gathered my mail and then added this little cherry. It was corroborated by a message from Cortland on the answering machine. (Cortland insisted on keeping his ancient landline so as not to arouse suspicion, and he had a cheap phone plan grandfathered in from the nineties that didn't include voicemail.) "Got a little call from the landlord," Cortland said. "Wanted to check in with you about it." Cortland, even though he was a writer, had an aver-sion to putting anything in writing. He refused to discuss any-thing about the apartment over email for fear of creating a paper trail. But I wasn't going to bother to figure out how to call Cortland in Europe. I was happy to play dumb and wait until he called me back.

The day after New Year's, Cortland's girlfriend asked to meet for giant lattes. She was already at the café when I arrived and had claimed a table for us by draping her coat and blanket-sized scarf over the extra chair. She was doodling in her journal, head bent down, her long, perfectly tousled hair fanning over her writing hand, and she didn't see me walk in. I ordered two coffees and set her tall cup on the table along with the padded envelope of rent cash. "Here you go," I said. I made a Boy Scout salute with the fingers of my free hand, curtsied, and pivoted to make my exit. Done and done.

"No, no, wait," she called in her high-pitched voice. She reached out and stroked my arm. "Let's sit," she said.

She moved her wraps off the empty chair to make room for me. I told her I didn't have a lot of time, but she acted like she didn't hear me. When all of her accoutrements were resituated, she closed her eyes and extended her arms across the table, like a cat stretching out its front paws. She reached a little farther and lightly held my wrists, taking my pulse or assessing my chi. When the mantra she was reciting in her head was complete, she released my hands and opened her eyes. "I have some difficult news to tell you," she said.

She stirred her latte with a wooden stick. She pulled it out and licked it. "Cortland is coming back," she said. "He's teaching here next semester. So, that's great. But he said he's had some problems with the landlord nosing around the apartment. And it's making him"—she scrunched her face, raised her hands, and seesawed her body side to side—"nervous."

She slurped the foam off her coffee and wiped her top lip with her bottom one. "Obviously he felt anxious about telling you this, which is why he's getting me to do his dirty business." She widened her eyes as she leaned back in her chair and pulled down her sweater. She picked at pieces of her bangs that felt out of place and fluffed up her long hair by gently massaging her scalp. Then she realized she was fidgeting and stretched her arms across the table again.

"Cortland's coming back. Well, I said that." She rolled her eyes at her own ridiculousness. "But he's going to take over the apartment again. He's going to use it as a writing studio. Until things blow over. Then maybe you can move back."

I was still. When I sat down with her it was only perfunctory, on the edge of the chair, my legs crossed, my body angled away from her, ready to get up and leave. I never took off my coat or let go of my paper cup. I opened my mouth slightly but didn't say anything. I uncrossed my legs and turned to face her.

"I know," she said. "I'm sorry if this is difficult for you."

"He's kicking me out?" I asked, purposefully filling the situation with drama.

"No," she said, crossing her hands at her wrists in front of her and overusing her lips to form words, a gesture she learned from her brief stint with Occupy Wall Street. "No. Not at all. He's just following your agreement."

"What?" I was half laughing, wondering if I could talk her out of this decision. Make her forget about us meeting and following Cortland's instructions for delivery of information. Buy her another latte and a chocolate croissant.

"You agreed that it would be open-ended, but that either of you could end it with a month's notice. So he asked me to give you a month's notice." For the last part she smiled with difficulty, exposing her teeth and looking at me with concern,

the way a student gives an answer in a classroom when unsure of the response, worried that she is saying something upsetting, but still wanting credit for giving the correct answer.

All I could say was "Fuck."

"I know," she said, looking at me, communicating that she
was sad to make me sad, and that she did not enjoy being the
deliverer of sad news one bit. I had moved into Cortland's
place when I broke up with my girlfriend, Noreen. Cortland
had been happy to help me out. "I know what it's like," he
said. "I've been there." When he split up with his second wife
he had nowhere to go and a friend in the building had gotten
him the apartment where I now lived, or used to live until
Cortland revoked my tenancy by girlfriend proxy. The girlfriend reached for my wrists again, inhaled, and let them go.
She looked at me for the cue that our tension was abating and
she could talk about something else fascinating that was going on in her life.

"Fuck," I said again. I had gotten myself into this situation.
It was my own fucking fault. It was probably because of the
mail that had accumulated while I was away. I should've had
a friend pick it up for me. I should've gotten a PO box when
I moved in. There was a place on First Avenue that would accept packages for you, which would've saved me from having
to haggle with the shoe-repair guy downstairs for performing that service. Then I could've avoided this whole thing.
Or not. Cortland must have known he was coming back: you
don't pick up a teaching gig that quickly. He must've been
thinking about this for a while, and then the snoopy landlord
was a convenient fault-free excuse to ask me to leave.

"So, February first?" she asked with an uptick in her voice.

I shrugged my surrender. She took a celebratory gulp of

her latte and quickly checked her phone. She was glad that was over.

I tried to force myself to drink my coffee, but my mind was already racing through my soon-to-be-homeless predicament, which couldn't have come at a worse time financially. Plus, trudging around in the cold waiting for no-show brokers was not going to be fun. Not that I could afford a broker. Not that I could afford anything. What I really needed was someone's cat to feed and a free place to stay for a month. That could get me back on my feet. Since I had just paid everything for January, my bank account was reset to zero and I had no money for a security deposit on a new place. I hated myself for being this age and still in this situation.

The girlfriend asked me if I would watch her stuff while she went to the bathroom. She got up and shook out her hair and walked to the back of the café in a way that made sure everyone would notice her. She was young and beautiful, with tight jeans and great hair. She wore a giant shapeless sweater but she telegraphed what was underneath. I laughed at myself as my eyes trailed her path. When she shut the door to the bathroom, I remembered the envelope of cash. It was still sitting there, half slid under her journal. I should take it back, I thought. What if I find a cat-sitting gig and move right away? Why should I pay for the whole month? Taking the money would be the immature and irresponsible thing to do. I chastised myself for considering it. Then I tried to rationalize things. I'll take it, and when I move out, I'll pay for however long I've stayed. If I stay the whole month, I'll give it all back. If I stay half the month, I'll pay half.

I slowly pulled the envelope free, folded it, and shoved it in my coat pocket. When the girlfriend came back to the table, I stood up before she had the chance to sit down. I said I had to go. She insisted on hugging me. I worried she would feel the bulk of the envelope in my pocket, but she threw her arms around my neck, letting her breasts press against my coat, anchoring herself by reaching her ass in the opposite direction. It was a bizarre pose. A gesture I wasn't used to.

"My only Hope!" I looked up from the hug with the girlfriend. My friend Jamie was standing over us with his coat on. He looked flushed, his fair cheeks stained pink from the cold. I hadn't seen Jamie in almost a year. Maybe more. "How *are* you?" he asked. He wasn't going to find his own table. He wanted an invitation to sit down. "I don't think I've seen you since you and Noreen came to my show at Performa. And that must have been over two years ago."

"Noreen and I broke up," I told him in case he hadn't heard through the grapevine.

"Yes, I know," he said.

The girlfriend smiled and glanced back at me. She felt out of place. "I should let you two catch up," she said. She gathered her journal and wrapped herself in several layers of hand-knit wool. She hefted her bag over her shoulder and didn't notice the envelope was missing. She gave me one last quick hug, sealing my guilt.

Jamie moved over to her seat, opposite me, and sloughed off his coat. He looked glum in contrast to his excitement at seeing me two minutes earlier. He didn't meet my eyes, and took a long time arranging his bag over the back of his chair. He dug his wallet out of his pocket and went up to the counter to order. When he came back to the table, I asked him what was wrong.

Jamie leaned forward, his hands cradling his freshly filled water glass. He tilted his head from side to side, eyes cast down, as if he was having a discussion with himself about how to divulge what was on his mind. When he came to a resolution, he looked up at me.

"I don't know how to tell you this, Hope," he said with an air of seriousness. "It's not the type of thing you want to tell someone you haven't seen in some time. And I'm sorry I haven't seen you in some time. I am. You're my dear friend and I don't see you enough." He rotated his glass of water a few times, then stopped. "Maybe you heard this from someone else already. I'm HIV positive."

I had heard this from someone else. But I didn't tell him that. As soon as he said, "I don't know how to tell you this," I knew what he was going to tell me. I waited until he looked up from his glass of water and I said, "I'm so sorry."

Jamie took a deep yogic inhale, filling his chest completely. He closed his eyes for a second and then slowly released his breath. He smiled ever so slightly and gave a faint nod.

"I've known for a few months," he said, reaching for a napkin and wiping his nose. "I just haven't seen you." The person at the counter called out Jamie's name, and Jamie stood up to fetch his order. He came back with a large coffee and said, "I come here all the time. It's near my gym." He sat down and took another deep inhalation. "Anyway" — he gave me a brief rundown on his health. He was doing a lot of holistic treatments. "I'm on meds," he said. "Even though I don't trust Big Pharma. They're the ones getting rich off the epidemic, and it's still an epidemic, by the way, even though it's not media-sexy anymore. Why do you think they never developed a cure or a vaccine? What's in it for them if we don't need to buy their drugs anymore? Gay is a market now. They're not about to give it up."

He took a sip of water. Something about Jamie was more off than usual. He seemed more manic, more twitchy. His eyes were searching me all over and couldn't stay put on any one point. "Are you sure you're okay?" I asked. Jamie closed his eyes and slightly shuddered his shoulders. "I know," he said, opening his eyes and restlessly scanning the room. "I'm an idiot for getting infected in this millennium, so late in the game."

"You've got to let that go," I said.

Jamie exhaled. "I don't want to trouble you, Hope. But I'm full of trouble these days. I don't even know where to begin. My health is the least of my short-term worries."

He took a sip of his coffee and blotted his lips with a napkin. "I made a foolish mistake that I'm really too old to be making. I hooked up with this young guy. You know, fresh off the boat from Nowheresville, USA. Just a hookup with a morning after. Or two or three. It was lovely. It was fun. I sent him on his way and didn't give it an ounce of thought. Then a week later the kid shows up on my doorstep. He's packed his bags and moved here from the backwaters of upper Michigan and has no place to go. What can I say? I have a heart. I was that kid once."

"We all were," I said.

"Some of us still are," Jamie said, and I didn't know if he meant himself or me. "The kid offered to pay rent," Jamie said, "which I needed. I was really strapped after my last show. So, okay. I made my deal with it. I made the bed, so to speak, and I slept in it, too.

"This was all around the same time I found out I was positive. And as soon as I found out, I told him. I said, You should get tested. Then he flips out and accuses me of knowingly infecting him. Now, in a normal person, I can understand that sentiment. You're angry. You lash out. You're looking for someone to blame. And of course I feel guilty. I feel terribly guilty." He paused, let go of his cup. "But I don't know if he did a test or not, so who knows?" he said. "Maybe I didn't infect him. But he just completely flipped out. He beat me up. Then I realized, this person is incredibly unstable. And how could I have not seen it? And now he's in my apartment. He has the keys."

Jamie sipped his coffee. "But I sort of decided to just tough it out since we had an understanding that he was only staying with me a month, until he found something else. On the flip side, I'm working with this new manager-fundraiser person and she's very well connected and she put together a benefit cocktail party for me. She thinks it's very important to build on the momentum from my *Times* review. 'This is how things happen,' she said. 'It's just one thing that tips it over and suddenly everyone loves you and everyone absolutely has to have you.'"

I knew the woman Jamie was talking about. I had emailed her once about getting on her roster. She wrote back a one-line message that said, "Oh, right, I know your work," and I never heard from her again. My friend Zara looked at her client list and said, "She only likes gay men and European women, of course she didn't take you."

Jamie went on: "She hooks me up with Julianne Moore. *Julianne Moore.* The Oscar winner. My manager puts together an evening and there's drinks and hors d'oeuvres and we do a short excerpt from last year's show — we restage it so we're dancing around the tables, in the aisles. It wasn't easy. And toward the end Julianne Moore breezes in and gives a short speech about the necessity of art in our lives. She probably gives the same speech for a zillion other little arts organizations she helps out, and she probably didn't write it, someone probably wrote it for her, because it's a gem, really, but it felt special to me. The whole thing was a great success. And I really believed that this could be something. This could be the thing that takes my work to the next level. I didn't have a thing to drink, but I am high that night. High on my own potential." Jamie glowed when he said that.

"When I got home, late, because I was doing everything at the benefit including the cleaning, I find my little friend waiting up for me. And he's been smoking. My entire body tensed and I said, 'I asked you not to smoke in the apartment. Please put it out and take the filthy dish you've been using as an ashtray, take it down the hall, throw out the ashes, and then come back and wash it. Twice. It's a dish. It's something you eat food off of. Don't be a disgusting piece of trash.'" Jamie said that as if it was a perfectly reasonable request given in a perfectly reasonable demeanor.

"He completely freaks out. Starts screaming at me. Saying if I infected him, he's going to sue me, and he has a lawyer, and just rambling on."

"That's ridiculous," I said.

"Ridiculous, I know, but that energy was in my apartment and I was so exhausted. I said, 'Christopher, do you know where I've been? I've been at my dance company's benefit with Julianne Moore. *Julianne* fucking *Moore*. I really can't deal with your imbecilic bullshit right now.' Does he stop?

No. Does that get through to him? No. He screams bloody murder. Loud. Eardrum-piercing screams. So I slapped him. I wasn't thinking. Maybe I was. I don't know. I'm not a violent person, but I slapped him right across the face and said, 'Christopher, you're hysterical. Calm down.' Then he hits me, full-on punches me, and pushes me against the wall, and my arm catches on something and I cut myself all the way from here"—he indicated his wrist—"to here"—his elbow. "The sight of blood sent him over the edge and he starts screaming, 'Stay away from me! Stay away from me with your infected blood! Don't touch me! Don't fucking touch me!' Somehow, in all of that, I don't even know how, I managed to shove him out of the apartment and into the hallway, and I locked the door and put the chain latch on. But he kept screaming and my neighbors called the police and the cops arrive and Christopher is going on about how *I* hit *him*. I beat him up and threw him out and he lives here and he pays rent. The cop asks me, 'Did you hit him?' I said, 'Officer, he has hit me many times, violently, as you can see.'" Jamie indicated the scar on his arm. "But the cop asked again, 'Did you hit him?' I said, 'Officer, he was hysterical, he was screaming, he was out of control, and I slapped him. I didn't hit him. I didn't punch him. I slapped him across the face with an open palm because he was hysterical. I was just trying to snap him out of it.'

"The cop was actually sympathetic. He looked at Christopher and said to me, 'We've gotten complaints about this one before.' So I'm just one person in a long line of suckers, I guess. The cop said, 'Look, if I take him in, I'm going to have to take both of you in, since you admit you assaulted him.' I said, 'What about me? He assaulted me.' But apparently, since I admitted it, I'm on the hook. 'Or,' the cop said, 'you can promise there won't be any more disturbances to-night and I'll walk away.' I said, 'I promise you, Officer, there won't be any more disturbances from us tonight.' So the cop said okay. And he tried to do his civil-servant duty and told me to take a long hard look at the reality of my relationship."

I told Jamie to get rid of him.

"I can't," he said. "I can't get rid of him. He paid me rent for the month and that money is gone now. I don't have it."

I asked if Christopher was still there.

"Yes," Jamie said. "He's there right now."

I was relieved that I had my own apartment dilemma to deal with. I didn't want to be the friend who helped Jamie change the locks on his apartment and sit vigil until the roomie came home. I didn't want to be the one to back him up as he knocked on the super's door and told him that it would be necessary to change the downstairs lock as well, and I didn't want to be the one to lend him the three hundred or so dollars the super would say it would cost to put in a new lock and make new keys for everyone in the building. The super would want more than three hundred bucks. That just covers the lock and the locksmith. What about me? My time? It would cost five hundred altogether. At least. Jamie didn't have it, and I didn't have that much to lend him and get back eight months later. Jamie always paid me back, but it always took him eons to do so. It was always long after I had forgotten about the money and no longer cared. Jamie had a habit of announcing repayment in front of other people, when we were out with a group of friends or at a dinner party. "It's important to me," he would say. It's what he said when he paid me back for stiffing me sixty dollars on the electric bill when we lived together one summer after college. He wrote me a check when my first play was produced and gave it to me at the cast party.

Jamie and I left the café together and said goodbye outside. He hugged me and looked down at me from his tall, graceful stature. He held on to my shoulders and rubbed them through my coat and smiled warmly, as though this entire conversation had been about my problems and making me feel better.

What happened to my friends? I wondered.

Jamie and I both started out as English-Theater double majors in college. We met in freshman acting class, where we were paired together in our final scene for the year. We were rehearsing in Jamie's dorm room one night, in the middle of our scene, when his phone rang. Our characters had been arguing. Jamie glared at me and picked up the phone, almost as a dare. "Hello?" he said angrily. He was quiet for a minute and then grew impatient. "I have to call you back," he said. Then louder, "I'm rehearsing a scene. I'm in character!" He slammed down the phone and began improvising. He said he hated me and I had no identity and that's why I glommed on to other people. "There's a word for people like you," he said. "And it's fag hag. Fag hag, fag hag, fag hag, fag hag." He got very close to my face and saliva flew out of his mouth and landed on my forehead. His eyes shifted. I could see him break character and the question run through his mind whether or not he should apologize. I pushed him away from me. I told him he was pathetic and would never amount to anything. *"You'll* never make it," I said and locked myself in his bathroom. I waited what I thought was a good amount of time for him to have a moment in the scene by himself and then poked my head out. With anyone else, that

would have been the time to break out laughing, but Jamie
held his chin in his hand. He wondered if our characters were
confused. He wondered if they could possibly make a go of
being straight together. Or if their identities were sealed.

In our sophomore year, Jamie left me a voicemail message
that I wish I had kept. "Hope, are you there? Where are you?
Where, oh where, are you? Call me back. I've something mo-
mentous to tell you. I've discovered something. And it's called
modern dance." Then he hung up.

When I got home, I took the rent envelope out of my coat
pocket and shoved it into a desk drawer.

I lay down in bed with my shoes still on. I didn't own any
chairs except for one wooden desk chair and the one-room
apartment was too small for a couch. Tomorrow the work-
week started up again and I had no work. January was always
dead for temping. I should have used December to hit a lot of
holiday cocktail parties and remind people that I was around.
I knew I should be making a list of people to email in the
morning to try to drum something up. See if my friend who
had a tech start-up needed someone to do something menial.
Root around and see if I had any half-finished ideas for plays
I could submit somewhere. I should've spent that week at my
dad's, writing. I knew I wouldn't have any messages tomorrow. I wondered how long it would take, if I stopped calling or emailing people, for people to stop contacting me altogether. How long would it take to completely disappear from
their memory?

I thought I could probably move out of Cortland's apartment with just a rented van or a couple trips in a cab. When
my girlfriend, Noreen, and I broke up I let her keep our apart-

ment and most of the furniture. Guilt will make you do that. Then, less than six months later, she moved in with her now wife. I wouldn't have been able to afford our old apartment on my own anyway. I threw out a lot of my belongings when I left. That upset Noreen. "You should have asked me," she said. She felt she had rights to my clothes and other personal things I didn't want. To old papers from my file cabinet. Old videotapes of me and Jamie from college. I dumped all of it when I moved out. I didn't like carrying around the past. I did too much of that as it was.

I glanced around my tiny illegal sublet. It wouldn't take me long to pack up everything I owned. I could do it tonight. I could do it tomorrow. Just say fuck it and ditch Cortland. He would threaten never to write another letter of recommendation for me. Ten years ago that would have terrified me. Cortland was the one who nominated my unpublished play for an award that got it produced. That's what got it produced in London. It was my one and only quote-unquote success. Ten years ago I didn't realize that Cortland was a hack like everyone else. Trying to hang on to a cheap, rent-stabilized apartment in case his girlfriend broke up with him while he wrote books on theater history that no one bought.

I can't say I'm that much different.

I picked up my phone and ordered food to be delivered. As soon as I hung up, the landline rang. I let the machine answer. It was the girlfriend asking if I had given her the envelope. "I hope you forgot, because I'm freaking out that I lost it. Or someone stole it from the café. I don't know what to do. I'm not going to tell Cortland until I hear from you. Ugh. So sorry to bother you again." I felt bad she was stressing out over it, but I needed a few days to figure out what I was doing.

I flipped through the pile of mail, separating mine from Cortland's and the person who used to sublet before me, which I trashed unless it looked important.

There was a letter from Gail. I opened it and found two thin envelopes inside. Gail had stuck a Post-it on the first one saying it had been forwarded to her. The envelope was addressed to me, but at my mother's house. The second envelope was addressed to Eden. "In case you're in touch with her" was written on the second Post-it.

The envelopes looked identical. They had the same return address: *Office of the District Attorney, Matoaka County, Virginia.*

"Shit," I muttered to myself.

The letter informed me that Larry was up for parole. And if I wanted to contact the parole board, I could. After that part was out of the way, the DA more cheerily introduced himself, stating that he was now in charge of this case. He said that while he was confident parole would be denied, there was a chance it could be granted because Larry had been an exemplary prisoner. In the next paragraph he got more serious and said he was trying to indict Larry for murdering a girl who was found dead two years before Eden and I got in Larry's truck. The DA said it had been a cold case because his predecessors didn't have enough evidence, and people were satisfied enough that Larry was in prison. Convicting him for the girl's murder would ensure that he wouldn't be released, the DA wrote. He wanted to talk to me. He wanted me to call anytime. He wanted me to make an appointment to come into his office.

I looked at the envelope again. My name neatly typed across the front. Eden and I were minors at the time. We lived with my mother. And therefore it was sent to her.

I never thought that Larry would get out of jail someday. I guess I should have realized that. Larry must be older now. He must be near my parents' age.

I crumpled the letter and threw it aside. It hit the floor and scuttled away from me.

I packed up my things the next day. I called my friend Zara, who was an artist with a big loft space out in Queens. She agreed to keep my boxes and my three pieces of furniture. I jokingly referred to Zara as my successful friend. Zara was a computer genius who dropped out of an advanced technology PhD program "because of the rampant misogyny" and because "it was basically a training program for the NSA." Now she was an artist, a "data sculptor," as she called it. I never quite understood it, but the computers dictate the sculpture and light installations, and as soon as she started showing her work, people started throwing money at her. Then she had a nervous breakdown, but that only helped her art career. People love a crazy, pretty girl. Zara sensed this and made a vow never to buy any new clothes, never to wear any makeup, and never to cut or brush her hair. Not that it did much good. Zara was gorgeous. The camera loved her. Magazines brought designer clothes to photograph her in and left them at her loft. She kept the basic stuff and sold the dresses on eBay when she had a slow month. She got terrible reviews for her last gallery show, and selling designer clothes and trinkets from swag bags kept her afloat. "It's like they're daring me to lose it again," she said. "My gallerist would love it if I had to be hospitalized again. You know, nothing permanent, just a little damage to give me a boost. Maybe a quick arrest or something involving drugs. Give my brand a jolt. It's incredibly fucked up." She was wrapping high-heeled shoes in tissue paper to ship out when I dropped off my stuff. "It's like the only things I can engage in economy-wise are female tropes," she said. "And no one gets the irony of it." I asked her how her hair-growing was going, because it didn't look all that long. "I know," she said. "It gets to a certain point and then breaks off."

I asked Zara if she wanted some money as a rent contribution. "No," she said, "you're my friend." "So what?" I said. I took a couple of hundreds out of my rent cash and passed it to her. She put up her hands. "I'm not touching it. I'm not having my friendships reduced to commercial transactions," she said. "Besides, you said you were broke and homeless. At least I'm house rich, even if I am cash poor at the moment. And you can take any of these clothes you want," she said.

"I didn't mean to insult you or anything," I said. "It's just that on top of all of this I got some weird news." Zara nodded. Zara understood weird news. Like, sorry your gallerist in France snorted a bunch of cocaine and took off for Morocco with your money, never to be heard from again. Or that your ex-girlfriend is now a sex worker in Florida with a blog and posts a lot of pictures of you. Or that your estranged mother was trying to shop a book deal about your fucked-up childhood. Or that some anonymous computer dude constantly spews hate about you online. Zara once said, "I should really be more famous if I'm going to have to deal with this kind of shit."

I told Zara how when I was a kid, my sister and I were witnesses to a crime and I recently got a letter from a lawyer saying they wanted to reopen the case. Zara didn't ask what kind of crime it was or what we saw. Zara never asked direct questions. She nodded her head and taped up a box. "That must've really affected you," she said. "Yeah," I said. "It sort of fucked up my whole family. I don't think my sister ever got over what happened to us."

Zara looked up from her package, a little perplexed because in the space of a few minutes I had changed my story. Now we weren't witnesses, we were victims. Or at least my sister was a victim. And maybe I was a witness. She digested my gaffe. It was more interesting to her than whatever she thought the real story might be. "You never told me any of that," she said.

4

The police delivered us to our father, who immediately drove us back to my mother. Eden and I had the same father but different mothers, but Eden had lived with my mother since she was really little, since before I was born. Eden shut herself in her room for a week. My mother left food outside her door on a small TV tray, but it went untouched. "She must sneak out at night," my mother whispered to our dad, who was sleeping on the downstairs couch, but he said he never heard anything. My mother always woke up early to work on her dissertation before she went to her job. She didn't like our dad staying over, but she tolerated it because she didn't want Eden alone in the house. Not that Eden seemed to care if anyone was in the house or not. She finally appeared at breakfast one day and said she wanted to go to the alternative boarding school that her friend Sharon went to in Pennsylvania.

My parents were dumbstruck. There was no way to afford something like that, but they both said, instinctively, "Whatever you need. Whatever you want."

My first day back at school the vice principal was standing outside at his usual spot on the front steps. He was out there every morning, arms folded across his wide chest, looking like a prison guard. He liked to show off his knack for remembering kids' names. "Nice hat, Lucas," he would say to one. "Salutations, Charmaine," to another. And to me that day he said, "It's a good day to be alive, Hope."

I went to the school office first. In part because I had lost most of my textbooks, and in part because it seemed the official thing to do after the event. I don't know why. The school secretaries were shocked to see me. They didn't get up right away. Then one of them came over and hugged me. "So glad to have you back in one piece," she said, pressing me to her gigantic breasts. She smelled of baby powder. I pulled out the folded blank check my mother had given me to pay for the lost books. That's when the other secretary stood up. "Don't be ridiculous," the other one said. "We'll fix it."

When I walked down the hall to class I felt strangely magnetic. I thought everyone must know what had happened to me. I had come back from the presumed dead. I must have supernatural powers, or be blessed by God or some animal spirit, or be really smart in situations like that. Fight-or-flight situations. Life-or-death situations. I must have good survival instincts. But no one asked about it. Their parents must've told them not to talk to me about it. Just act like everything is normal when you see her, they probably said. No one came up to me the way they did to the kid with the bald head who had cancer. When you get cancer, a community snaps into gear, raises money for your parents to stay at the Ronald Mc-Donald house, fixes the family car, drops off casseroles on the doorstep, and cuts your grass for you. People shave their head in solidarity with you. Everyone roots for you.

A few kids stared at me. I thought some of them whispered or stopped talking when I walked by.

The second day back at school my homeroom teacher handed me a slip of paper that said I was supposed to go see the guidance counselor. I never had to see the guidance counselor before, except for an obligatory "Hey, it's not too early to think about college!" meeting. Or once, when the female health teacher was out sick the day they split the girls up from the boys to talk about birth control and safe sex, they sent the girls to the guidance counselor instead. She passed around a fishbowl of condoms at the end of the class and said we could take as many as we wanted and the bowl would always be available in her office. We were all too embarrassed to take any, except for this girl Layla, who was last in the circle. She grabbed a few and stuck them in her pocket. The rest of us were doing our best not to laugh from discomfort. Layla looked like she didn't give a shit. Then this girl Amy asked why we could get free condoms but we couldn't get free tampons. She did that to one-up Layla.

I dutifully showed up at the appointed time and knocked on the guidance counselor's frosted glass door. She sang out, "Come on in!" I sat down in the chair in front of her desk. She said, "Wait just a sec," and went to hang a DO NOT DISTURB sign on her office doorknob.

"How is everything?" she asked when she sat back down.

"Fine," I said.

"Everything okay being back here? You okay catching up with classes?"

She was acting like I had missed a month of school. But I had only missed one week. I was confused. I thought maybe she had mixed up her files and was thinking I was the kid who had mono. But I didn't know how to respond, so I just said, "It's fine."

She smiled at me. Her desk had lots of stacks of folders. The sun beaming in through the window behind her back made her look hazy. "I think we should talk about what happened," she said. "Is that okay?" she asked with a concerned look and using a girly voice. It was a voice you used with little kids who hurt themselves on the playground. I found the whole situation bizarre. I said, "Sure, but I guess, you know, everything turned out for the best."

"What do you mean by that?" she asked.

"I mean, it all worked out in the end. They caught the guy. And we're okay."

"I'm glad," she said. She waited a minute and then said, "Is your sister okay? She hasn't been back to school yet." I said, "I think she just hasn't been feeling well."

"Was there something else that happened to her?"

"No. I mean, we were together the whole time."

The guidance counselor smiled and said, "Hmm." She said, "It's good you have each other to talk to. I grew up with three brothers and I always wanted a sister."

"Right," I said, and then thought it was a weird thing to say. I thought maybe the guidance counselor has to check in with students when something like this happens. She has to fill out a form that says she met with me. It's just this one time and I just have to get through it.

"Sometimes," she said, "when something major happens to us, we don't react until some time has passed. Maybe it's a week. Maybe it's a couple of months. Sometimes we don't feel all of our feelings right away and then they start coming out when we don't expect them. So if that happens to you, you can always come talk to me."

"Sure," I said. I had no intention of ever coming to her office unless I suddenly needed condoms. Or to have her go over my college applications when I was a senior.

The bell rang and I instinctively reached for my backpack, but I didn't have one because I had left it at Larry's. I was carrying stuff around by hand until my mom and I could go shopping. The guidance counselor nodded at me that I could go.

I didn't get summoned to have a follow-up session with the guidance counselor, but she did go out of her way to say hello to me in the hall or the cafeteria and ask me lame questions about movies or TV. No one else at school asked me directly about it, but I could feel people were curious. They wanted more details than what was in the newspaper. They wanted me to make a public statement about it. Get up in front of class and read my essay about it. They wanted to give me an award, a savings bond for not dying. Each day that I got home unscathed by questions, it only felt closer to when people would start to ask. Then, as if an internal timer went off, people would think that enough time had passed and I seemed to be doing fine and it would be okay to start asking me about what happened. But the school absorbed my silence and no one asked me anything. My parents didn't bring it up either. And Eden left for boarding school not long after that.

Larry cut a deal. He pleaded guilty. Eden and I didn't have to go to court. The lawyer said we could go to trial and he was sure Larry would go down with the maximum sentence, because the bus station ticket guy said he had seen Larry hanging around a lot and therefore it looked premeditated, like he had seen our dad picking us up before and that's why he said what he did. But my mother thought we shouldn't have to go through all of that. Especially Eden. No one asked me and Eden what we thought. I didn't know that a trial was an option until after it was over and done.

I stopped going out to visit my dad. Now he would drive into Charlottesville and spend the day with me. Sometimes he would sleep over at a friend's and see me again the next day. He stopped complaining about all the driving. His girlfriend at the time had broken up with him. Her name was Luce, short for Lucinda. I ran into her on the Downtown Mall one day after school. She apologized for leaving my dad. "It was too much negative energy for me," she said. "I'm not as strong as you girls." She went inside herself when she said that and seemed spaced out and far away. Then she came back to me and sort of tried to smile. I correctly guessed (having gotten confirmation from my father) that she had been through a lot of therapy. "Luce had other problems," my father said.

A few months later, Luce moved to North Carolina, but she and my mom stayed friends. "Why wouldn't I be friends with Luce?" my mother said. "She's not the reason your father and I split up." My mother was friends with many of my father's ex-partners, and she was best friends with Eden's mom, Suriya. People would say that it was interesting that Eden chose to live with my mom, but it really wasn't a choice at all. There wasn't ever a question about where Eden would live. No one expected her to leave everything and move out to the middle of nowhere with my dad. And Suriya was a free spirit. She went to India almost every winter for three months or longer. One time she was gone for a year. She spent the summers traveling around with a guy who sold T-shirts at music festivals. In between she would sometimes live with us, or with a lover if she had one. Eden's mom was a lesbian. Some people thought she and my mom were lovers, but they weren't. Boys in middle school used to tease Eden about her mom. They'd say something like "Your mom's a dyke and you're a dyke too." Eden was good at dealing with it. She would say, "You don't even know what that means." And the boys would protest that they did. "Oh, really?" Eden would say. "What does it mean, then?" "It means you're a muff-diver," they said. "How do you muff-dive?" Eden asked. "You should know," the boys said. "But I don't," Eden said, "so you should tell me, since you know." She would zero in on one boy and make him turn red and explain what exactly a muff was and what one did with it when diving. She would finally get him to say, "And then you smell it. And you lick it, like a dog does." One time Eden made a sixth-grade boy wet his pants, challenging him to say it.

Eden easily immersed herself in the clique of liberal, well-off smart girls who go to expensive progressive boarding schools. Other girls at her school had mothers who lived in ashrams, but they usually had a family trust fund behind them. Unlike other scholarship kids, the ones plucked for their ability to appear in brochure photos and make the school look better and feel better about itself, Eden's poverty, and her mother's rejection of both heterosexuality and capitalism, secured her social status. "Her mother truly is liberated," one of her friends said.

Eden rarely came home on weekends. She didn't come home for Christmas break because she got invited to go to a friend's ski lodge in Vermont. My parents felt odd about it because neither of them skied and no one we knew skied. My mother worried that it would be expensive: "They have to buy those tickets and things. And the equipment." Eden said they didn't have to worry about it. She would go directly from school to her friend's house, and the same friend would drive her back to school in January. She didn't come home for spring break either, because she was working on a "community engagement project." She spent the summer with her mother, traveling around New England, and then stayed with Luce down in North Carolina and worked at a music festival. My mother was a little hurt that Eden never came home. My father didn't think it was a big deal. "She has too much of Suriya in her," he said. "You can't pin people like that down. Believe me, I tried."

Eden went to the boarding school for less than a year. Then my mother received her high school diploma in the mail. It was the beginning of Eden's senior year. She was seventeen. Apparently, she had completed all the state requirements and elected to graduate early. I thought my mother would be glad that they wouldn't have to pay for another year of tuition, but she was immediately on the phone to my dad, livid, asking if he knew anything about it, which he didn't. "Then where is she?" my mother asked. And looking at the date on the diploma she asked, "And where has she been for the past two months?"

My parents called Eden's friends, but they wouldn't say where she was or they pretended not to know. They called the school, but the school had no idea. Her adviser had signed off on her early graduation, but neglected to tell anyone else. And now the adviser no longer worked there. My dad asked if he had been fired, but the school wasn't at liberty to say. "That means he was fired," my dad said. "If he wasn't fired, they would've effusively said no. You only cover up when it's something bad."

My father and I drove up to Pennsylvania in The Camper to get Eden. He didn't want to stop for lunch, relenting to my hunger only when it reduced me to being annoying and grouchy, and only because we needed gas and there was a drive-thru without a line. We made no stops other than that and drove the rest of the six hours straight to the school. My father parked in a spot reserved for faculty, and when I pointed out that he couldn't park there he said, "I don't give a fuck." He got out of the car and race-walked up the steps to the school with me scurrying after him, my new backpack bouncing against my spine as I tried to catch up.

My dad bolted into the school office like a cowboy, pushing open the double doors with no announcement, not caring whom he bulldozed over and left stranded in his wake. He didn't stop until he got to the desk and said, "Get me the principal." The back-to-the-land female teachers, unused to such outbursts and unused to strangers, smiled at him and said their school had no principal; it was nonhierarchical and was cooperatively administered by the faculty. To which my father responded, "Bring me whoever the fuck's in charge or I'm calling the police."

I could tell my father was nervous. He was putting on a tough-guy act but he kept nodding his head, his overgrown curls jiggling free around his ears, his glasses sliding down his nose on nervy sweat. He fiddled with his fingers a lot and his hands flew up to his lips and he bit his nails. Then he realized he was doing it and dropped his hands to the desk and clenched his fists to keep them there. This whole thing was weird. No one used to worry about Eden at all. No one minded that she went on walkabout last summer, sleeping in the back of a van with Suriya and the T-shirt guy she worked for. But now my father desperately needed to know where Eden was and what she was doing. He was putting all of his parental chips on this one moment. So that he could save Eden from whatever this was, this minor dilemma, this small-time infraction. It was his golden heroic opportunity.

I was directed to wait in an old overstuffed armchair. Kids at this school waited in comfortable chairs before having a talk with whoever was democratically elected by the cooperative to deal with a student who was a contrarian in an unproductive or disruptive manner. I watched students wander in and out. There was a large card catalog against the wall opposite me, and students and teachers regularly went up to it and pulled open drawers, then pushed them shut and went on their way. When there was a lull in foot traffic, I got up and went to inspect it. Each drawer had someone's name on it. I followed the drawer labels with my eyes, some of them decorated with stickers or ancient graffiti, until I found one with Eden's name and slid it open. There were no library index cards inside. It was a mailbox. Inside was a letter I had written Eden a month ago. My own handwriting stared up at me, the envelope slightly crinkled and worn and postmarked, as if a part of myself had gone away somewhere, traveled to some-place I had never been, and sent word from afar.

I had written Eden on the anniversary of what happened with Larry. I always thought on anniversaries you should do exactly what you did the year before and see what was differ-ent. You should wear the same thing, re-create your day, eat the same thing for lunch if you can remember. But I didn't take the bus to my dad's anymore. A few months ago I had started going out to his house again, but my mom offered to drop me off because she was driving to DC. On the phone the day before, my dad said that we should go to the apple festival, and I said sure. I packed my backpack without think-ing about it, because we always went out to my dad's for the apple festival. It was one of the dorky things we enjoyed do-ing. We picked apples and brought them to a cider mill. My dad fermented his own hard cider in the basement. I packed my bag thinking it was just any other year we went to the ap-ple festival, any other weekend I went to my dad's. My mom dropped me off, and Sunday my dad drove me home because he said he had to do something in Charlottesville. I don't know if that was true or not, or if taking me to the same bus station where Larry picked us up freaked him out. I didn't re-member it was the first time back at his house until I went to bed and Eden wasn't in the room with me. That's what I wrote her in the letter. It seemed sentimental and dumb now, and I could see Eden rolling her eyes at it or getting mad at me about it. She probably didn't want to talk about it. Her life was so different now. Eden didn't go back to anything. That's when I realized she was already gone. That she would never move home again. She would probably go straight to college and never visit and move someplace far away, like France or something. She had talked about wanting to go to Amsterdam or Thailand or San Francisco or Seattle. I thought about taking the letter. Folding it in half. Shoving it into my jeans pocket. I was sort of embarrassed that it was there, like a little kid's letter to Santa. A school project mailed to a soldier somewhere. My handwriting looked younger, even though I had written the letter only a month ago. I felt older staring down at it in the narrow wooden drawer.

I shut the card catalog drawer with the letter still inside. Eden might turn up if she needed something. This place obviously had an open-door policy. Everything was communal. They had unisex bathrooms. There was barely any distinction between student and teacher.

"Come on," my dad said, reappearing and making a beeline for the door.

We marched back to our ill-parked car and got inside. "Find this on the map," he said, throwing me a yellow Post-it. "You're good at that." He started up The Camper and backed out of the parking lot. "Un-fucking-believable. They're lucky I'm not suing them. I should sue them. How could you sanction something like that? You know, your teachers are *in loco parentis*," he said, throwing around some eighth-grade Latin and one year of pre-law. "They are your parents when you're at school. They are legally responsible for your kids while they're in school. Fuck, I probably signed something saying I couldn't sue when we enrolled her. Fuck. Fucking arbitration or some other bullshit. Dammit."

I gave directions. We went uphill and the wholesome farm-land turned into forest. The woods grew denser. Small, interspersed towns sprang up, shaved out of the growth. It got cloudy. And dark green.

We turned a corner at a house with a pool table sitting in the front yard. It was surrounded by the type of people I tried to avoid at school. The boys all wore baseball caps and the girls wore bleached jeans and too much makeup. One of them playfully leaned across the table and pulled a pool cue out of a guy's hands. She had to half climb on the table to get it, and she used it as a pole to slide back to the ground. She squatted when she landed and stuck her ass out. Then she laughed at herself.

The road wound through a neighborhood of tiny cottages and trailers. It probably used to be a summer community, but now it looked like people lived here full-time. We came to a mailbox that listed the number on the Post-it my father had thrown at me. "This is it," I said. He stopped The Camper in the middle of the road without bothering to park or turn into the driveway. He got out and started walking up the dirt-and-gravel slope toward a double-wide trailer. He was halfway up before he said to me, "Wait in the car." I opened my mouth to protest, but my father sensed this and repeated, "Back in the car."

I stopped walking and watched him continue up to the house. He pulled open a screen door and banged the orna-mental knocker.

No one answered. He knocked again. Metal attacking

metal reverberated through the neighborhood, the sound bouncing off the mountains and echoing through the open air. When he reached to knock a third time, I heard him say, "Open up or I'm calling the cops!"

I leaned against The Camper instead of climbing back inside. Up at the trailer house, the front door opened. "Get my daughter," I heard my father say without a hello. I couldn't hear what the person who answered the door said back. I could tell it was a guy, but he was speaking softly, and maybe he was just a kid, because his voice didn't carry the weight of an adult. "I don't give a shit," my dad said in reply. The person went on about something and then I saw my dad push his way inside.

There was a camouflage tarp over a lean-to in the side yard. I thought it was covering up firewood, but I saw the sheeting separate and a young guy emerged. He was my age or a few years older. His clothes were rumpled as if he had slept in them for weeks. He looked up at the house where my dad was arguing with whoever was inside and saying he was going to call the cops and public health and shut this whole thing down. The kid wiped his nose with his sleeve and ducked back under the tarp. He came out shouldering a hiker's framed backpack and squeezing a sleeping bag under one arm. He looked around behind his shelter and pulled a towel off of a tree branch. He slung it over his shoulder and headed down the driveway. I expected him to say hi or hey as he passed by, but he kept his eyes on the ground. He dragged his feet as he walked. He had beat-up boots held together by strips of dirty duct tape.

"Let go of me!" Eden shrieked. She had kicked open the screen door and escaped. Her long hair flicked around her neck and floated up behind her in streams as she ran down the front steps. I hadn't seen her in months. She looked thinner and more grown up. Before I could really see her face, she turned back to the house, surprised that no one had followed her.

My dad held open the screen door. "Get your things," he said. Eden walked backwards slowly, digging the toes of her sneakers into the loose gravel. "I don't want any *things*," she said. My dad yelled something back into the house that I couldn't hear. He turned to Eden and said again, "Get your stuff." "If I go back in there," Eden said, "I'm not coming out again." "Eden—" my dad started to yell. "And stop yelling at my friends!" she said, bending over, her arms rammed straight and ending in fists reaching toward the dirt. My dad stared at her. "Fine," he said and let go of the screen door.

My dad walked down the steps and said, "Let's go." He looked tired, worn out by being Mr. Macho with the people inside the house and earlier at the school. Eden stood there waiting for something else. None of her mythical friends emerged to say a teary goodbye. No concerned neighbors were intervening. I wasn't sure if I was supposed to do anything, if I was supposed to go up and give her a hug and tell her I missed her, which I wasn't sure was true. I had gotten used to not having her around. And being around my dad was sort of easier with her not there. I wasn't sure if Eden had seen me. I didn't know if it would change anything about how she felt. On the other hand, I was starting to think that's why my dad had brought me along. Think of your sister, he could throw out, as if I were much younger than my actual age, still clutching a teddy bear and easily reduced to tears.

"Fine," Eden said, walking back to the porch. "I'll get my

stuff." She stomped up the stairs and back inside. My father tried to catch the door and follow right behind her, but he missed it and had to open it again. It banged shut behind him.

I walked a few steps up the driveway and turned around and looked back at the street. The Camper was blocking the driveway and a good portion of the road. There was a small ranch house across the street that looked tidy, with a fenced-in garden on the front lawn. Two little Asian girls were sitting at a picnic bench under the shade of the roof. They had a collection of leaves they were sorting and cutting up with pink school scissors. The older one would stack the pieces like she was getting ready to shuffle a deck of cards. Then she carefully placed her leaf collection in a pink plastic briefcase and snapped it shut.

"I changed my mind!" Eden screamed from the house. I heard other people arguing now, and my dad repeated Eden's name over and over, trying to get a word in edgewise. The two of them burst onto the porch, my dad holding Eden by the elbow and yelling at whoever was inside to back off or he was calling the cops. "Call them!" said a guy inside. "I'm sure they'll bring family services into it and that'll really help mend fences. You're providing such a stellar example of parenting." My dad pointed his car keys at the screen door. "Just try it," my dad said. "I'm sure everyone camping out here is over eighteen." Then he turned to Eden and said, "Come on."

Eden shook her arm free. "I said, I'm not going!" she yelled. She was carrying an old shopping bag in her other hand. I wondered where she got it, because it was from a fancy department store and probably no one in this neighborhood would shop at a place like that. A guy came out onto the porch and walked down the steps. I guess he was about my dad's age or maybe younger. He was wearing cheap flip-flops and he jogged with little coordination, trying to catch up to my dad and Eden. He was skinny, except for a potbelly, and had glasses and a beard. He was wearing sweatpants and a really old T-shirt that had been washed too many times and was almost see-through. He was trying to be diplomatic. "I'm just asking," he said as he caught up to my dad and Eden. "Look, hey, maybe there's an alternative solution to this. Maybe we're letting our emotions get in the way of clear thinking."

"Back off," my dad said. "Maybe you should've been thinking clearly before you slept with my underage daughter." "No, hey," the guy said, putting up a palm and looking at my dad over his glasses. "She's got her own space here. She's an autonomous person." "She's a minor," my dad said. "She's my daughter and she belongs to me." "I am not a fucking object!" Eden yelled. "Shut up," my dad said.

Suddenly the flip-flops-and-glasses guy looked sad. I thought he might cry. His face wrenched up and he looked like a powerless kindergartner. He gasped a little and said, "Eden," in a whimpering voice. He extended his arms toward her to give her a hug and then my dad punched him. I don't think I had ever seen someone punch someone except on television. At first I wasn't entirely sure my dad had hit him; it looked more like he accidentally knocked him down. But the guy was clutching his face, and my dad was saying something stolen out of a movie: "You want some more?" or "You're not stopping me" or something like that.

The guy was down on the pavement, trying to sit up. "Oh, that's great," he said, patting for the glasses that had been knocked off his face. I was worried they would be broken, but he picked them out of the pebbles in one piece. "Using violence. Great way to communicate with someone. Great way to get your daughter to respect you as a human being."

"What makes you think human beings aren't violent?" my dad said.

When the guy made it up to his feet and took his hands away from his face, we could all see he had a bloody nose. Eden dropped her shopping bag and started crying. She said, "Oh my god, Eric," and started moving toward him, but my dad pushed her down the driveway and said, "Get in the car." Eric turned away and said, "You better go. You better get in the car. I'm sorry, Eden." He walked back toward his double-wide trailer. There were a couple of other high school kids waiting for him on the porch and looking out the window. Eden watched him go, still quietly crying, and let my dad tug her toward The Camper.

"Hi," I said to Eden, but she didn't seem to notice me. I was going to relinquish the front seat, but she walked around the side and yanked open the sliding door to the back. I guessed she didn't want to sit next to my dad. She lay down on the back couch and wedged her shopping bag against the window as a pillow. My dad started the engine and pulled into the driveway to turn The Camper around.

"Eden!" Eric came running down the driveway. He tripped over something in his flip-flops and fell forward on his hands and knees. He got up, rubbed his knee, and kept coming toward us. He still had blood on his face and it had dribbled down his T-shirt. "Shit," my dad said. He put The Camper in reverse.

"Eden!" Eric made it to The Camper and was banging on the window. Eden sat up and brushed the curtains aside. "You should become an emancipated minor!" Eden tried to crank open the window but the lever broke off in her hand. She put her palms on the slatted glass. "Become an emancipated minor!" he said again. "Un-fucking-believable," my dad said. He shifted into gear and drove out of there.

We stopped at a gas station twenty minutes later. When Eden got out of The Camper, my dad yelled at her to stay inside. "People have to urinate, you know," she said. "Or are you going to deprive me of that, too?" My dad picked up the gas nozzle. He gestured at me with it. "Go with her," he said.

I followed Eden into the mini-mart and toward the back. A mop and bucket blocked the entrance to the restroom. Eden kicked it out of the way and went inside. She slammed the door and I heard her latch the lock.

I wondered if there was a small window in the bathroom that Eden could crawl out of. It probably faced the back of the building and my dad wouldn't see her. She could run into the brush and out to a different road and hitchhike. She could get picked up easily. But the only place she had to go was back to that guy Eric's trailer and we would know where to find her.

She came out of the bathroom, ignoring the fact that I was right there. I was torn whether or not to use the bathroom, but I decided it was okay since Eden was now in my dad's sight.

Out at the car, Eden leaned against the driver's door and said, "I can drive if you want. I know how to drive stick." "Oh, you are not driving," my dad said. Eden walked around and climbed in the back. We drove a few hours more and stayed in a motel. "Why are we stopping?" Eden asked. My dad said because it was dark and one of his taillights was out and he didn't want to get a ticket. "Wouldn't a ticket be cheaper than a motel?" Eden asked. My dad didn't say anything. "Are we getting food, or is that not in the budget?" My dad called the motel office and asked if there was a place that delivered pizza. The motel room was dim, with flat, worn-out carpeting and a framed poster from Matisse's cut-out book *Jazz*. It looked like a guy doing an awkward dance at night. My dad was about to claim one of the two double beds for himself and have me and Eden share one, but then he changed his mind. He said we could each have our own bed. He took a pillow and one of the scratchy polyester quilts and spread a towel out on the floor in front of the door to prevent Eden from running off.

Our dad deposited us at my mom's. He sat on the couch fidgeting with his car keys, wanting to know what my mother was going to do about the situation, as if it were all her fault and as if she had to have the solution for everything. My mother usually did have the solution for everything. She had already figured out what to do with Eden. She couldn't go back to school because she had already graduated, and it was too late to enroll her in college, or even community college, where she would surely be bored. Instead my mother had called a friend and gotten information about sending Eden to Costa Rica. "You can study environmental science in Costa Rica," my mother said. "It's an ecological research center in the rain forest. They have a program for people like you." "People like me?" Eden asked. "What exactly am I like? Who are my people?" "People taking time off between high school and college," my mother said. "I'm not going to college," Eden said. "We can decide that later," our dad piped in. "This is a bribe,"

Eden said. "It's hush money to forget everything that's happened." My mother didn't take the bait. "How often do you get the chance to go to Costa Rica?" she asked.

Later that night I tapped softly on the door to Eden's room. There was no response so I poked my head inside to see if she was there. Eden was smoking a cigarette next to the open window and hadn't heard my knock. She looked at me and then turned back to the window. Since she didn't yell at me, I assumed it was okay to come into her room.

"Shut the door at least," she said. I did as I was told. Eden sucked on her cigarette. "It's not good for you," I said. She rolled her eyes and stubbed out the cigarette inside the window frame. "I thought everyone would be happy," she said. "Graduating high school is supposed to be an accomplishment and I did it in less time than most people. I also saved them a shitload in tuition. But I get dragged back here instead. And banished to Central America. Fucking indentured servitude. I should get a lawyer."

"What would you do with a lawyer?" I asked. "How would you pay for it?"

"Did you know that you and I could've sued, but they decided we shouldn't?"

"Sue who?"

Eden shook her head. She went over and flopped down on her bed. "What were you doing out there?" I asked. "Living," she said. "Just living. Suddenly that's a crime. I just want my life to mean something. I just want them to leave me alone and let me do what I want. I don't need to be taken care of."

I thought Eden had made out pretty well. I never went skiing and no one was offering to send me to Costa Rica. I was the one who had to live at home and deal with the parents. I was the one who had to deal with everyone knowing what happened to us, whereas Eden got to go to a new school and reinvent herself where no one knew anything about her. And now she could do it again in Costa Rica.

Eden used to include me more when we were younger. I was quieter than she was. I was more awkward. I wasn't as pretty. Eden took care of me. One summer she taught me how to dive. It took forever because I was scared of choking on water and I wasn't a great swimmer to begin with. I was hoping she would be the one to give me driving lessons next year instead of our dad, who would probably end up yelling at me in frustration. And my mom was always busy working on her dissertation. I was the furthest thing from anyone's mind.

I crawled into her bed and stretched out next to her. Eden didn't move. She just stared at the ceiling. "I don't have any rights," she said. "I'm just their slave." She didn't say anything for a while and I watched her stomach rise and fall with her breath. I turned on my side and curled into her. "Do you ever think about what happened?" I asked.

She didn't answer, and I wondered if I really said it or if I only thought it inside my head.

The next morning I woke up to people arguing. I wandered downstairs and found Eden, Suriya, and my mother in the living room. Suriya's giant backpack was propped against the couch. My mother was on the verge of yelling something when Suriya saw me and said, "Woo-hoo!" and enveloped me in a hug. She smelled like sandalwood and sweat. Her long hair hung down her back in a thick braid, which she must've made days ago because it was frizzy and dandruff dotted the top of her head. Suriya kept an arm draped over my shoulders and held me close, as if we were old army buddies, maybe because my mom was looking at me like she really didn't want me to be a part of this conversation, whatever it might be. Eden was sitting astride the arm of the couch eating a bowl of cereal. "It's only five months until my birthday," Eden said, breaking the standoff. "And she is my mother. In case anyone forgot." My mother walked out of the room. I asked what was going on. Suriya frowned. "First of all," she said to Eden, "that wasn't very nice. Karen's your mother too. Don't go grabbing at conventions just because they happen to suit you." Eden walked to the kitchen. "She doesn't really want to go to Costa Rica," Suriya said to me. "It's a nice idea and all, but maybe not for her." Suriya and I went to the kitchen. Eden was standing in front of the refrigerator, peering inside. She took out the milk and made herself another bowl of cereal.

"What?" she said, already annoyed with me. She munched spoonfuls of cereal. "What are you going to do?" I asked. Suriya said, "She's going to come stay with me for a while. Give your mom a break. She'll do some independent study. I know some people who were a part of the Free University and they can be mentor types. If we make enough money this fall we can get to India. Or maybe Thailand." "You want to go to Thailand but you don't want to go to Costa Rica?" I asked. "I don't want to be a part of any system. I want to make my own choices," Eden said and put her bowl in the sink.

I followed Eden up to her room. She was pulling the clothes she brought with her out of the old shopping bag and smelling them. She packed a big duffel bag with fresh clothes from her dresser, then went to her closet and pulled out a winter coat that she hadn't worn in ages. My mother had bought it for her in the eighth grade. It was puffy and expensive, but once Eden had started high school she considered it uncool and never wore it. Now she was looking at her backpack and dubbing the coat too big. "Where's my leather jacket?" she asked. "I have it," I said. I had been wearing it since she left. "Do you want it back?" "No," she said. "You can have it." She opened a drawer in her desk and took out a Band-Aid tin. Inside was a wad of bills. She thumbed through the cash. "Got any money?" she asked.

"I don't know. Maybe twenty dollars," I said.

"Could I have it?"

"Sure," I said. This was part of the deal for the leather jacket, I thought. Or I assumed. And twenty dollars for a cool jacket was not that much. Although it was better to just find a cool jacket or have your older sister give it to you.

I went to my room and got my twenty dollars. I also had a jar of loose change, but I figured she wouldn't want that. I gave the money to Eden and told her I could ask my mother for more. "Never mind," she said.

A car horn beeped outside. Suriya called upstairs for her. Eden didn't say goodbye. She rumbled down the stairs like she was heading off to school on a normal day. My mother had emerged and was talking to Suriya, who swung her giant backpack over her shoulder and pulled her braid free. She asked my mom if there was anything she had to sign, or any papers she needed for Eden. My mother shook her head. "I have a copy of her birth certificate if you need it," she said. "Nah, you hang on to it for safekeeping," Suriya said. She hugged my mother even though my mother obviously didn't want to be hugged and didn't hug her back. Instead, she be-grudgingly bent her arms and lightly touched Suriya's waist. "I'm sorry about all this. You know I love everything you've done for her," Suriya said. "Some people just got to go their own way."

I followed Suriya onto the front porch. There was some older hippie guy with a bushy white Santa Claus beard lean-ing against the car. He helped Eden push her duffel bag into the trunk. She had taken the puffy winter coat with her and shoved that in too. A tall, thin woman got out of the car and walked up to the porch. She looked like a man dressed as a woman, with a sinewy body and a bluntly cut bob of over-processed blonde hair that had been dyed too many times and looked brittle. She wore a cropped white denim jacket and a prairie skirt that were both out of style. She asked if she could use the bathroom.

"Sure," I said, "it's in the back." She thanked me and dis-appeared into the house, her clog sandals clomping on the floor. When she came back out, she said, "Sorry," with a hand on her chest. She walked halfway down the porch steps so there wasn't so much of a height difference between us and extended her arm to me. "I'm Chrissy," she said.

I shook her hand. "I'm Hope."

Chrissy sat down on the porch steps, daintily tucking her skirt around her legs and angling her shins to one side. She rummaged through her woven purse for sunglasses, then tilted her face to the sun and closed her eyes behind her am-ber shades. She acted like a movie star. I wondered if she had once been famous. She looked over to the car where Suriya was changing her shirt, stripping down to a threadbare tank top in the middle of the street and putting on a short-sleeve blouse that she left unbuttoned. Suriya never wore a bra. I thought it was interesting that she was friends with a drag queen like Chrissy.

"Chrissy!" the Santa Claus hippie called. Chrissy stretched out her legs and dragged herself to her feet. She took off her sunglasses, folded them, and deposited them back in her purse. She extended her hand to me again, but this time she leaned in closer to me. She air-kissed me on both cheeks. "I'm sorry you can't come with us," she said.

I watched her walk down to the car. I heard the screen door open behind me and my mom came out onto the porch. Suriya gave us a peace-sign salute before she got inside. Eden was in the back seat next to Chrissy. Santa Claus started the car and looked over his shoulder to see if anyone was coming behind him before he pulled out into the street. "Bye," I yelled, feeling kind of weird about it, like maybe no one was going to say it if I didn't. Eden stuck her hand out of the window and waved.

5

called the number listed on the district attorney's letter-head. I gave my name to an assistant and she asked what it was in reference to. I said I was responding to a letter about Larry's case. She asked me what my relationship was to the case. I paused. I thought everyone would know who I was. After all, they were the ones who sent the letter. I was silent. Maybe her other lines were lighting up, because she prodded me. "Are you a lawyer for a party involved?" she asked.

"No," I said.

"Can you tell me your relationship to the case?"

"It's my case," I said. "I am the case."

There was a moment while she sorted through her confusion.

"Are you the victim?" she asked quietly.

It was strange to have to say yes. I didn't like the word "victim." At various points in my life I had read self-help books about people who had been through traumatic events. "It's not your fault!" they always said. "You're the victim!" I guess I was the victim, but acknowledging it never made me feel any better. I didn't see why I had to relinquish control over my life a second time.

I was placed on hold. Then the woman picked up and made an appointment for me to come to the office and speak with the district attorney. She sounded excited.

"Of course you're going," Zara said. "Wouldn't you donate a kidney if you could keep someone from dying?" I said I didn't know. I guess I would. "It's not that big a deal," Zara said. "You only need one. Like testicles." "But this girl is already dead," I said. "Someone else might not be," Zara said. She got up and walked across the loft to get more tape for her boxes. "If it were me," she said, "my gallerist would make me do it. She'd get a fashion magazine to publish my crappily written essay about it." I winced. "Isn't that kind of gross?" I asked. Zara shrugged. "Being an artist is inherently gross," she said. "We're self-commoditizing savages." "That's rather harsh," I said. "But you are considering going," Zara said, "and not necessarily for purely altruistic reasons." "What do you mean?" I asked. "You're bored," Zara said. "You've got nothing to do and nothing going on. You haven't put up a play in a long time. This is the best thing to happen to you in years. The tragedy of life is raw material. And you could use some new material." "My mother just died," I said. "Isn't that enough to work with?" Zara shrugged again. "Everyone's mother dies," she said. "It's relatable, but not terribly dramatic. This is better. In the big sense. If you want to make a splash." "Now I really feel gross," I said.

One of Zara's computers woke up and its screen began

flickering lines of code. She went to tend to it. "It's up to you," she said as she sat down at her desk.

I debated taking the train, but the bus was so much cheaper. I packed a small backpack and a tote bag. I told Zara I might only be gone for the day. I could take a late-night bus back to New York. "Or I might stay at my dad's," I said, although I hadn't told him I was coming. My bus left the Port Authority at one in the morning. I used to do this when I was a college student; I hated the idea of wasting a day traveling. The overnight buses were never late because there was less traffic, and no one tried to talk to you — everyone was asleep. Everybody I knew hated the bus, but I didn't mind it. I had grown up on one, more or less.

I didn't feel tired so I took out my notebook and pen and flipped through the pages. Zara was right: I didn't have anything going on. I had a couple of scraps of ideas for different plays, but mostly they were fragments. I hadn't had a play produced in a long time because I hadn't finished a play in a long time. *A play that takes place on a bus,* I wrote sloppily as the ride joggled my pen, *where everyone is asleep.* I stared at my scraggy handwriting, unsure if it was a good idea or not. *Something to do with who is really awake and who is just drifting through life.* I tapped my pen. It would be expensive to do a play on a real bus. It would require extra insurance or permits or something. Where would it park? Where would it go? Can anyone drive a bus, or do you need a special license? How many sleeping actors would I need? And then how many seats would be left over for the audience?

I scratched out the page. It was a random idea. I didn't know what it was about.

I woke up at six. The scenery had changed. The bus began to curl onto the Beltway. I debated using the onboard bathroom and decided against it. The guy sitting in front of me woke up, stretched, and began methodically cracking his knuckles. Poor people and students take the bus. I guess I'm one of the poor people. For a brief period, I had a job as a content writer at an Internet start-up and I made good money and got out of debt. But immediately after the company ran through its seed capital, one of the partners gathered us for a meeting where he sat on the edge of his desk and said he was moving on to work on an exciting new project. "I like starting things," he said, "that's my strength. And you guys are doing great. You don't really need me anymore." He had brought in a keg of beer and ordered us pizza. This was a happy occasion, he tried to convince us. Two weeks later they laid off half the staff. My emails to coworkers bounced back. The cubicles slowly emptied out until I was one of the few people left. Technically I was a freelancer, so technically they couldn't fire me. After another few weeks I couldn't take it anymore. I went into the remaining partner's office and asked for an end date. He said he didn't know. He was still hoping things could turn around. I felt bad for him. I said, "Why don't we say till the end of the month?" He acknowledged his defeat. He said, "I might still call you after that," but he never did.

I could have built on that experience and made it into something resembling a sustainable career, but I fell back into the same precarious financial position I had been in since I was a college student. I knew someone who worked as a branding strategist, whatever that was. I could've done something like that. I wondered that out loud to Zara before I left. "You weren't interested in it," Zara said. I asked her what she

meant. Why wouldn't I be interested in it? "Because you decided your life was about writing plays and trying to get at
the truth of something by bringing people together and sitting in a dark theater for an hour. And now that's who you
are. You put all your chips in that basket long ago." I wasn't
sure what to say to that. I didn't remember ever consciously
making such a decision. I wondered if anyone actually did.
Maybe I did. I wasn't sure if that's what my life was about, or
if that's just what my life happened to be. Zara said, "You're
sort of like a junkie. You use what's in front of you to pay for
your fix." I asked what my fix was. What was I addicted to?
"To continuing," she said.

At the Matoaka County district attorney's office I was directed to sit next to a large copy machine, and when I did, my
head was below the level of the receptionist's desk divider.
The receptionist leaned out to the side of her partition every
now and then to check on me, to make sure I was still there.
Finally, after the phone rang, she led me a few steps down the
hall to a conference room and said, "He'll be right in."

The oversized table left little room to move around behind
the chairs. There were boxes stacked haphazardly against the
walls.

The door opened and the DA entered carrying a stack of
file folders. He looked overworked. He was short, out of
shape, and slightly out of breath. He shook my hand and sat
down. "Happy you contacted us," he said.

"Did you write to the parole board?" he asked. I said I
hadn't. I didn't know the address or whom to write to, and I
didn't know what to say, exactly. He said it was okay. "We still
have the football," he said. He flipped through some of his

folders, then closed them and rested his forearms on top of them. He said that we had an interesting case.

He coughed into his hand to begin his speech.

"When you were picked up by the police, you said you hadn't been raped." He looked down when he said that and paused. I wondered if he was trained to do that. To not appear aggressive when talking about rape. Maybe he had to take a seminar on it and someone, somewhere, produces training videos for lawyers on how to talk about rape. And they suggested putting in these little pauses in order to give the interviewee some space while discussing potentially upsetting subjects. I said, "Right." He looked up at me and said, "Right." He opened a folder and skimmed it quickly, like an actor cheating, looking at his lines scribbled inside a prop because he can't remember them word for word. "They did a . . . an exam on you at the hospital and didn't find anything specific. And Larry burned your possessions that were left at the scene. So we didn't have a lot of physical evidence. Your sister, however, wouldn't say anything one way or the other and refused to submit to a physical exam. The file says they sent in counselors, but she didn't say a word, wouldn't budge, and your mother didn't force the issue. And I don't blame her. What you went through was horrific. It's amazing that you got out of there in one piece and are sitting here today. I don't know if I would've done any different if it were my daughters."

He cleared his throat, leaned back in his chair, and called out to the receptionist down the hall. He asked her to bring in some water. "Would you like a glass of water or anything?" he asked. I said I didn't. He drank half his cup right away. He was gearing himself up for something.

"Is there anything different about this that you would like to tell me? About the whole experience? Anything that you remember after the fact? Something you might not have told the police at the time? You know, sometimes things come back to you later on."

I shook my head. "No," I said. "I don't think so."

"I understand what your parents did," he said. "They just wanted this horror show to end and get you girls back to normal life and healed up. And considering the evidence they had on hand and the technology at the time, and considering the mental welfare of you girls, I think they made a reasonable decision. So, here's the thing: your sister, you, you're adults now. And you can make your own decisions. We would like you to consider revising your statements, adding information you might not have mentioned. We would like to establish a pattern that would connect Larry to another case."

He waited for me to say something. He reached for his water cup and drained it.

I said there really wasn't anything else to say. I said I was sure I told them everything at the time and said everything there was to say.

"We would really be interested in hearing from your sister," he said. He refilled his cup from the plastic pitcher. I laughed. "So would I," I said. He sipped some more water and swallowed. "You're not in contact with her?" he asked. I said I hadn't seen her in years. And I didn't know where she was living. And my family didn't either.

He looked down at his folders. He rearranged them, reordered them, picked one up and tapped it against the table. "Do you remember the last time you did see her? Or your parents saw her?" "Not really," I said. "Okay," he said. He paused, unsure of how to proceed. He folded his arms over his stomach and leaned back in his chair. He pulled his arms apart and wove his fingers together. He looked up at the ceiling.

"But you know what happened," he said. "You were a witness to your sister's assault. Often that's more valuable in court than a statement from the actual victim."

My only interaction with the legal system in my adult life had been a *voir dire* for jury duty where I got excused by saying I had been abducted as a child. Everyone thought I was lying, and one of the lawyers laughed at the preposterousness of my claim. But the judge either took pity on me or didn't want to waste time asking me specifics, and she let me go. Now I squinted at the DA. I was confused and trying not to smile from nervousness. He was rewriting my story, or at least I think he was. I think he was asking me to lie, or to bend the truth, or to tell the truth as he wanted to hear it. Because I hadn't seen everything that happened to Eden. But it would be perfect for me to say I had. I felt like I had walked into an intricate role-playing game and didn't know how seriously we were playing. An actor in one of my plays once told me he got his Equity card by working at a Renaissance fair, and some people got way too into it, refusing to relinquish their Shakespearean accents at the end of the day for the van ride home.

"Would that be legal?" I asked.

"I was hoping we could help each other. I'm just a small-town district attorney trying to keep my community safe. That's what my concerns are. Here." He pushed one of the files over to me and it slid across the table. "That's a copy for you. Some information on the girl Larry grabbed who didn't get away. Was not much older than you were, but not near

as lucky. She's got a mama and a daddy and a sister too."
He stood up. "I'd very much appreciate it if you could get
in touch with your sister and tell her to give me a call." He
picked up the rest of his folders and walked out. The door
was left open and he said something to the receptionist,
leaning one elbow on the cubicle divider and crossing his ankles. He slapped his file folders against the side of his thigh.
Then he walked down the hall and disappeared into an office.

Outside, the sun was blinding. It was freakishly warm for
winter. I stared at the intersection. I crossed to the opposite
side and sat down on the bus stop bench. I had to wait almost
forty minutes for a bus to take me to another bus that could
return me to a Metro station so I could get back into the city.
The squat, square-shaped county office building stared back
at me, emotionless, from across the street.

I texted Noreen and said I was in DC and maybe we could
meet up. I wandered around town killing time until I heard
back from her. I ate a sandwich at a café near Dupont Circle.
Next to me, a power lunch was in session. A young guy was
doing all the talking. He worked for a think tank. It sounded
like it was about education, but I couldn't be sure. It might
have been about technology. Or technology in education. He
knew a lot of people. He wanted to network. He's probably younger than me, I thought. He probably doesn't consis-
tently roll over credit card debt. He's barely thirty and probably owns a condo. "We're about helping people," he said to
his new connection.

———

I pulled open the glass doors of Noreen's office suite, which was located not far from the tourist strip of the Hard Rock Cafe and Madame Tussauds wax museum, a fact I found strangely fitting for Noreen as a recent transplant from New York. I didn't say anything to the clean-cut interns in khaki pants earning their college credits. I could tell they debated stopping me and asking if they could help. I was wearing jeans and boots and Eden's old leather jacket. I was out of place among the novice career climbers of nonprofit corporate culture. They probably thought I was a messenger. Or a case study. Or Noreen's pot dealer.

Noreen waved me into her glassed-in office and motioned for me to close the door. She was talking on the phone and didn't miss a beat of her conversation, which had something to do with "impending legislation." She wore an earpiece and typed quickly on the computer as she talked. At one point, someone knocked on the door and delivered papers, which Noreen eyeballed while her associate stood there, waiting for approval.

When she finally got off the phone, she came around and hugged me. Then she returned to sit behind her desk. "How are you?" she asked. "How'd everything go at your mom's?"

"Fine. Her friend took care of most of it."

"Oh, that's right," Noreen said. "Gail emailed me." Noreen still kept in touch with my family, a fact I found annoying.

Noreen began clicking something on her computer. Her eyes scanned the screen. "How's your dad?"

I could tell Noreen didn't really care what my answers were. She was only asking questions to keep me occupied while she finished whatever it was she had to do. "He's fine. He has a new girlfriend," I said.

"Of course," Noreen said. "What are you working on these days? Do you have a new play coming up?"

"I'm sort of in between projects right now," I said. I didn't want to talk about my writing with Noreen and I hoped she took the hint. I looked over at the windowsill next to her desk that was filled with framed pictures. When Noreen and I lived together, we had an apartment with an old nonworking fireplace. It had been bricked up long before we moved in, but the crumbling ornate mantel was still there. Noreen framed photos of us and sprinkled them across the mantel, in front of books on bookshelves, on top of the stereo speakers. Noreen and I were together for almost eight years. Right after we broke up she had a whirlwind romance, got married, got inseminated, got pregnant, and got a killer job in DC. It had been only two years, but already there were more pictures of her new wife and the baby than there ever were of me. And this was just her office.

Noreen gave a final triumphant tap on her keyboard. She stood up and said, "Let's go out."

We walked a few blocks to the Mall and sat down on a bench in front of the National Gallery. Across the grass, a double line of schoolkids trailed toward the Smithsonian's Air and Space Museum. A teacher waited for the stragglers to catch up to the group. "Let's go!" she shouted a couple of times, wheeling her arm in the direction she wanted them to move, but the kids refused to pick up their pace.

"How's your dad?" Noreen asked me again. She didn't remember asking me in her office. "He's fine," I answered. "Oh, that's right," she said. She laughed a little and shook her head. "You told me. He has a new girlfriend."

Noreen stretched her legs out in front of her and crossed

her ankles. She had nice shoes. Nicer than she could have afforded when we were together. And fancier than she would have worn at her old job as a social worker. ("I can't look too nice or people will think I look down on them. And I can't look too schlumpy or they'll comment on it and it'll be a distraction. I have to look very neutral.") But now she had to look like she could handle large financial donations for the protection of reproductive rights.

She pulled her feet back under the bench. "Everything okay with him? Or is this just a random guilt visit?"

"No," I said. I hesitated to tell Noreen what was going on because she had a way of co-opting my ideas. Once you told her an idea or a possible plan, you were committing to it, and she would follow up on it and hound you about it, even if it was the vaguest of inklings in your head. I learned to keep quiet around her, which didn't work either. She felt that I didn't share enough. That she wasn't included enough in my life. That I didn't think what she had to contribute was important. It would surprise most people who knew Noreen to hear that she was that insecure. Everyone always thought it would be Noreen who broke up with me, and not the other way around.

"I think I'm going to try and find Eden," I said. Noreen raised her eyebrows and said, "Huh," with seemingly little interest. I relayed what happened with the DA, and Noreen folded her arms across her chest. Her sunglasses rested halfway down her nose. She stretched her legs out again and looked at her feet. "I don't know why you would bother doing that," she said, "but I've never been a big fan of the myth of Eden." She turned and looked at me. I didn't know what Noreen wanted from me. I happened to be in town and I thought maybe we could have a simple coffee or lunch and she could give me some advice, since she knew the whole story and had some experience dealing with the legal system from her social worker days. It wasn't my intention to give her an opportunity to subtly undermine me and talk me out of it.

"How do you intend to find her?" Noreen asked. "Didn't you try to do that once before?"

"Not really," I said.

"But didn't you used to Google her every now and then?"

"This is different," I said. The truth was, other than deep Internet sleuthing, I had no idea how to find Eden. I had never once gotten an email from her. As far as I knew, she had never had an email address. My previous searches never turned up anything. I assumed finding Eden would involve trying to find her old friends or asking at her old commune, both approaches probably futile and fruitless. And Noreen already knew this.

"It seems to me that sometimes you use Eden as a way of not getting on with your life. Like you fetishize her. I'm not saying you fetishize what happened when you were kids. In fact, I think you've done remarkable work on yourself getting beyond that. But there is something about Eden that holds you back. Or that you hold on to. Maybe it's because Eden never got over it. Or who knows if she did or she didn't, since she's elected to be incommunicado." Noreen tucked a wisp of hair behind her ear. "I got to hand it to her, she really has a sweet setup. I'd love to have that kind of freedom. And that humongous sense of self-importance."

I tried to play it down. "She probably has a normal life," I said. "She's probably just not on the Internet."

Noreen's phone buzzed. She dug it out of her purse. "It's in-

teresting," Noreen said, squinting at the screen and quickly text-
ing something, "because I've been thinking a lot about Eden
lately. About you and Eden. Maybe it's because of my job and
that we just started this new program for at-risk youth. Not
that you or Eden were what we call at-risk." She finished her
text and dropped her phone back in her bag. She pursed her
lips, which she did when she was thinking about how to say
something. "You had middle-class parents, you weren't hungry or abused, but your parents were rather uninterested in
your lives. Especially Eden's mom. It's a lot for a kid to digest,
you know, the fact that they are a burden to their parents. Everyone's a burden to their parents, I guess. I don't mean you
were a burden in terms of money or school or childcare. I
mean, maybe you were, but I think you and Eden were a burden to your parents because you were a burden to their identities. It's like they had children before they knew who they
were or what they wanted. Before they even thought about
whether they wanted children or not. Everything just happened, and now they can never make an objective, honest decision about it. And they have to deal with that. Unless, of
course, you're Eden's mom and you just drop your baby off
with a kind stranger."

"My mom wasn't a stranger," I said. I knew I shouldn't engage with her on this, but I couldn't help myself. "It wasn't
like that."

"Suddenly you're defending your family?"

"I'm trying to do the right thing, that's all. I'd rather not
lie in court."

Noreen pushed her sunglasses up on top of her head.
"What would happen," she said, "if you didn't look for Eden?
If you simply accepted the fact that you're never going to see

her again?" Noreen looked at me, expecting a response. She widened her eyes and jutted her chin to get me to say something.

"Maybe it's something I have to do for my own moral code," I said. "To feel I did the right thing in this situation."

Noreen sighed and turned back to the grassy expanse of the Mall. "Your moral code has nothing to do with it. That DA wants to make a career move and he wants you to do the work for him. He took a shot in the dark, you answered, and he got lucky. He's not going to let go of you now. You walked into that one. You should've told me about it before you went."

Another group of schoolkids crossed toward the Washington Monument. Sullen teenagers slumped from the weight of their backpacks. They moved twice as slowly as the elementary kids skipping in the opposite direction.

"I just feel like you allow yourself to get hung up on Eden," Noreen said. "It prevents you from getting on with your life. And it doesn't have to." Her phone buzzed from inside her purse, but she didn't bother to retrieve it. She hugged her purse tightly to her body, trying to smother the interruption. "I should probably get back," she said. She slipped her hands under her breasts. "I have to pump."

I walked with her back to her office building. The conversation changed to chitchat about people we knew in New York and how Noreen's cat was adjusting to the baby. She stopped me on the corner and pointed me toward the Metro. We hugged goodbye. Noreen's hugs were both strangely clingy and light, and I was always the one who moved away first.

"I'm sorry about your mom," she said. "Remember, you have friends. Don't isolate yourself. I know you do that." She had her sunglasses back on and I couldn't see whatever look she was giving me. If it was concern or pity or some remnant of love. We both turned and walked in opposite directions.

On the Metro I flipped through the folder the DA had given me. The girl in the other case had just turned eighteen. She was a senior in high school and lived with a foster family. She wasn't from around my dad's area but from someplace near Chesapeake. She had been in town visiting a friend on her own. It was unclear how she got there, because she didn't have a driver's license. She was last seen at a shopping mall, leaving with a man in a truck. She had six foster siblings, and her foster parents didn't report her missing for three days. And since she was eighteen, she wasn't considered a juvenile. It happened a couple of years before me and Eden.

The DA included the girl's obituary in the file. It described her life with her foster family, how she babysat all of her little foster siblings, how they all went to church regularly, how she sang in the youth choir and volunteered in the community. As if being abandoned or an orphan was an idyllic life.

The police speculated that the girl's body had been dumped in a wooded area and that her assailant assumed she was dead, or nearly so. She had been stripped to her underwear as we had. She had been sexually assaulted. The night before she was found, the temperature dropped and it was very cold. The girl somehow made it to her feet and walked through the freezing woods in only her underwear. She was close to a highway. She was found on the sloping embankment where she had crawled out of the drainage ditch on the side of the road, one arm reaching forward toward the pavement. She died of exposure. She had almost made it.

I wondered why I had never heard the story of this girl, but my dad lived in the rural no-man's-land that wasn't covered by the DC or the Richmond papers. I wondered if the DA back then just wanted Larry off the street, in prison, and used our case, since there were two people who could testify and that's why Larry pled guilty to kidnapping.

The girl smiled at me from a photocopy of her senior-year portrait. She had worn a plaid button-down shirt for the occasion. She smiled in front of a marbled background; a tiny gold cross peeked through from where her top button was unbuttoned. Her hair looked shiny and clean.

6

After she left my mom's house with Suriya, Eden moved out to a commune about an hour or so from where my dad lived. For the rest of high school I saw her only occasionally. If it were up to Eden, I wouldn't have seen her at all. Eden was busy. She was trying to live. She didn't have time to make the rounds to visit me and the various parents, and maybe she didn't want to. So I always visited Eden, and Eden never visited me. She sort of apologized. She said the whole purpose of living in an alternative community was to be intentionally alternative and not beholden to the outside world, and she included me as part of the outside world.

Her teacher Eric, the guy my dad punched, moved to the commune too. Eden didn't tell me that directly, but I saw him hanging out in the little town where Eden and I would arrange to meet. I assumed she didn't want my dad to know about him and that's why she never mentioned it. I didn't know if he was her boyfriend or not.

"Thought I would come see you," I wrote in a letter, "because I'm leaving for college soon. I'm moving to New York." Visitors weren't allowed on the grounds of Eden's commune. "It's not a commune, it's a community," Eden said the first time I met her out there. "It's not about being a tourist attraction for liberals who want to day-trip off the grid." "Sorry," I had said as we drove into town. "It's not a zoo," Eden said. "And there isn't really anything interesting to see. If you're really interested, I'll give you something to read." At the end of the hour Eden had allotted me at the local diner or library or park, I asked her for the reading materials. Instead of giving me a pamphlet, Eden wrote down a list of books. "There are some here I've read," I said. "Then read the ones you haven't read," Eden said. "It's always more telling what you haven't read, isn't it? Who cares what your favorite book is? It's the book you've never heard of that's important." She turned away from my car, not wanting a ride home, and walked off into the middle of nowhere.

I sent a follow-up to my letter with an exact date. I had a summer job and was leaving at the end of August and there wasn't a lot of time. A whole day was needed to try and see Eden, because it would depend on when she could get a free moment and if she had luck hitchhiking into town or had to walk all the way. I would wait where I always waited, by the small park square with the dry fountain, or in the diner, or at a table near the window in the tiny public library.

Eden didn't show up. I waited at the library until lunchtime and then went to the diner. Then I went back to the library. The librarian asked me to leave at seven. "We're open until eight," she said, "but only for returns and express check-out." Express checkout was a collection of battered trashy novels and the video collection that was kept behind the desk. A group of teenagers flipped through a binder of laminated movie covers trying to pick something out. A middle-aged guy plunked a pile of science-fiction novels on the counter.

It was still light out. I weighed my options in this small intersection that called itself a town. There was only a post office, which was now closed, a gas station with a convenience store about a block away, and on a side street, a store selling handmade crafts that looked abandoned. There was a church that I never saw anyone enter, but someone must stop by because the front lawn was neatly trimmed. I crossed the square back over to the diner.

There weren't many customers so I slid into a booth, claiming it for myself. The waitress put the same menu I had seen at lunchtime in front of me, along with a glass of ice water.

"You got a no-show?" the guy behind the counter asked. I smiled meekly. There was no way to hide it.

"Guess so," I said.

"From the commune place, right?" he asked.

"Yeah," I said.

"You know how to get there? I'll take you there if you want," said a customer at the counter. He was hunched over a bowl of soup. He had a baseball cap pulled over his forehead and his stringy goatee was slick with steam.

"I don't think they allow visitors," I said.

"Depends," he said as he slurped another spoonful. He reached for a napkin from the dispenser. His hands were shaky, as if he hadn't eaten for days. "Depends who you are and who you know." He wiped his mouth. "But I'll take you there. Not a problem."

I looked over at the man behind the counter. He met my eyes briefly and then looked down at the dishes he needed to bus. "Sure," I said to the other guy.

We walked out to the parking lot together. He told me his name was Steve and said I could follow him most of the way and then either we could walk in or he could drive. I said, "Isn't it easier if we just take your car?" He stopped and looked over at me, nervously nodding. "It's fine with me," I said, defusing any weirdness about it, "as long as you can drive me back here."

Most people must think that I have an aversion to getting into cars with people I don't know. That after what happened to me and Eden, I would never accept a ride from a stranger again, even if it was from someone as unthreatening as another kid's parent. But in reality, after what happened, I was more prone to accept rides from strangers, to get into cars with friends I knew were drunk, and to fool around with people I had just met and had no intention of ever seeing again. I was testing something, daring something, but I wasn't sure what.

Steve's car was dirty. It smelled like smoke. It had a kid's car seat in the back. He lit a cigarette before he got in, and after he pulled out of the parking lot, he took it out of his mouth and held it far out of the window. He asked if it bothered me, and I shook my head and said no. The sun was setting and the road was dark. He flicked on his high beams. A little stuffed elephant dangled from the rearview mirror.

"Ever been up there before?" he asked.

"No," I said. "She always told me to meet her in town."

"Yeah, they do that. That's their thing." He wound the steering wheel and the car turned off down a dirt road. We shook back and forth in our seats as the car descended a small hill. He slowed down to avoid deep ruts, winding the steering wheel with one hand.

"Do you live there?" I asked.

"Me? No." He didn't give any explanation other than that. We were quiet for the rest of the drive until he stopped the car in front of a gate. "This isn't their gate," he said. "But you gotta go through the neighbor's property to get there. There's no . . . what do you call it? When there's no road. No way in. They're boxed in by other properties."

He got out of the car to open the gate and rehitched it after we passed through. When he got back in the car he said, "I really shouldn't bring you up here, but I saw you were waiting all day and I know tomorrow they're all leaving."

"What do you mean?"

"Yeah," he said. "They're shutting down here for a while. Going somewhere else. Maybe Pennsylvania? They got some friends there. I don't know what it's about. But I thought, if you were trying to get in touch with someone, and you sent a letter tomorrow, they'd never get it."

We arrived at a second gate. He stopped the car. Up on a hill was a small farmhouse with porch lights on.

"Look," he said. "They're real particular. You should wait here and I'll go in and ask for you. And you know I can't promise if anyone will come out or not. Whoever you're looking for might have left already."

"I understand."

"Who you looking for again?"

"Eden," I said.

"And whom do I say is calling?"

"Hope."

He said, "Okay," and got out of the car. He walked to the gate and unhitched it just enough to slip to the other side. I heard him trudge through the grass as he disappeared into a black patch on his way up to the house. And then all I heard was the whir of late-summer insects.

I was conscious that I was leaning forward and looking intently over the dashboard. People can smell desperation on you, my friend Layla told me before I interviewed for a summer internship I didn't get. I leaned back in my seat and exhaled. I wished I smoked cigarettes at times like this. When you were trying to make like you didn't care.

I put one foot up on the dashboard. It was a junky car anyway.

A screen door slammed against a rickety wood frame. I fought the urge to sit up.

Steve was walking back down the hill with a woman. But I could tell, even from this far away, that it wasn't Eden. Too tall, too thin. When they made it to the front of the car, the two of them split up and each came around to a side door. The woman bent down to my window. It was the drag queen, Chrissy, who drove away with Eden and Suriya a few years before. She smiled at me.

"Hi," I said.

"Your friend's not there," Steve said as he got in the car.

"Where did she go?" I asked.

"We're all going to different places," Chrissy said. "I don't know what I can tell you. I only know where I'm going."

"Why is everyone splitting up?" I asked.

"Oh, that is a long story. I wish I had time to explain it."

"Are you going to be coming back here sometime later?"

Chrissy stood up and arched backwards, rubbing her sacrum with her hands. The shirt she was wearing rode up and exposed a strip of her belly. "Hmm," she said and looked up at the farmhouse. "That's a good question." She turned back to me. "I'm not sure," she said. "I hope so." She stared across the dark field. Then she leaned back down to the car window like it was causing her great effort to do so. "I'm sorry you came all this way."

I turned and looked through the windshield at the pool of light from the car's headlights. The hippie flip thing is like an *Alice in Wonderland* verbal riddle. They keep repeating the same thing with a look on their face like they are thinking deeper thoughts than you, until you finally hit on something that proves to them that you can think for yourself (or that you think like them) and that you aren't working for the feds or a cult deprogrammer. "All deprogrammers do is rape you and retraumatize you," Eden said to me once, right after she told me that if I ever showed up with someone, she would never talk to me again. I had forgotten about that when I accepted the ride.

"Could I leave a message?" I asked.

"Oh, sure," Chrissy said.

I didn't have anything to write with. I never carried a purse; purses felt ridiculous to me, something to slow you down. Whatever I couldn't fit in my pockets, I didn't need. Eden always had a sack with her. It was like her long hair. All these things used to create a cloud around her, to distract you from looking directly at her. Not long after the thing with Larry, I saw a movie on cable with a sex scene where the man held the woman down and then grabbed her long, loose hair and fucked her from behind. After that, I cut my hair very short. I liked how it made me look androgynous. I liked having nothing to hide behind, nothing to pin me down. I've had short hair ever since.

I didn't have a pen or a notebook or anything to write on. Neither did Steve. He rooted around the back seat, but only came up with a gnawed crayon.

Chrissy squatted down by the window. "Just tell it to me," she said. "I'll remember." She closed her eyes and had a holy smile. She wore eyeliner and was older than I thought she was. She looked like she expected me to kiss her.

"Tell her Hope came to talk to her. To see her. Because I'm moving to New York for college in a few weeks." I added the last part so Eden wouldn't take her usual glacial pace of getting back to me.

Chrissy opened her eyes and said, "Who couldn't use a little hope?" She stood up and shook my hand goodbye. I watched her go through the gate and walk up the hill. Steve stretched his arm over my headrest as he backed the car out of the dirt road until it was wide enough to turn around.

He drove me back to the town square and waited until he saw that my car started up. I knew he would. I have a knack for picking out nondangerous people. It's like I couldn't get into trouble if I tried. And I'm always a little let down by it.

7

ey, it's Hope," I said into my phone. It wasn't my dad
but his girlfriend, Beth. She perked right up. "Oh, hi!"
she said cheerily. Beth was always cheery. It was annoying. She tried too hard to be friends and never noticed my ob-
vious disinterest in her. I said I was coming to visit. Maybe
for a while. I said I had trouble with my apartment so I was
between places. I was already in DC. "Oh, that's great!" she
said. "Your dad is going to be so happy to see you. He got
some bad news recently and this will cheer him up." I asked
what it was, but Beth said, "Oh, I'm sure he'll tell you about
it when he sees you."

Beth asked me if I ate chicken. "You know your dad's supposed to cut down on salt." And then she prattled on about
something, something that was bad for the environment, or
someone who was unnecessarily rude to her at the store, or
someone who just didn't get it, whatever "it" was. With Beth,

either everything was astonishment that people had opinions that differed from hers, or everything was "just great," and "just great" included everything she didn't quite understand, or didn't understand enough to have an opinion about.

"Do you drink herbal tea?" Beth asked. She had made some from her garden. "I dry the plants myself and make different blends. I can make you your own blend if you want. You just have to tell me what you like in your tea. People tell me I should start a business with it, but I don't know. I'd have to get a website. It seems like a lot of work. But you never know." My dad's previous girlfriend had been a ceramist who had her own business and showed her work in galleries. She wanted to move to New Mexico and my dad did not, so she broke up with him. Beth always felt inferior, which she made up for by being really nice. The first time we met I asked her what she did. She said, "Oh, I'm just a person with a job. I'm not very interesting."

Beth went on about what she was going to plant this year and how she was going to start a lot of seedlings in the den because it got the most sun. "I think it will be really nice once spring gets here," she said.

My dad was waiting for me when I walked out of the Metro station at the end of the line in the Virginia suburbs. He leaned out of his car and waved his baseball hat so I could find him.

"Downsizing?" he asked, looking at my lack of luggage. I didn't answer. "How long are you staying?" he asked. "Not sure yet," I said. "I see," he said. He wore old jeans and new sneakers and an old sweatshirt that used to say something, but the design had flecked off. He shifted gears and his fingers rubbed the knob, itching for a cigarette he stubbed out two decades ago. I was making him nervous. This is every parent's nightmare. Their adult child returns home for an unspecified amount of time. With only a backpack. And no voiced plans.

"Shit," he said. He quickly turned his head, worried, and made an abrupt move into the turning lane. "Yeah, yeah." He waved off another car honking at him. "Sorry, I need to pick something up."

We pulled into a grocery store parking lot. "You want to stay here? I'll just be a sec." He didn't wait for my answer and was halfway out of the car when I said, "Sure." He hurried to the store. The automatic glass doors parted for him and exhaled as they sealed him inside.

I wondered if this was worth it. If instead I should've coughed up the money and looked online for a cheap hotel room. I knew my dad didn't know where Eden was, but he might know something. He might remember someone's name. My father never threw anything away. He still had The Camper. I didn't have enough money to rent a car. And to find Eden, wherever she was, I needed a car.

When he emerged from the store, he was carrying a bottle of wine in a brown paper bag and a pint carton of cream. He stopped to talk to someone on the curb and gestured loftily with the carton. His friend said, "Take care" and walked on. My father stood there for a moment, squinting into the distance. He shifted the wine to his other hand, dug into his pocket for his cell phone, and dialed a number. He put on his sunglasses, the kind with a Velcro band around the back, the sporty version of a librarian's spectacles on a chain hanging from her neck. He paced back and forth while he talked, cradling the wine and cream against his hip. Every now and then he would pause and look down at his feet, his whole body sagging into a curve.

He's avoiding me, I thought.

He finally got back in the car and hastily deposited his purchases at my feet.

"Okay," he said. "Sorry about that."

"Who'd you have to call?"

"Nobody," he said. "No one important." He jammed the brakes to avoid hitting a slow-moving shopper pushing a cart. He was about to yell obscenities but controlled himself enough to wave her on. "We might actually make it out of here alive," he said as we rolled to a short pause at the parking lot exit.

I never thought I made my father nervous, but he seemed unable to contain himself. He tapped on the steering wheel. He wiped his sunglasses at stoplights. He fiddled with the radio that never worked properly. He scrolled through his cell phone numbers while waiting for the light to change. And then he said, "Whenever you want to tell me what you're doing here, let me know."

"Really?" I said, too annoyed not to get sucked in. "I need a reason to visit you?"

"Oh, come on, Hope. You're dropping in out of the blue. You were just here for Christmas, which is the only time you visit. No one's sick. I'm not dying. Okay. I'm sorry. I'm sorry about your mother. But you knew for a long time it was terminal. I'm sorry if that seems unkind, or that I'm lacking in compassion for one of the mothers of my children, but you had some time to prepare. You knew the situation. Now, you tell Beth you've lost your apartment, and I assume your job,

or whatever you were doing for money. I think I deserve a little explanation."

"You've answered all your own questions. I really don't
have any more information to give you."

He rested his elbow on the edge of the window, steering
with one hand until it proved too awkward a position for him.
"What do you intend to do? Are you moving in with us while
you get back on your feet? Are you going to lie on the couch
all day and watch TV again? Get a job in the local lesbian
bar? I don't even know if there is one. Am I supposed to give
you money for doing chores around the house? Or maybe I'm
supposed to pay you for copyediting my book."

"What book?" My father hadn't published anything since
I was a kid.

"What do you mean, what book? I'm a writer. I'm working on a book. And they take a long time. And they require
quiet and intense concentration and not a lot of disruptions
to routine. I don't know, Hope. I thought you had an idea of
what you were doing with your life. You were involved in the
arts community. You got some play with your theater things.
You wrote a little here and there. I know some people don't
get any gigs, but you got some. You just never seemed able
to do anything with it. Or you never met the right people.
Everything is always just within your reach, Hope, but you
bail out before anything can happen. You switch what you're
working on. You quit your job. You decide you don't want to
be a filmmaker or a journalist or a playwright or whatever it
was. Just when you're about to get there, you drop the ball.
You know, I thought you had a niche. And it's smart to have
a niche. Then you can be the big fish in the small pond, even

when you're in an ocean like New York." He lifted both hands off the steering wheel in defeat and let them fall back down. "I don't know. I expected you would win an award or something by now."

"I did win an award," I said.

"I mean something else. Another award. Not just a first-timer, starting-out award."

"That's your marker for success? A display case of awards?"

"You have to mark it somehow. You have to determine whether you've failed or whether you're on the right track somehow. Okay, sure. It's petty and it's bourgeois, but yes, I think an award is a mark of success."

"Exactly which award was I supposed to have won by now?"

"Hey, I don't know, Hope. An award. A good review. A good paycheck. You fold that into a teaching job. Or editor. You get asked to do things. Fuck, I don't even know what I'm talking about because I don't know what you do or what you care about. If you cared so much about your plays or whatever, I think you would have sent them to us to read or invited us up to see them sometimes."

"Like you would come."

"I would. I would come."

"Suddenly you're going to be the supportive parent?"

"I've always supported you, Hope. I've always supported you. I've always encouraged you. I paid for college. I helped you—"

"Oh, I see, your mortgage on me is paid off."

"Hope, I didn't say that. But I think I have a right, yes, as a parent, but also as coadults here in this situation, I think I have a right to ask you what is going on with your life rather than just sucking it up and pretending that everything's okay. I know your mom just passed, and that was sad and she was too young and we're all still mourning her. She was a wonderful, beautiful, brutally honest woman and she was very important to me. She was your mother and she was a big part of my life. But you know, I was much younger than you when both my parents died, and life goes on. You have to go on, Hope. You have to go on." He paused for a moment and then jumped back in. "I mean, maybe I'm making too much of it all. Maybe I'm too involved or maybe I'm projecting too much onto you. Maybe you really don't have a very interesting life. Maybe you're just a zombie walking through the whole thing, in which case you probably need some therapy. You know, because you're not like other adults your age, Hope."

"No," I said. "I'm not."

"And don't go throwing that at me," he said. "I know the most horrible thing imaginable happened to you and Eden, but guess what? A lot of people have been through a lot worse and come out the other side. And don't think you're the only one who has ever experienced something like that. And don't think I don't know why you're really here. I know why you're here. I know you got the same call I did from some lawyer for the county, wanting to open the whole thing up again. And you know what? You're too late, because I already talked to him and told him to go fuck himself. You're not the only one involved in this situation, Hope. You know, out of everyone involved, everyone in this hodgepodge family of ours, out of all of us, you got off easy, Hope." He was gesturing wildly with his hands and almost missed turning into his own driveway. He swung hard and the car jostled over the gravel and up the incline. "You know, don't think it wasn't hard for me, don't think I haven't suffered every day of my life thinking that I'm a failure as a father, that I couldn't protect you, that I fucked up. Because I did, Hope. I fucked up. I was supposed to be there to pick you up and I wasn't. And I'm sorry. You know, I'm sorry."

My father was crying now. He turned off the engine and opened the door to get out of the car as fast as possible, but he forgot the groceries at my feet. He climbed back inside and herded them into his arms, his sunglasses falling off his face and dangling there around his neck, caught by their Velcro strap. He slammed the car door and marched up to the house.

Beth was out on the deck. "Hey!" she called as I got out of the car and stood up. "Great to see you!"

My father shook his head as he passed her.

"I want to borrow the van," I said before he got inside. He stopped in his tracks and sank a bit. He looked at me and said, "The Camper?" like I was asking to borrow his prized toy. I was the grade school bully. I would take it and never give it back and he didn't have the power to say no. He didn't know what to say. He stood hurt, his mouth agape, before turning to go inside.

Beth looked at me quizzically, but did her best to stay upbeat. She peeked in the window, trying to assess my dad's state, if he wanted to be alone or not. I got my bag out of the back seat.

When I closed the car door my father came back outside, walking so fast his ankle got caught on the edge of the screen door, which hadn't opened wide enough yet. He stumbled and immediately got back up, determined not to slow down.

He extended his arm out in front of him, offering me the keys but not wanting to touch me. He wanted me to go away. He was worried I might bite. I took the keys from his fingers. He dropped his arm, then turned around and said, "I can't promise that it'll start. If it breaks down, I'm not responsible. I don't want to be involved with whatever it is you're doing."

He marched into the house and Beth followed him. I wondered if he wanted me to get in The Camper and drive off right then and there. But it was late and I didn't have a plan, so I went inside the house.

My father was behind the kitchen island counter pouring himself a shot of vodka. Beth was unsure how to approach him. She stayed on the other side of the counter. The drinking of hard liquor repulsed and scared her. He drank half the shot, coughed, and then drank the rest. He poured another and screwed the top back on the bottle.

"I need to find her," I said.

"Let her go, Hope," he said, not looking up from his glass. He stared at the clear liquid, unsure if he really wanted it. "She's a ghost." He took a sip and put the vodka bottle back in the freezer, still avoiding my eyes. "She lives on another planet. She never came out of the woods, so to speak, if I may use such a terrible metaphor. About my own child." He took hold of his glass again. His body hunched over it, awkwardly swaying over the kitchen sink.

"Maybe I just want to find her because I want to find her. She's my sister."

"She's my daughter. Don't you think I want to find her too?"

I know it's incredibly immature, but I always felt that my dad loved Eden more than me. Sometimes it seemed like my mother was our common parent and Eden was the only one who belonged to our dad.

"What about the other case?" I asked. "They could connect him to another case if she provided some evidence. Then he wouldn't get out of jail."

"What makes you think she has evidence to give?" He took another sip and wiped his mouth with the back of his fingers. "Maybe nothing's there. Maybe she said everything that happened to her and there's nothing else to tell."

"I guess that would be easier for you."

"That would be easier for Eden. Do you wish she suffered more? Does that make you feel better in some twisted way? I'm sorry." He put out his free hand like a stop sign. A retraction. He closed his eyes. He dropped his hand. His mouth started to torque into a grimace. "It would be easier for me. It was my fault, Hope," he said, making a grand sweep with his vodka glass to cover his sloppy emotions. "It was *my fault*," he said again. But he couldn't keep up the act. He grasped his face with his free hand and started to sob in retching cries. "I got the weekends mixed up," he said in a high-pitched voice that was out of his control. It sounded womanly and in pain. It seared out of his body, scorching wounds as it went. "I was at this stupid party. It was a reception for Woodward's new book and a lot of people were going to be there and I thought it would be a good opportunity to approach his agent because mine had just retired and no one had picked me up. I was going to be left out in the cold. I needed to go to that party and get my name back out there. I completely forgot. It was just a mistake." He was gasping now and losing his breath. "I should've been there." He turned his shielded face away from me, toward Beth. She reached out to hug him, but he pushed past her, setting his glass on the counter and then accidentally knocking it to the floor as he left the kitchen. Beth reached down to pick it up and followed him out.

I stayed upstairs in my and Eden's old room until I heard the car start up. Out the window I saw them drive to the main road. I crept down to the kitchen, where a note was left for me in Beth's handwriting saying they went out for dinner, but there was plenty of stuff in the fridge. She signed the note with a heart and a B.

I was back in my room when they came home. I expected my father to come up the stairs and softly knock. One of us would say, "I'm sorry," and the other would say, "I'm sorry too," and we wouldn't talk much more about it. Noreen and I would always have long-drawn-out emotional discussions or fights or misunderstandings that wouldn't resolve until one of us was crying, the other one teared up too, and then we had sex. And what the whole fight was about in the first place or how it was actually resolved, I couldn't tell you.

My father didn't stop in. He came upstairs with Beth, two sets of shoes thumping up the steps, past my room, and into their bedroom. I heard the faint sounds of a TV talk show and bathroom water running.

My dad had written a magazine article about what happened to me and Eden, but, according to him, "they edited the fuck out of it." It came out about a year after it happened, around the time Eden took off in the car with Suriya. He tried to parlay the article into a book, but got no takers. An editor told him that the story needed more of him in it. "If you somehow saved the girls, or went after the kidnapper, or nursed them back to life from a subsequent drug habit, that would've been good." The story needed something like that, the editor said.

I once temped for that same editor, purely by chance. On my first day, she stared at my name and then asked me if I was related to my dad. When I said I was his daughter, I watched her face as she remembered the story. She looked at me, half in awe that a person who had been through something like that was standing in her office in cheap career clothes from a thrift store trying to look "nice," and half pitying me that obviously I had never gotten it together to be successful and was working a temp job because I had been so traumatized. She bought me lunch later that week and told me that if I ever wanted to write about "the event," as she called it, she would be happy to read it, and that she thought it would make a great book. I never told my father that. I never told him I had worked for her.

The next morning, I woke up around six. I decided I didn't want any more confrontations. My bag was still packed. I slung it over my shoulder and went outside.

When my dad used to pick us up at the bus station, he always came in The Camper. Sometime after Eden took off, he finally got a new car. But he never sold The Camper. It stood in the carport my father had cobbled together out of a falling-down old barn. He only parked The Camper under it, never a car, and when the structure finally collapsed, he would probably leave it there, entombed.

I unlocked the driver's door and climbed in. The seat was almost the size of an armchair. I had to slide it all the way forward to reach the pedals. The stick shift stood at attention and looked like it would take two hands to move. I stooped into the main area of The Camper and shoved open all the curtains. There were two butterscotch vinyl couches that faced each other like a booth in a diner. A table between them hinged up and stabilized with a single pole leg. That was where Eden and I sat and played games or did home-work on long rides. Next to the sliding side door was a sink that never worked and a small refrigerator that was basically a built-in cooler. I climbed over the second couch into the way-back, the area that would be my bed, and tied up the curtains so I could see out the rear window.

My father opened the side door as I crawled back over the couch. "How's inspection going?" he asked. "Fine," I said. He took a sip from his coffee mug. I pulled aside the last curtain, next to the passenger seat, and sat behind the wheel. "I don't know what kind of gear is still in here," he said. "You can use whatever you find. Might be a raincoat or something in there. Do you need a tent?" "No," I said. He looked down into his coffee. "Is there a sleeping bag in there for you?" He didn't wait for me to answer. He put his free hand on the edge of the nonworking sink and hoisted himself inside. He knelt on the couch and peered in the back. "Yeah, there is. We used to use two, but I guess you can use just one. Can't say how clean it is." He backed off the couch and squatted on the floor. He set aside his coffee mug and opened a storage compartment un-derneath the couch. He got down on his hands and knees to search inside. I looked at him in the rearview mirror. He was wearing a washed-out denim shirt and an old pair of jeans. He pulled out a couple of plastic tubes. Then he dragged out a long green sack with metal poles clanking together inside. He stood up with his find. "I think this is a chair," he said. "If you need it." He tossed it on the couch. He reached down, swiped his coffee mug off the floor, and walked up to the front. He sat in the passenger seat and balanced the mug on his lap.

"Kind of strange," he said after a quiet minute. He pointed at me. "I'm used to being in that seat." He opened the black plastic glove compartment and sorted through the papers inside. "Oh, this'll be useful," he said, flapping an owner's manual from the seventies at me. "In case you break down. Some younger mechanics probably won't know what to do." He smushed the papers back inside. "Everything's there," he said.

I put the key in the ignition and tried to start it up. It wheezed a bit and didn't do much. My father laughed. "I warned you," he said. It did the same thing a second time. "Got it in neutral?" he asked. "Yes, I have it in neutral," I said. "I know how to drive." "Well, it's stick. When's the last time you drove stick?" I didn't say anything. "Maybe the engine's dry and it needs a little gas. Just pump it a few times before you start it again, but don't flood it."

It finally started. The gearshift was so hard to move I thought it might snap off. I got it into reverse and started to back out. My father said, "Hang on," jumped out, and pulled the sliding door shut. He came back around to the passenger door and put his hand on the seat, as if he was going to climb aboard and go along with me on a father-daughter road-trip adventure. Then he realized he had walked into a fantasy and took a step back, leaning his weight away from The Camper, stretching his arms out between the door and the frame, not wanting to let go of his prized motor vehicle, or maybe not wanting to let go of me, whether I was prized or not. The engine percolated beneath me. The monster van vibrated violently. The Camper didn't like standing still; it felt like it would cut out at any moment. You were either coming along or you weren't, but The Camper wasn't going to wait. My father let his eyes fall to the dusty black floor under the glove compartment. Then he looked up at me and said, "Okay" and shut the door. He kept a hand on the outside and then gave it a few pats and let go. I backed the van out the rest of the way and turned it to face the driveway. My father followed my path with slow steps, never drifting far from the passenger window. I shifted into first and it stalled. My father dropped his head and laughed to himself.

"Try it again," he said. It started right away, huffing and bubbling like a dune buggy. My father walked slowly around the front to my side. I rolled down the window. "Do you have any idea where I can find Suriya?" I asked. "Do you still keep in touch with her?" He smiled. "I see Suriya now and then," he said. "You might find her over at Piney Cove. It's sort of a farm retreat. A lot of artists. It's a couple hours from here. Sometimes she camps out there before she leaves for India. But usually"—he grinned and looked down at his cup—"Suriya finds you. I was out in the yard one day, and when I turned around, there was Suriya. The first time Beth stayed over, Suriya knocked on the door in the middle of the night. Scared Beth half to death."

The Camper cut out again. I shifted and restarted the engine.

"I hope it's okay to drive," he said. "Guess you'll find out." "Guess so," I said. He took his wallet out of his back pocket and held his coffee mug against his body with one arm. He pulled out his AAA card and gave it to me. "Always good to have, just in case," he said. "Thanks," I said. He slipped his wallet back into his jeans pocket. He reached through the open window and put his hand on my shoulder, sort of clamping it. He shook my shoulder a few times and then released me with a few pats, the way, I imagined, fathers said goodbye to sons. He turned around and walked back toward the house. In the rearview mirror I saw him dump out the rest of his coffee on the driveway gravel.

8

I would have missed the turn for Suriya's compound had there not been a bouquet of deflated balloons drifting off a signpost. It marked a teasingly paved road that ended in dirt as soon as you couldn't see the way out anymore. The road bumped you downhill and around a bend, then opened up to a large dirt patch next to a meadow. On one side stood a modern house with solar panels and a gated driveway with a stern NO TRESPASSING sign. On the other was a sprawling clapboard house with many additions and trim painted a mismatched rainbow of colors. There were cars parked in two clusters on either end of the muddy lot, as if the two parties wanted nothing to do with each other. I headed toward the ramshackle property, which seemed more like Suriya's kind of place.

An old dead tree in the yard had several hooks hammered into it. Large pots and pans sprouted as stainless steel branches and leaves that shined in the sun.

I walked around and opened a door and popped my head inside. "Hello?" I called at an uncommitted volume. I always felt self-conscious walking into an empty house that wasn't mine. People in the country do this all the time. My father did this too, leaving notes on someone's kitchen counter when he stopped by. I asked him why he did that. He said, "Wouldn't you want to know if someone had been in your house? It's polite," he said, though politesse didn't concern him in most other situations. I stepped inside and called out again, "Hello?" No answer.

I circled the outside of the house and found a path. I walked by a wrecked, wintered-over vegetable garden, a field of dead grass, a few droopy tents. The path took me into the woods. I passed some barrels for collecting rainwater or concocting home brews. There were sheds professing to be workshops, with the cutesy-cozy hand lettering you see at coffee shops.

The path delivered me to a flooded quarry. THE EMERALD CITY, a sign proclaimed, which also said, SWIM AT YOUR OWN RISK. There was a shed near the embankment, and I thought I heard voices coming from inside. It oozed smoke. Or steam. It fogged from its cracks like a giant ice cube made of rapidly defrosting wood. Another hand-lettered sign said, IF YOU LIVED IN THE MERRY OLD LAND OF OZ, YOU'D BE HOME BY NOW.

I went up to knock, but before my knuckles landed on the door, it swung open, nearly knocking me over. A naked guy leaped out, his furry body hair slicked down with sweat. He ran toward the quarry followed by a handful of people whooping and sweating, odoriferous and cooked slightly

pink. Steam was sucked out of the hut. I wasn't sure if anyone had seen me, and if they did, I doubt my presence was
alarming. They were jumping and skipping to the ice-cold
quarry pond. High on high temperatures. All naked. All different body types. At the back of the pack I saw Suriya's
short, round form scurrying to keep up, her long, rough hair
streaked gray in irregular patterns, not quite long enough to
cover her bare ass.

"Suriya," I called out, and I couldn't help laughing, finding her like this. She turned around, naked except for the
necklaces she always wore. She let out a little yelp, hopped
over, and slapped me on the shoulder. Then she turned back
around and caught up with her mates. She ran out on a
wooden plank diving board and cannonballed into the water.

Everyone hooted and howled. Exhilarated. In awe of nature. Of the sensations of having a body. They cawed at the
afternoon setting sun. At the emerald-green pine trees that
must give this place its name. One guy swam to shore and
pulled himself out. I couldn't help looking at his penis, which
was considerably shrunken by the cold. He saw me looking
and smiled, like it was so funny that it could be so small. He
ran toward the main building, his wet feet padding against the
dirt path. The rest of the gang reached a consensus that they
should get out too. "Dip's over," someone said. "Don't let
yourself cramp up." And they all came ashore. They hurried
over to the side of the shed, wrapped themselves in blankets,
and picked clothing from leafless bushes. Suriya squeezed the
water out of her long hair. She coiled a sweatshirt around
her head as a turban and threw a blanket over her shoulders. "Hope," she said, appearing rather regal in her getup.
"Come."

The group walked toward the house. A bonfire was lit in the yard. Suriya led me over to sit on a log. "This is Hope," she said to the group. "One of my daughters," she added, rubbing my back. "Hi, Hope," the group sang in response, like a trippy, outdoorsy AA meeting. More people gathered around, not just the ones who had gone skinny-dipping. Clothed, dry people. A young, tall guy with bushy, grown-out hair had a big laugh. An older guy doffed his blanket and put on a cap, air-drying the rest of his naked body in the fire's warmth. Someone lit up a joint.

"Okay," Suriya said, stepping over the log and sitting down. "I ask you all the usual questions. How are you? How are things? How's your mom? How's your dad? How's New York? How's love and life? And you say back, 'Fine.'"

I opened my mouth, unsure of what to say. Suriya looked at me out of the corner of her eye as if I had not gotten the joke. She elbowed me in jest. "You know, my mom just passed away," I said.

Suriya squinted at me. "The cancer," she said. "Nasty business. I'll miss her." She looked back at the fire. "When your time's up, your time's up. Her spirit's here, though. Heh, probably telling me not to believe in spirits. She was a bossy one, your mom. I was going to go see her out there next summer. Good soul. She fought the good fight." Suriya put an arm around my shoulders and hugged me to her. "You still got me," she said and laughed. "You came all the way here to tell me that?"

"I need to find Eden," I said.

Suriya closed her eyes for a moment and thought on the matter. "I don't know where she is. Wish I did. No." She scrunched her brow, eyes still shut. "That was reflexive," she said. "I don't need to know where she is. I'm guessing she doesn't want me to know. I hope she's happy and well and all good. That's my wishing." She opened her eyes and turned to face me, proud of her rationale. "What good would it do me or her, knowing where she is? What would be different?"

"It would be easier for me at the moment," I said, trying to make a joke.

Suriya smiled. Maybe a little disappointed with me for not going deeper. "It's hard being a parent. Most kids these days don't know left from right," she said. "Can't take a shit without it being scheduled and don't know how to wipe their own behind. As you can hear, I worked in a school recently." She gave me a strict look, warning me never to take up this occupation. "Just all so desperate, those moms and dads. And for what? To get into some college. To cheat on a test. To have a chance. That's what they all said to me. All the parents. 'I just want him to have a chance. The best chance.' Can you imagine? They had no idea who their kids were. I tried to say, You know, kids are like flowers. You water them a little and watch them grow. A flower knows intrinsically, internally, instinctively how to grow. You see what happens. See if the plant can figure it out. Find the sun. Of course they would be horrified to learn what my kids are up to."

"Thanks a lot," I said.

Suriya laughed. "I'm gossiping," she said. "That's not good. Anyway, I'm not doing that job now. I didn't do it for very long."

There was a slight breeze and the flames licked toward us. The smoke started blowing our way. Suriya waved it back with a blanketed arm. Eden always flaunted that she was part Native American on Suriya's side, and Suriya looked more that way as she had aged. Or maybe it was this setup. Sitting around a fire.

"It reminded me too much of being a mother," Suriya said. I must've looked confused because she added, "That job." Suriya unwound the sweatshirt from her head and slipped it on, reaching her arms through the long sleeves and pulling it down over her naked breasts. She resituated the blanket as a toga skirt around her hips and shook out her damp hair. "That was a big decision for me. When I took off and left your dad. I didn't want to be a wife or mother anymore. I went on the road. And when I say on the road, I mean *on the road*. Hitchhiking. Riding the rails. Digging for food. Trying to stay safe, looking for like-minded people. Trying to find a temple of enlightenment, which is hard to do in this country. That's why, when someone said, Try India, I went on over. Collected a lot of recycling cans and bought a ticket."

Suriya laughed.

"I can't say there was more enlightenment in India, but if you wanted to find it, there was more of a structure to help you out. Which has its goods and its bads. Beautiful there, though. Beautiful people. Lots of poverty. So much more than you can imagine. You come back from there with an awareness of privilege. Even when you think you have such a hardscrabble life here, there it's something else. It's strange. So many beautiful colors there, though. That's what I always try to take back with me. All the colors.

"Maybe Eden's like me." Suriya shook her head and touched her forehead lightly with her hand. "You try so hard not to be a mother. To just let your kids come through you and not stamp your identity on top of them. But part of you always claims them. And someone out there can claim you. Frightening, isn't it?" She looked at me. I didn't say anything. "Some people like it that way. They feel less alone. I didn't care so much about being alone or not, I just wanted to feel like me. I didn't want anyone to have to depend on me, and I didn't want to depend on anyone. That was what I was out to accomplish. You know"—she gestured toward the fire with an arm—"maybe Eden's trying to free herself from all that."

Suriya picked up some dirt and tossed it into the fire. "Events can be like families. Places can be that way too. Everything can be a person trying to claim you. I think Eden had a revelation similar to mine. I didn't want to be a wife and mother. And Eden didn't want to be Eden, the girl who all that happened to."

"You want to try?" A young woman with wet hair in strings stuck to her face slid between me and Suriya with a stack of earthenware cups and crouched down. Suriya took one. "Try it," the woman said to me. Her eyes were very wide. She gave me an empty cup. "It's wine. He made it." She stood back up and walked around the circle. The tall, bushy-haired guy came around with a pitcher. He poured us each a glass, then bowed like a waiter and ducked out. I got the feeling he didn't speak English.

The wine was very fruity. Way too sweet. I wanted to tell Suriya about the other kidnapping case, with the girl who died, but then I thought, She doesn't want to know. That's the way Suriya wanted it. That was her freedom.

Someone lit a torch from the bonfire. A small group scurried out into the meadow. They ran past the torch holder, disappeared into the darkness, and reappeared carrying giant papier-mâché hands on sticks. They swayed the puppet

hands left and right and twirled around. Someone near the
fire started banging on bongos. An older woman, around Suriya's age, played a recorder. She got up to dance along as
she played, picking up her feet and pointing them balletically
in different directions, prancing a few steps like a faun. One
of the giant puppet hands got a little too close to the torch.
"Oh! Watch out!" a girl said and brought her hands to both of
her cheeks. She laughed and gasped and clasped her hands in
front of her chest. I think she was high.

The puppeteers organized themselves into a semicircle.
The group faced the house, shook their giant papier-mâché hands, and chanted. A young woman emerged from the
doorway and someone swooped in and picked her up. She
shrieked. She was carried by three or four people working
to keep her aloft as she surfed above the crowd. The puppet
hands followed her around the meadow, peeling out of their
line in a massive version of the Virginia reel. Someone said,
"Hello, home!" Everyone around the fire got up and walked
into the field, repeating, "Hello, home!" Suriya kissed the
top of my head and joined them. She waved at me to follow
her. I wandered into the revelry that swayed and chanted and
hopped up and down. The group lurched toward the main
building. When the front of the pack reached the doorstep,
the bongos guy yelled out, "Welcome home!" and everyone
plunged inside. The current carried me indoors. People were
jumping around me, touching me, hugging me happily as
they dashed around the house, not going anywhere in particular, but only interested in touching doors and windows and
ceilings if they could reach them. As if the group itself was
a gust of fresh air blowing through the communal dwelling.
Maybe that was the point of it all.

I found Suriya back outside, exchanging the blanket wrapped around her waist for a loose pair of pants. She turned around and saw me as she was pulling up her pants. Suriya never wore underwear. "First thing any of us ever saw," she said, gesturing to her bush.

I cringed and looked at the ground. Suriya laughed at my modesty, or the modesty I wished she had. "It's safe to look now. You're safe from Oedipus or Electra or Doctor Freud," she said. "At least I can still put a smile on your face. Come on." She led me to an old trailer hidden behind the main house. Inside, a bed took up most of the space. A hole was drilled into the ceiling for the smokestack of a tiny wood stove. Her hovel smelled of mildew. Suriya pulled out a box from underneath the bed, lit an oil lamp, and put on glasses. She looked much older now.

"Someone who used to live here knew Eden when she was a kid. Well, you know, not a kid, but younger. Years ago, when she was living on that farm. He helped out around here sometimes too. He was a doctor who did a lot of community work. Gave us a deal. We could pay him in chicken eggs. He might know where she's been. But you'll have to find him yourself." She took a large envelope out of the box and dumped its contents on the bed quilt. She picked through business cards and scraps of paper. "He gave me his card last time he was here. Was years ago. I kept it. You never know when you might need a doctor friend. Here." She handed me a business card. *Dr. Marshall Westmoreland,* it said. Other than his grand southern name, it only had an email address. "He's on the Internet," Suriya said. "I guess that's the place to be."

Suriya offered to share her bunk with me. I told her I had driven The Camper and could sleep in there. "That old girl's still running?" She cackled. "It's getting cold. I got a wood stove in here, what do you have?" she asked. "A sleeping bag," I said. "Well, if you get too cold, you can sleep on the floor in the big room. Why don't you just do that? Save me the worry of finding you a Popsicle in the morning and sick as a dog."

I carried my sleeping bag inside. A small group of young communards had spread bedrolls near a large iron wood stove. I hesitated to join them. I dropped my things in the far corner. A girl saw me and shuffled over in thick hand-knit socks. "Come over with us," she said. "It's warmer." I said I was okay, but she told me that the bathroom was right on the other side of my wall and I would be up all night listening to the plumbing. She was so nice about it. She was so friendly. She said, "My name is Penny." She was cradling her pregnant belly, which I hadn't noticed at first. I felt bashful, but I rolled up my sleeping bag and followed her across the room.

The group was sitting on their blankets, looking at the fire. "We really should shut the stove door," a guy said. "Oh, not yet," Penny said. "I like to watch it. It calms me down." "What are you worried about?" I asked. "Oh," she said, "many things. All the tomorrows. All the yesterdays. All the things that happened to me or could happen to me. All the things I can't erase or control." She smiled and glanced over at me, wanting me to like her. "Everything, really," she said. Her round cheeks were swollen and pinked from being too close to the heat. I could see it was work for her to maintain her pleasant hippie balance. She was terrified of something. She asked me how long I was staying. "Just tonight," I said. "Oh," she said and looked down at her quilt, disappointed. She slid her index finger under a loose thread. "I hope you come back sometime," she said, weaving her finger further into her blanket. I said I would, that I came to visit Suriya. "Oh, I love Suriya," she said, excited again. Relieved. "Suriya said she would stay for the birth and be my doula. I love Suriya."

I fished the business card Suriya had given me out of my pocket, but I couldn't get any signal on my phone. I asked Penny if they had an Internet connection here. "Oh, yes," she said. "This is a good time to use it, when everyone's asleep." She got to her feet and led me through the warren of rooms to a dark office that housed mismatched, jury-rigged PCs. They were all somewhat out of date, probably salvaged from the dumpster of a local government office after it finally got the funds to upgrade. A solitary guy sat in the dark in front of a screen. He had studious wire-rim glasses and a shaved head and wore a tie-dyed T-shirt. He spun around in his scavenged office chair to welcome us. "We do indexing here," Penny said. "To bring in some money. Especially off season. It's boring," she said. "But some people like it. He'll help you if you need it," Penny said, and she shuffled away.

I found Marshall Westmoreland's bio on the website of a small rural hospital. Marshall was a surgeon. After he graduated from medical school he worked for a charity that sent doctors into war zones. He did time in Bosnia and Rwanda and a part of Asia I couldn't quite place. He had published a magazine article about his experiences. Then at some point he dropped out of the adventure game and became a country doctor in an idyllic mountainside community off the Blue Ridge Parkway known for its hot springs.

I wrote him a message asking if he had heard from Eden recently. I said I was her sister and needed to get in touch with her. He wrote back almost immediately and said, *I'm sorry, I don't know the person to whom you are referring.* I responded that Suriya had given me his name. *Terribly sorry,* he wrote. *I'm afraid it's not ringing any bells.*

"Fuck," I mumbled to myself. I kept trying: Eden was Suriya's daughter. Eden was from Charlottesville. She had gone to a boarding school in Pennsylvania where she lived with her teacher Eric, I wrote, suddenly remembering the whole Dad punching incident, and later they all lived on a communal farm.

Oh, yes, Eric! Eric Piper! he replied. *Now there's a genealogical connection I remember well, metaphorically speaking.* I asked if I could meet him tomorrow to ask a few questions. *Tomorrow is fine. You're a journalist?* I decided to be vague. I said I was a writer. He said to call him when I got to town and wished me a good night.

I made my way back to the indoor campout. Penny had positioned herself next to my sleeping bag. When I lay down she spooned around me and nuzzled her forehead into the nape of my neck. If I turned around, she would want me to kiss her. She would want me to stay. She draped her calf over my shins. On the far side of the room, a couple trickled across the floor, hand in hand, and climbed up into the loft over the bathroom, and I could hear them begin to have muffled sex.

I woke up early and slipped out.

9

My sophomore year in New York, I didn't go home for Christmas break. My dorm had emptied out almost completely except for me and Jamie, who never went home and didn't speak to his parents. His college education was being financed by his great-aunt, who was a semifamous stage actress in Dublin. "I come from a theater dynasty," Jamie liked to say, even though it appeared to skip generations and be a dynasty of only two.

It was freezing outside and I didn't have a real winter coat, only a thick Icelandic sweater that I had taken from my mother and Eden's old leather jacket. I had a ski hat I had found abandoned in a classroom. I was underdressed for bitter January. Classes hadn't started back up yet from winter break and the cafeteria was closed. I didn't have any money from my work-study job and I was broke. I spent a lot of my time in the library, where there was a snack machine that was easy to reach into if there was anything left in stock on the lower rows. I figured out when the man came to restock it and waited until he was done. Sometimes he took pity on me and handed me packets of peanut butter crackers for free.

When I got bored at the library I would hang out in the lounge of the dance department. I could usually find Jamie there. Even though it was winter break, the dancers still reported to the studios, working by themselves or in small groups. I liked being around them. I liked their seriousness.

I saw a sign tacked on the bulletin board. *Looking for models,* it said. *Dancers or similar body types. Professional artist with gallery representation. Good pay.* And just so you'd believe him, his flyer included a drawing of a dancer sitting on a stool, Degas style. I thought it was corny, but I thought I could fake it. I called him and made an appointment. "Why don't we try a session and see if we like each other," he said. "I'll pay you for it. Bring your dance clothes, tights and things."

When I buzzed his Upper East Side apartment intercom and gave my name, he paused and then said, "No, I don't think we said we were to meet today." "Oh," I said, "I'm pretty sure we did." "Well," he said. He seemed to think it over. "Just come in," and he buzzed the door open.

He lived in a building with low ceilings that must've felt modern in the fifties, but now felt claustrophobic and sterile. It smelled of cats. He said, "I think we've gotten the dates mixed up. I have an appointment with a friend. I have to leave in less than an hour. But why don't we . . ." He looked nervously at the kitchen clock. "Why don't we do just twenty minutes or so. I really can't do more than that today. This will be our trial session, only briefer."

I said it was okay. I assumed he would pay me half, but I

didn't say anything. I put my bag and jacket and sweater on the couch. He asked what I brought to wear. I showed him that I was wearing a tank top under a worn-out long-sleeved shirt. It used to be a turtleneck, but I had cut the neck off when the seam ripped. I said I was wearing tights under my jeans because it was so cold. He didn't say anything at first. He was holding a pencil that he twittered anxiously. I wasn't what he expected or wanted. He wanted a girl with long hair swept up in a bun with a few loose strands dangling down her neck. A girl wearing a leotard and a see-through skirt. I could tell because he had his chalk and pastel drawings framed all over the apartment. I unbuckled my pants and pulled off my jeans. He crossed the room and sat behind a drafting table and looked at me. I draped my jeans over my backpack on the couch.

"Why don't you take one of the stools there." He pointed to stools around a breakfast bar. I moved one to the center of the room and sat on it with one foot hitched up on a rung. "That's good," he said. He made some sketches. I tried to be still.

He flipped his pad over. "Could you twist a little?" he asked. "And turn your head." He was frustrated with his work. He went through several pages on his pad. Then he asked me to take off my top. "Both of them?" I asked. "I think so," he said.

He was an old guy. I had dubbed him harmless. Weak. Sure, he had "gallery representation," but the gallery was probably out on Long Island, run by a friend of his as a retirement hobby. And this is what suburban retirees like to buy: romantic pictures of young dancers in repose. I pulled my shirts off over my head and tossed them on the couch. I wasn't wearing a bra.

I think he was staring at me, but his desk was in front of the window and sunlight blared in, making it hard for me not to squint. He got up, went over to a chest of drawers, and pulled out a piece of sheer pink fabric. It unfurled and its wavy edge brushed the floor. He brought it over to me, and I could see that it was a gauzy wraparound dancer's skirt. The kind the uptight girls in Jamie's ballet class sometimes wore. As if wearing a leotard and tights weren't enough to represent their femininity, they had to put on a little skirt, too. The old guy floated it over my bare shoulders and adjusted it around my neck like a cape. He let go of the ties. Then he said, "Look, you're a big girl. If I do something you don't like, you let me know." I think I said okay. He studied me. He picked up one of the ties and moved it to fall over my nipple. The other one was hanging in front of my sternum. He brushed it across my other breast so it disappeared in the fold of my armpit.

He went back to his desk and drew a little while longer. After ten minutes he replaced his chalks and pastels into a case and said, "I'm afraid that's all I have time for today." I pulled the skirt off of me and put my clothes back on. He said, "You can change in the bathroom if you want." But I said, "It's fine." I was already done.

I put on my jacket and my hat and picked up my bag. He was puttering around in the kitchen. I waited by the door. "I'll be in touch," he said. "Again, sorry we didn't have much time." I thought, He is going to stiff me. I should've gone to the bathroom and stolen something. Toothpaste or Tylenol or something I could use. I glanced around the apartment wondering what else would be worth stealing. A few books, maybe. He had some coffee-table books I could sell at the

Strand. But what was I going to do? Grab them and run out? He'd follow me down to the lobby and say, "Stop that girl. She took something from my apartment." It would be easier for me to take a few cans of food and shove them in my bag. Clean him out of some dry goods. I would have to wait for him to go into the other room. But he was standing in front of me, about to open the front door. He handed me a folded ten-dollar bill. Then he opened the door and I dutifully walked into the hallway.

I pushed the button for the elevator. I unfolded the money, thinking maybe there was another bill inside, but there wasn't. Still, in terms of time worked, it wasn't that bad for a college student. I had thought getting naked would get you more money, but maybe it didn't.

I wandered downtown. I didn't want to spend the money to take the subway. Every now and then I would duck into a store to get warm. I would rifle around clothing racks pretending to be looking for a certain size until a salesperson asked if I needed help. Then I would leave, but not too quickly. I wasn't going to steal anything, but if I left too quickly they would think I was a thief. So I would take my time moving toward the door. Or sometimes I would pretend to look at my watch and act like I was late.

I walked for over an hour. I crossed Times Square and went down Seventh Avenue on the West Side. I stopped outside a gay and lesbian bookstore that had a HELP WANTED sign in the window.

I didn't ask about the job at first. I walked around looking at books, pulling a few off the shelves and reading the back covers. After a while I went up to the cash register and asked about the job. Noreen was working there. Noreen was five years older than me. She was already in grad school to become a social worker. She seemed to take pity on me. I said I was a student and had never worked in a bookstore before. But I had a work-study job in a dean's office. She asked if I would have enough time to do both. "I think so," I said. She must've thought I was lying. I looked like a homeless queer kid even though I didn't know I was queer yet, exactly. I thought I might be, but I hadn't had sex with a girl yet. I had slept with a few boys my senior year in high school and my first semester of college, and then I became uninterested. Jamie accused me of being a dyke for hanging out in the dance lounge where the girls were not shy about changing their clothes in public. He said, "Why don't you try it sometime? Then you can see if you like it or not." I asked, "Are people like food?" And Jamie said, "Yes. You see what tastes good." And then he laughed his big bellowy laugh. You wondered how such a big laugh could come out of his skinny body.

I could've shown Noreen my college ID. That would've made me more hirable. But she didn't ask to see it. She let me fill out an application form and said she would give it to the manager when she got in. "They'll call you," she said. They never did.

I didn't see Noreen again until six years later at a party. I recognized her right away from the bookstore but didn't say anything. It was a dinner party for my old girlfriend Lana, who technically wasn't my girlfriend—we just slept together. Lana was also sleeping with a guy, Max, but she didn't want anyone to know about it. "It just happened," she told me. "I don't know what it is." In my coven of lesbian friends, Max was our pet straight male friend, the kind of straight male friend who

double-majored in women's studies and fine art. We would
have dubbed him as creepy, but he had an amazing girlfriend
and we were all hot for her. Her name was Kate, and she
came from old money. Kate had amazing clothes, amazing
boots. She smoked. She told us she had been shipped off to a
Swiss boarding school as a teenager. She ran away and lived
in Istanbul for months before anyone figured it out. "It was
my own fault," she said. "I ran out of money and asked my
dad's ex-wife to wire me some, and she turned me in to my
parents."

"It just happened" was how I was sleeping with Lana too.
She was designing the postcards for one of my plays, so I was
hanging out at her apartment. The first night we had sex,
Max buzzed the intercom as I was getting dressed. I chatted
with him when he came upstairs. I talked for an inordinate
amount of time, something I usually don't do. I didn't want
to leave, because if I left, I knew what would happen next.
Lana's eyes were wild and bright, like the situation of having
us both there was turning her on. She wanted to see what we
would do. I stopped sleeping with Lana later that summer
when she went to a crafters' workshop in Maine. I agreed
to cat-sit for her while she was away. When she came back
in August, she dumped everyone she had been sleeping with
in New York and announced she had fallen in love with her
glass-blowing instructor and was moving to Northampton.

Noreen came to Lana's going-away dinner. She came with
Kate; Max was mysteriously absent. It was sort of odd that
Noreen would be invited to a going-away dinner for someone she didn't know. But as we were leaving to go to a bar afterward, Lana threw her arms around Noreen and said, "It's
so great that you're here. This is such good energy to have a

new person here as I'm starting on a new journey." I rolled my eyes when Lana said that and Noreen saw me do it. Noreen was a little stoned. She smiled at Lana and said, "It's good you're leaving."

I sat with Noreen at the bar, watching Lana dance with Kate. "Did those two have a thing?" Noreen asked me. "Not that I know of," I said. I must've said it sarcastically, because Noreen asked, "Did you two have a thing?" "Briefly," I said. Noreen dropped her hand on top of mine. She stroked it a bit and then hooked my pinkie with hers. She leaned into me and nestled her head on my shoulder, and I moved my arm out of the way to drape it over her. It made me feel powerful. It made me feel wanted. I watched Lana gyrate her hips against Kate, and Kate lean in and lick Lana's sternum.

"Where do you live?" Noreen asked.

"Not far," I said. "What about you?"

"A lot farther," she said. She rubbed my thigh. She said, "Let's go to your place."

We passed a newsstand that also made egg creams. Noreen was still high so she ordered an egg cream and an ice cream sundae, and an old guy made it for us while screaming something in Russian to a kid working in the back. When we got to my apartment, we drank tap water to rehydrate from all the alcohol and dairy products. Noreen's eyelids were heavy, held open only by her assured smiles. Someone upstairs was having a party and Noreen looked up at the ceiling, closed her eyes, and swayed to the music that seeped through the floors. She snaked her arms around my neck and we danced with our foreheads pressed together. We stayed like that, stuck together with sweat, until there was a loud thud from upstairs. A girl started yelling. "Oops," Noreen said, smiling, and she closed her eyes again and kissed me. And we kissed like that, standing up in my narrow kitchen, for a long time.

Afterward we lay on my futon, naked and glistening and slicked. It was the end of August and I didn't have an air conditioner, only a window fan. "You didn't tell me you didn't have AC," Noreen said. She sat up and said she had to go. "You can totally stay if you want," I said. Noreen said, "It's okay. I don't want anything serious. I just got out of something serious." "I just got out of something frivolous," I said. Noreen laughed. "It's just not what I need right now. I'm still kind of raw. I've been through a lot." "Me too," I said.

Noreen started getting dressed. She seemed pissed off. "Are you okay?" I asked. "Fine," she said. "You're sure you don't want to stay? You're sure you can get home okay this late?" She said, "I'm an adult. I know how to get a cab." "Is something wrong?" I asked. "You know"—she was angry—"I've been through quite a lot lately. I'm really stressed out. I just wanted to have some fun. I don't need to be trivialized." "Whatever I said," I said, "I didn't mean it like that. I'm sorry if it came across as uncaring. I really wish you would stay," I said. "I like you a lot."

Noreen started crying. She was holding one sock in her hand. She covered her face with it. I stood up and wrapped my arms around her. I was still naked and her belt buckle pressed into my stomach and it felt good and cool in contrast to the nighttime heat. Noreen let me hug her, then she pulled away. She sat back down on my futon. She seemed calmer, and I thought she was deciding whether or not to stay, and I didn't want to push her so I sat on my desk chair and the vinyl stuck to my thighs. "What's your big thing that you've been through?" she asked. "It can't be Lana leaving." I laughed.

"No, I just mean some childhood stuff," I said. "Lana and I were never that serious. It was just for fun, I guess."

Noreen stretched her legs out, pushing the sheet down to the foot of the bed. "What kind of childhood stuff?" she asked.

I looked around my bedroom at the piles of paper on my desk and my clothes heaped on the floor. I wished I had cleaned up. I needed to do laundry. I needed to buy a file cabinet. "My sister and I went through some stuff," I said.

"Does she know you're gay?"

I knew Noreen was thinking I must have come from a conservative family who didn't take too well to me coming out. That my sister must be a religious nut who didn't accept me. Of course none of that was true. But I was caught off guard by her question. And I didn't know the answer.

"I don't know," I said. "We haven't spoken in a long time."

10

'd forgotten how wide Virginia was on the southern border of its triangle. It took five hours to drive The Camper down deep to where the Blue Ridge Mountains begin to merge with North Carolina and Tennessee. I had no cell phone service in Marshall-the-doctor's small town. I spotted a pay phone outside a laundromat and called his number. "Yes, yes, yes," he answered. He was more of a chatterbox than I had imagined. "I got your email. So you're tracking down Eric and the whole gang! Wonderful! Where are you?"

Marshall gave me directions to his office in a building adjacent to the small local hospital. He was standing outside with a friend as I drove into the parking lot. "Hello!" he sang when I got out of The Camper. I was a bit worried he would hug me, but he extended his hand, his southern manners preceding him. "So nice to meet you. Can you believe this weather? In January? What a wonderful day! Come inside." It was Saturday and his office was closed. The hospital felt deserted, as if all the patients had been discharged for the weekend. Marshall introduced his friend, Phil. Phil shook my hand and didn't say much. He wore a baseball hat and mirrored sunglasses that he didn't take off indoors.

Marshall prattled on about this and that, about his plans for the day, meeting up with his wife to go hiking since it was unseasonably warm, maybe even warm enough to eat outdoors. He paused to politely ask me if I would be staying for lunch. "You're staying for lunch?" He asked in a way to make me feel good about my imposition, as if he had invited me here and always expected me to stay for lunch. I declined. Lunch was always too much of a commitment. Lunch always led to, Why don't you stay for dinner; you're welcome to spend the night.

"Oh, that's too bad. So we don't have much time. Right," he said. He exhaled, revealing an inner exasperation that neither I nor his friend understood. "Right," he said, fingering an anatomical display and then straightening up some free literature provided by a pharmaceutical company. "Okay, here's what we'll do—oh, by the way, this is my office." He gestured left and right like a stewardess, curtsying a bit to each side. He was wearing a sweatshirt and belted baggy shorts that exposed his slender, feminine knees. "Sorry if I talk a lot. I'm a nervous talker. But that's because I'm *always* nervous." He let out a "Ha" and dropped a hand onto a metal paper-towel dispenser that echoed like it wanted to be refilled. Marshall was pale and needed a haircut. Overgrown blonde tendrils escaped from his limp baseball cap and he looked as if he was about to start sweating profusely even though his office felt air-conditioned. I began to wonder if he was on drugs.

"Okay, here's what we'll do. Phil," he said to his friend, "you'll take my car and I'll go with Hope and we'll drive out to the farm. Phil, you'll follow us since you don't really know the way. He's just visiting," he said to me, touching my arm with the back of his hand. "He lives in Florida."

"Or we could just talk here," I said, but Marshall said, "No, no, no," and shooed us out of the office.

Marshall bent over and sorted through his keys. He locked one lock, tested the doorknob, and decided it was sufficient. We walked to The Camper. "Oh, yes," Marshall said, stroking The Camper's flank. "The old VW bus. This takes me back."

Phil stood by the office door not saying anything. "Phil, you're taking my car," Marshall said. And then, as if Phil was deaf or didn't understand English, he overenunciated: "You're *driving* my car."

Phil's mustache widened, exposing his teeth. "I need the keys," he said.

"Oh!" Marshall patted down his pockets, fished out his keys, and briefly stared at the abundance of them before tossing the whole lot to Phil. "You got it," Marshall said. Then he nodded to me to get in The Camper.

Marshall directed me back to the main road. He chattered on about his wife. About how they decided to move out here. They wanted a simple life now. "I've seen more than my share of excitement in this lifetime."

Marshall had worked with Doctors Without Borders in Rwanda in the nineties. He posted his daily journal entries to a dial-up message board and a friend of his in Seattle printed them out and tacked them up on the wall in a coffee shop. An editor saw them and published them in *Rolling Stone.* Marshall was in Rwanda during the genocide. The wire-rim-glasses guy at Suriya's had given me a university login so I could read the archived article. I had assumed Marshall was hiding out here in the western edge of Virginia, suffering from post-traumatic stress disorder or smoking a lot of pot in a log cabin, disconnected from the real world. Seeing him in person, he looked like he wouldn't survive two days in Africa.

"Yes, well," he said, "we're a far cry from Africa now. Or Rwanda." He stared out the passenger window as the mountain scenery sped by. It was a muggy gray day that smelled like rain. The clouds hung low in horizontal strips against the foothills.

In his dispatches, Marshall wrote about a German nurse who was the de facto manager of their hospital, if you could call it a hospital; it was more like *something out of a* M*A*S*H *episode, only more dysfunctional, and of course, lacking the humor.* The German nurse (*I'll call her Hot Lips to protect her identity*) was in charge because everyone else was sick, dead, or catatonic. *But also,* Marshall wrote, *because she had a maniacal urgency to save the world. Maybe it was being German,* he wrote. *Maybe she was making up for her grandparents' war crimes, or their blind-eye passivity.* She refused to see that the situation in Rwanda was becoming severely unsafe for aid workers and that all of them could be hacked to death by a machete gang at any moment. She yelled at Marshall when he came down with a fever and had to stay in bed to rest. That meant they were without a surgeon for the day. *"People are dying because you are too lazy to get out of bed," she said.* Marshall self-medicated with sedatives so he would fall asleep and not have to listen to her. And if the machete gangs attacked, they would think he was already dead. Still, Marshall knew, she had tried to drag him out of bed, because he woke up on the floor the next day. When he returned for duty, she mentioned nothing about it. If she had wept or was distraught over who had died because of his sick day, she didn't show it. All that would slow her down. She was one nurse administrator standing against a tide of slaughter. It was washing over her, drowning her, and she refused to see it. As Marshall wrote: *She couldn't keep people off the trains heading for certain death. And she couldn't admit that work, in fact, could not make her free.*

Eventually the medical team was evacuated. The next thing Marshall knew, he was in the Brussels airport. *And everything was so clean,* he wrote. *Everything was so white. I was in outer space. I was in orbit. And I could no longer hear the screams down below. Only static.*

A few dots of rain speckled The Camper's windshield.

"Did you see Eric again when you got back from Rwanda?" I asked.

Marshall shook his hand in front of his face, as if waving away gnats. "Maybe?" he said. "When I first got back I didn't know where I was. Literally, mentally, physically, *metaphysi-cally.* I was just so strung out on . . . stress!" he said, shaking his hands around his ears and then dropping them back into his lap. "And Valium. And I was drinking. The period right after Rwanda is a total blur. I don't remember much of it at all."

He paused and tapped his fingertips on the window ledge.

"I often find myself in situations," he said, "of transforma-tion. Where it's inevitable. Transformation is just inevitable. It's the only way out. Sometimes you know where the escape hatch is and you fling the door open and jump through, but more often than not, you have no idea where the escape hatch is. And someone is pushing you through a door and then you're somewhere else entirely and you've no idea how you got there." He turned toward me and smiled with excited eyes. "It's as though the hand of God reached in and got you." He chuckled a little to himself and looked out his window again. "Oh, but you don't care about all of that. All of that, just old news. On a strip of microfiche somewhere.

"Here we are," he said. "On the left. Left-hand turn. Left, left, left," he repeated, worried that I'd miss it despite already being in the correct lane.

Marshall was building a house. "We're not living here yet. We're renting another house until it's done. So much work. Ugh. But it's the perfect spot."

The half-finished house sat alongside a narrow creek, and on the opposite side, a steep hill led up to a ridge. A rail fence stretched around a meadow by the dirt road where we left The Camper. "Now where are they?" Marshall said. "Where are my babies?" He strode up to the fence and put one foot on the lower rung, exposing a knee and part of a pale thigh. "Phil!" he called as Phil got out of Marshall's car. "Go up over the hill and bring the cows down." "Why me?" Phil asked. He spoke so little it was odd to hear his voice. "Because we're talking here. We're having an interview. Of sorts," he said to me more quietly, in confidence, as if we were two girls gabbing and billing the office for drinks.

Phil ducked between the fence rails and made his way up the hill. When he got near the top, he was out of sight.

"Did you keep in touch with Eric?" I asked.

"You know, I really didn't know Eric very well on a deeply personal level. We were all squatting on this abandoned farmland. I did it because I needed a cheap place to live. And you can't get cheaper than free. But Eric kept company with a younger crowd, and I guess, I guess I just wasn't that interested. Of course I was interested in what he was talking about. Self-sufficiency. Sustainability. Life and death and the meaning of life and death and all that. Who isn't interested in that? Well, I guess some people aren't. Some people don't want to know how small and insignificant their lives are. It's too painful for them. Much too painful. It's like being a doctor. Some people just don't want to know how sick they are. They don't want to know that even after surgery they will still have to lose weight and stop eating anything fried. Otherwise they'll be back on my operating table in six months. There are only so many stents you can shove in someone's heart. When I met Eric I had just gone through a divorce. I married way too young. It was the thing to do back then. So at that time, after the divorce, I was more interested in putting my life back together than taking things apart. Eric really wanted me to be more a part of his inner circle. And I don't blame him."

I couldn't help but laugh. Marshall playfully slapped my shoulder. "I mean that I was useful to them. I was good at plumbing and electricity and that sort of thing. Plus, I had medical training. I think I gave Eric some unofficial stitches back then. And I could get drugs. Not those kind of drugs." He leaned into me again, working the same joke. "Basic prescription medications. Antibiotics. I could pilfer some here and there. Samples. That sort of thing. You're not recording this, are you? Because I'm not entirely sure what the statute of limitations is for ethical violations. Not that I'm saying it was an ethical violation. First, do no harm." He turned toward the hill. "Here they come."

Silhouettes of cows appeared on the ridge and carefully loped down toward us. Phil followed them. "Try not to fall on your ass, Phil. But sometimes there's no other way to do it. You might just have to fall. You might have to scoot down the rest of the way on your ass." Phil cupped an ear, indicating he couldn't hear. "On your *behind*, Phil," Marshall yelled, grabbing his own ass and shaking it a little.

Phil sidestepped down, digging the edges of his feet into the incline to make little stairs. He looked like he was climbing down a ladder sideways. "Good job, Phil," Marshall said.

"Here she comes," Marshall said, smiling at a large brown cow. "Here comes Big Mama. That's her name. She was our first one. And here's little Buttercup. And here," he said, thumping the side of a young male, "is Einstein. Our first thought when we moved out here was that we would raise dairy cows, but, ugh, so much work. And then you have to store the milk and sterilize it. So much equipment. We decided on just a few cows that we would raise for us. Einstein here will be number one."

I was confused. "I thought Big Mama was your first cow."

"Yes," he said. "But we're going to eat Einstein. You only need one bull, and we've got Romeo here." He tossed some feed in a bucket and a large bull dove his head in after it. "I'm afraid we don't have a job for Einstein. I castrated him myself."

I couldn't picture Marshall dodging genocidal warfare in Rwanda or Congo or the former Yugoslavia. However, I could picture him castrating a cow. I could see how he liked it out here, working at the small hospital. Renovating a farmhouse the same way he did a rural squat or an aortic valve. Carving up Einstein and throwing him on the grill and enjoying it with his absent, fanciful wife. And then one day he will wake up someplace else, having fallen through another escape hatch he didn't know he was looking for. Something will pull him from here and make him want to run to a different corner of the earth. Hurl his body into the flux of the next bloody struggle. He won't last long here. At the very least, I imagined he would form a drug habit, self-medicating with anesthesia to survive this anesthetized life. He can't handle the quaint country existence for long. The dividends of peace are far too boring for him.

That's how Noreen would diagnose me, I thought. She accused me of writing impenetrable plays to purposely remain obscure. Of purposely sabotaging job interviews by being late or not smiling enough. "Why can't you admit that you survived?" she asked. "And now you can have a normal life? It's not so terrible. Why can't you accept peace?"

Sometimes I regretted ever telling Noreen what happened to me and Eden.

"What did you do there, Phil? Oh, good Lord, you stepped in cowshit. Walk around, scrape it off. Walk around on the grass. Or maybe not. You'll just step in more. Well, don't get back in the car with those shoes on. Take them off. You can drive barefoot. You're from Florida. You all live barefoot down there on the beach."

Marshall unlocked a storage shed. "This is where I keep my past," he said. He pulled a string and a lightbulb popped on. The shed was filled with boxes and file cabinets. He patted his breast pockets. "Lord, give me sight," he said. He found his reading glasses and put them on, balancing the bridge halfway down his nose. They made him look like a grandmother. "Let me think"—he put a finger up to his lips—"because I had a system at one point." He turned in place, reached for a file drawer, and yanked it open. He took one look and said, "No." He pushed the drawer shut. "Unfortunately, I think what we're searching for is in the era of boxes, or things I wouldn't mind being vanquished in a nuclear holocaust." He dragged a stack of boxes out to the center of the dirt floor. From one of them he pulled out an old spiral-bound address book. "I should put all of this on a computer somewhere. One of the many projects I'll never get to." He flipped through the pages. "People who might have known one Eric Piper." He licked a finger and turned a page of the book.

"Do you remember a girl named Eden?" I asked.

"Eden," he said closing his little black book on his lap and folding his hands on top of it like a napkin. "Yes, she was very smart. Very attractive, though I made no forays there. Eric had a coterie of young women flitting about. Usually they didn't stay long. The serious ones did, though. Eden. You know, I think she and Eric were lovers. Have you tracked her down?"

I said I hadn't, that he was the first one I found. He smiled. "It was that article," he said. "Sometimes I wish that magazine editor had never stopped into that café. Anonymity is precious these days. I'm afraid what you've chosen to research is rather difficult. It was the last era when people could vanish. The last era in which anyone *considered* vanishing. People are terrified to be alone now. Even if you decide to live isolated and off the grid, you've got to have some blog about it."

Marshall gave me some names and what he thought were probably outdated phone numbers. "Do be careful," he said. "There were some people who were involved in" — he twirled his hand in the air above his head — "drugs, and I imagine other things that might walk the blurry line of legality. Best wishes for tracking down the story," he said and shook my hand, and I left him there under the bare bulb of the shed.

I drove south and pulled The Camper into a motel parking lot. It was late and the motel office was dark. I didn't want to spend the money for a room anyway. I closed all the curtains in The Camper and climbed into the way-back with a flashlight and a pocket knife.

Everything you need is always right there in front of you. That's what Cortland used to say in playwriting class when someone was stuck. "Nine times out of ten," he said, "you don't have to create anything new. It is all already there."

I called Zara and asked her if she could find me some information online because I was in the middle of nowhere. "As long as it's legal," she said, "since you're calling me on a cell phone." Zara was paranoid about surveillance. At various points in her academic and artistic careers she had been approached by "government security assholes" and "corporate black-ops types," both of which, she said, were looking to earn double points by recruiting women into the industry. Their appearances had leveled off since her mental health issues had been publicized by her gallerist, but they still showed up every now and then at a Q&A and would try to chat her up afterward. "One guy went so far as to try and seduce me. Literally," she said.

I asked her to look up a few names Marshall had given me. She could only find the email address for one person, a guy named Ron Sandy. I wrote to him on my phone. I said I was looking for a girl named Eden or anyone who knew her. She lived in a sort of commune with an older guy named Eric. And a person named Chrissy. That they were friends with a doctor named Marshall.

TO: Hope
FROM: Ron Sandy

Sure. I knew some of those people. I don't know any of them now. They were going for their chance at Utopia, trying to figure shit out. But like all human attempts at mimicking paradise, eventually it fails and everyone gets kicked out. It was great while it lasted, but it didn't last long. Like I said, I don't know any of them now. If they're not dead, I wish them well.

Mostly I knew Eric. Eric the Pied Piper. Eden was his girlfriend. Real good-looking. Don't know how he managed that one because I wouldn't call Eric a handsome fella. I had a house a couple miles from their place. Forget how I first met Eric, but he made himself known. Always propositioning favors. He used people. Like for instance, he would come over to my house, take a dump, leave. I live out in the country. I don't always lock the door. Sometimes you would come home to that in progress. Or unfinished. Or unflushed. Can't say it was pleasant. He preferred my place to do his business because his place was a shithole.

Also, Eric liked me because my aunt owned a diner and I would help out there sometimes. At the end of the day we had to throw out all the bread and other stuff the health department keeps tabs on. I hooked it all up. Told my aunt it was for my friends who volunteered helping homeless people. I didn't tell her that my friends actually were the homeless people. That all worked until she died and my asshole cousin took over. He asked for receipts. Said he wanted a letter from the homeless shelter saying it was a donation for his taxes. I think we doctored one up using a copy machine. That worked until he did his tax return and the H&R Block dude wanted an ID number. Decided he could fire me over that. Cut me off. Three years later he ran the whole place into the ground.

After that, I told Eric, you live on a farm, why don't you grow your own food. It's not terribly difficult. But he wasn't interested. All he and his clique were interested in was The Cause. They liked calling their liberal do-goodery philosophy club The Cause because all the Civil War Daughters of the Confederacy grannies still keep the term alive. Like from *Gone with the Wind*. "It's for The Cause." Scarlett O'Hara said that. I had an uncle who referred to Robert E. Lee as "The Man." People live in the past. The Cause. Great slogan, actually. So vague it could mean anything. Of course they said "It's for The Cause" in *Gone with the Wind*, because they couldn't say "It's for preserving slavery, brutality, crimes against humanity, and industrial fascism." But, wink wink, everyone knew what it was. Even back when I was in school, they taught us that The Cause and the Civil War wasn't about slavery, it was about "states' rights." That's another beautifully vague term. It can mean whatever you want it to. That's how advertisers do it. They "just do it." Get it? Got Milk? Where's the Beef? It's all so simple. It has something for everyone. Everyone can have a Coke and a smile. And get out there to be all they can be. We can be heroes just for one day. Eric was big on pointing all that out. He was good at blowing your mind. Good at exploding preconceived beliefs. But he had nothing to patch up the hole.

I drove by one day and they were all gone. Just up and split. Heard Eric was living with an old college buddy who worked for the CIA as an accountant or something. Wouldn't be surprised if Eric sold out and started working for the CIA too. Might be the reason why he dropped off the face of the planet. Can't find much of him on the Internet. Never heard from any of them again.

Didn't surprise me that they pulled the plug on their operation. They were misguided into thinking they could have made a difference with their little Starship Enterprise. America is bogged down with special interest groups and the illuminati. The world is run by powers so big, you and I can't understand it. These people are corrupt beyond your wildest dreams and they make test-tube babies to carry on their work in future generations. They have an army of them in secret bunkers ready to be shot with sperm and sprung into action. You and I and everyone we know, we're just cogs in a wheel. But that's what people want to be. They want to be told how to live and how to eat and how to fuck, or should I say "make love"? How to invest their sorry little paycheck. How to raise their kids. People want to be subservient to something. Like the Hale-Bopp comet guy who made all his followers castrate themselves and wear purple sneakers. People want to be defined. How do you think the global powers got to where they are in the first place? Everyone thinks they'd never let it happen. Everyone would have fought against the Nazis. Everyone would have hidden Jews in their attic or runaway slaves in the Underground Railroad. Everyone would love their gay son and get up there and rah rah rah with their pink ribbons and red ribbons or whatever the ribbon color du jour is for the social cause du

jour. As if tacking a ribbon on your cheap suit does anything. What a load of crap.

Glad I finally figured out the answer, something Eric &
Co. was never able to do. It's a dream, you don't exist. Cling-
ing and grasping at a transient material world only leads to
suffering. It's all dream dust. Logic and concepts will never
take you to understanding because it's just mucking around
in the illusion. We're all transients. That's the harsh world
of karmic tangles, spiraling forever from one dream world
to the next. Doomed to keep repeating the same old story
to the same old song.

I sense this is some sort of quest for you, needing some
sort of closure. Sorry I can't be of more help to you, Hope.
But keep on keeping on. The best thing you have going for
you is your name.

11

I still had my backpack on when Eden and I were riding in the back of the truck. It was sort of uncomfortable, but I worried about crawling around too much while the truck was in motion. It's not like there were seat belts in the back of the truck. Eden had tossed her backpack into the corner and she didn't seem to care if it flew out if we happened to whip around a curve. She had her headphones on and her Walkman in her hands, her thumbs resting on the side buttons. I could hear the music escape from the foam cushioning of her headphones. Eden leaned her head back against the truck cab and looked up at the dark sky, immersed in her personal soundtrack to the galaxy. When we stopped at a red light, I inched forward and took off my backpack. I pulled it around in front of me and put it between my legs, holding down one strap with my foot.

The wind lashed my hair around my face. I kept retucking it behind my ears. I wished I had a ponytail holder so it wouldn't get completely messed up. That's what I always did in the summer when we went with my mom on the annual eleven-hour drive to Michigan to visit our grandparents. Our car didn't have air conditioning, so the windows were always rolled down unless it was raining. Eden never seemed to mind. Her hair was long enough and thick enough to be wound in a knot and stay there without barrettes. If it did bother her, she used her headphones as a headband.

We turned off the main road with the strip malls and the big grocery store. We went through a hilly neighborhood of small houses. We passed the big combined junior-senior high school where Eden and I would've gone if we lived full-time with our dad.

I thought we were going a different way than my dad usually drove us. We normally passed a gated community called The Pines, which Eden called the Last Outpost of Civilization. Last summer Eden figured out how to sneak into the pool at The Pines. We went there every day until this guy started talking to Eden. He thought she was older than she was. He was trying to pick her up. It went on until a lady and her kids came by and saw that this guy wasn't leaving us alone, and she decided to get involved. She asked if he was bothering us. Eden didn't say anything, so the woman asked if he was bothering me. I said, "He's kind of being weird and he always does this." "Does what?" she asked. "Talks to us," I said. "Inappropriately?" she asked me, quietly, so he couldn't hear. "It's just weird. It's not really a big deal," I said. The guy said, "Hey, I live here, I pay my HOA fees, I can use the pool and sit where I want, no one's bothering anyone." The woman said to us, "What's your house number? I want to talk to your parents about what's going on." Eden got up with her towel and walked away and I had to follow her. We didn't go back there anymore. Eden never said anything to me about it except "I could've handled it," as we walked back to our dad's that day.

The truck slowed down and wound through curvy side streets lined with little box houses that all looked like they had been built at the same time. And then the houses got farther and farther apart and we were out in the country. We pulled into a driveway and then off the paved part and onto the back lawn. I looked at Eden. She pressed the STOP button on her Walkman and scooted to the foot of the truck bed. Larry got out of the cab. "Come on in," he said and headed to the back-door steps without checking to see if we were following him or not.

Eden and I walked into his kitchen. The fluorescent light buzzed overhead. Everything was kind of run-down. The linoleum kitchen counters were stained with coffee cup rings. There was a bag of trash tied up on the floor next to the garbage can that was leaking something brown onto the floor. A box of Trix cereal sat on top of the garbage can lid. I was hungry. We hadn't eaten dinner and I actually liked eating cereal for dinner if my mom wasn't cooking because she was teaching a class that night. There was usually plenty of stuff for me and Eden to cook, or there were always burritos or Stouffer's French-bread pizzas in the freezer that we could microwave, but on those nights I usually ate cereal. My mom never bought Trix. I only ate it when I used to go to slumber parties at other people's houses when I was younger.

Larry switched on the lights in the living room. "Make yourself at home," he said. Eden plopped down on the couch and put a foot up on Larry's coffee table. Larry went back into the kitchen and opened the fridge. "You girls drink beer?" he asked. "You want one?" "Yeah, I'll have one," Eden said. I gave Eden a look that meant, What are you doing, you shouldn't drink beer with this guy. But Eden ignored me. She surveyed the room, which was just the crappy couch and crappy coffee table and two old grandpa-style recliners. A mirror with *Budweiser* etched into it hung above the fireplace. There was a china cabinet that fit into a corner and was filled with porcelain Disney figurines, the kind you see advertised in the back pages of *Parade*. You have to cut out the little coupon and mail in a check. Or subscribe and get the first doll free and then they send you one a month unless you remember to cancel your subscription, but everyone always forgets, and then you get all those dolls and a big bill. My friends and I would do the same thing with the eight-CDs-for-a-penny Columbia House Record Club, but you have to remember to cancel your membership or you end up with a bunch of stuff you don't want and you have to pay full price. I once saw Layla at school filling out the mail-in form and choosing a lot of Christian rock. She wrote in the name and address of a girl she was mad at.

Larry came back slurping a beer and slinging two more cans hanging off a six-pack plastic ring. He dangled the cans in front of Eden's face, his finger stretching out the plastic loop. He stood there for a bit, waiting to see if Eden would reach out for it, but Eden never fell for stuff like that. She hated games. She didn't like playing along with things. Larry smiled. He lowered his arm and let the beers land on the coffee table and sat down on one of the recliners. Eden leaned forward and pulled out one of the beers. "Your sister can have one too," Larry said. "No drinking age here." I had drunk beer before, but I said, "No thanks." I knew my dad would be pissed off if he found me and Eden drinking beer with his friend. Also, if Larry was supposed to drive us to our dad's, now he was drinking, so now he shouldn't drive, and now we were stuck here. Or maybe this was always the plan. Our dad was going to pick us up from Larry's. Or Luce was. Since our dad now didn't have a working car.

"Are we waiting here?" I asked.

"Yeah," Larry said. "You're waiting here."

"Shouldn't we call Luce?" I asked Eden quietly.

Eden popped open her beer. "She knows to come," she said.

"Tell you what," Larry said. "You seem like liberal-leaning folk." He got up and rummaged around in a corner behind his recliner. He pulled out a bong and a plastic zipper-lock bag. "TGIF, am I right?"

"So true," Eden said.

"True ee-nough," Larry said. He packed the bong with pot from the plastic bag. "Wait, I have ladies here. This demands some hygiene." He went into the bathroom and returned with a streamer of toilet paper. He wiped the rim of the bong and then dropped the toilet paper on the floor. "You know how to use it?" he asked Eden.

Eden picked up the bong and set it on the crappy coffee table while she dug into her backpack for a lighter. Eden seemed perfectly at ease in this situation, but it was making me nervous. It wasn't like we were at a party. It wasn't like we were over at someone's house while their parents were working the night shift or out of town. In the eighth grade, I always hung out at my friend Ellie's house because her mom worked for the local TV station's news program and her shift was the eleven o'clock news, so she never got home before one a.m. Sometimes Ellie would make us rum and Cokes from the liquor cabinet, but it was kind of boring. I never understood drinking if you were just going to watch TV. It seemed better if there were more people around.

Eden held the base of the bong between her knees, leaned over, and sucked on the tube. It gurgled from deep in her lap. She sat up and passed it back to Larry. She exhaled the smoke in a long, ruffly current and then lit up one of her cloves. The familiar perfume wafted out of her mouth. We are going to get in so much trouble, I thought. I didn't know why Eden wanted to hang out with Larry like this. I thought he was pretty gross. He must be one of those guys who doesn't have a real job and is always hanging around and that's why my dad called him because he couldn't get in touch with anyone else. Larry didn't seem like he would be friends with my dad. He was more like a guy who fixed things. Sometimes my dad hung out with those guys and acted like they were his friends even though they were so different because my dad had gone to college and been a journalist and now taught at a college. But usually it was my dad hanging out with them at a bar and playing darts. Or a few of them were on his Frisbee golf team. He never invited them over to his house. Or if he did invite them, they never came.

Eden took another bong hit. I sat down next to her on the couch. "You want some, little sister?" Larry asked. "She doesn't smoke," Eden said. "She's pretty straight-edge." "I'm not straight-edge," I said, "that's something entirely different." "How is it entirely different?" Eden asked, half rolling her eyes at me, looking at me like a teacher who knows you are about to say the wrong answer. "Because sometimes I drink," I said. Eden kind of hiccup-laughed. She coughed on the smoke of her clove and took a slurp of beer.

"Don't make fun of little sister," Larry said. "She's trying to make something of herself in this life."

The front door opened and another guy came in. He was chunkier than Larry. He wore tan work boots and jeans and a jean jacket. He looked at me and Eden like he was pissed off we were there. "Y'all drinking all my beer again," he said kind of quietly. Eden suddenly looked upset. "He said it was okay," Eden said. The guy took the last beer that was still on the coffee table. He sat in the other recliner and pulled the plastic six-pack rings off. He opened the beer and looked at us. "Y'all friends with my cousin?" "No," I said. Eden elbowed me. "He gave us a ride," Eden said. "Uh-huh," the cousin said.

Larry looked serious, like he didn't want his cousin coming home and being judgmental. Like he was waiting for him to go upstairs to his room and leave him alone. "You girls old enough to be drinking beer?" the cousin asked. "It's a free country," Eden said. "That means you're not," he said. "Oh, like you didn't touch a drop until you were twenty-one," Larry said. "Excuse Mr. High and Mighty here." "It's not cool," the cousin said. "They're college girls," Larry said. "That one's thirteen," Larry's cousin said, nodding at me. "I'm fourteen," I said. "Case closed," his cousin said. He got up and went upstairs.

"See now, that's why she's not drinking," Larry called after him. "Because younger sis here is only fourteen. And a responsible fourteen at that." A door closed above us.

"Sorry, didn't mean for that to happen," Larry said.

"Can I use your phone?" I asked.

"Why do you want to use the phone?"

"I just want to call home."

"Your dad knows where you are."

"I just thought I would call Luce."

"Why do you want to call them?"

"Because she could pick us up if our dad can't."

"She probably went to pick up Dad," Eden said.

"Yeah, exactly," Larry said. " 'Cause your dad's car is toast."

"I just want to leave a message on the machine. She can check it."

"Luce never checks messages," Eden said. It was true, Luce never did call in to check the machine. It was our dad doing that all the time from pay phones. He was always so worried he would miss an important call. He tried having a beeper, but he could never figure it out and he ended up returning it. Or as my mom said, "He was probably disappointed that it didn't beep all that much." Luce didn't have an answering machine before she moved in with my dad. She said it was too much responsibility to call all those people back.

"She doesn't know how to use an answering machine?" Larry asked. "That's just sad."

Eden sucked on her clove. "It's very sad," she said. She dropped her cigarette butt into her empty beer can and set it on the coffee table. "Got any more beer?" she asked.

"I thought you wanted to eat dinner," I said, remembering how he was urging us to go because it was late.

"Dinner?" Larry went into the kitchen and came back with the box of Trix and a bag of white sandwich bread. He twirled the bag and let it fly in a loop-de-loop to the coffee table, where it landed, deflated and smushed. He kept the Trix, opened it, and grabbed a fistful of cereal. He held the box by the cardboard tab of its folding lid, like he was sort of debating sharing it with us. "Maybe I got some mustard for that bread," he said and sat down in the recliner with the cereal box.

"Disgusting," Eden said.

"Think I'm disgusting?" he asked.

Eden smiled. "Think I'm disgusting?" he asked again, playfully. Eden smiled like she was trying not to laugh out loud. She covered her mouth with her hand like she was still smoking a cigarette. "Yes," she said.

"I see now," Larry said. "Have you seen a lot of disgusting things? Or are you a virgin?"

Eden snapped out of her giggly thing. She put on her "I'm tough" face. Her "I know everything" face. I didn't know if Eden was a virgin or not.

Larry repacked the bong and put it on the table for Eden. Eden didn't move. Larry leaned forward and pushed the bong a couple inches across the table toward Eden. But Eden didn't budge. She was good at that. She could be super-stubborn if she wanted to. It would drive our dad crazy. Larry gave the bong another nudge, pushing it with one finger along the table until it got to the edge of our side. "Oh, go on," Larry said.

"I think I'll call Luce," I said. "That way you won't have to drive us."

Larry didn't say anything. He looked at Eden like he was waiting to see what she was going to do. "Fuck you," Eden muttered. She leaned over and sucked on the bong.

Larry looked at Eden. "I'll take you to your dad's," he said.

"I'm sure Luce can pick us up," I said.

"No. I'm going to do it. I just needed a moment. To get myself together. To think about things."

"What did you have to think about?"

"Grown-up stuff. Just needed a little adult time. Also, thought I needed to take a crap, didn't want to do it at your dad's. Only on my home turf. I'm peculiar that way. But that ship has sailed. Won't dock till morning now. So we're free to go. We just need to give your sister a little time."

"A little time for what?"

"A little time for dreaming," he said.

I looked over and Eden was resting her head in her hand with her eyes closed. The heel of her hand was mushing her cheek, making her face look fatter than it was. Her lips separated and she began to drool a bit. I shook her arm. "Are you asleep?" I asked her. Eden slumped to the side. Her arm flopped free and her head rolled onto the shoulder of the couch.

And then everything went black.

12

I drove The Camper over the border of North Carolina and stopped outside the town of Boone, where Luce had lived ever since she broke up with my dad. My mom and I had driven down and visited her a few times. I had grown up with Luce. It seemed I had grown up with most of my father's partners. Maybe that was why Beth irked me so much. It felt like she was an outsider. Everyone else had been around, had known me and Eden when the thing with Larry happened. But with Beth, my father had to tell her at some point. Thinking about that moment was worse than thinking about them having sex.

Luce lived in a drafty nineteenth-century farmhouse. "It's not really my style," she said when I showed up, "but it's still standing." The house was painted dull brown and stood across the lane from a bigger, nicer farmhouse freshly painted white. The big house was mounted imperiously atop a sloping meadow. It got all the good light. Luce's brown house backed into the woods. "It was where the brother of the landowner had lived," Luce said. "The one who didn't want to inherit the farm. I think he was a vet," she said. "I think he drank himself to death."

The inside of her house reminded me of home. My father liked these quasi-hippie women who threw pots, ran unions, and dried herbs. Luce was a painter and a retired social worker. She had retired from social work when she lived with my father. "All social workers retire before forty," she once said. "Most don't make it past thirty." Luce taught afterschool art classes for kids. She conducted art therapy workshops in hospitals. She foraged for mushrooms and ramps in the woods behind her house. She wore her hair long and gray and pinned back at the sides with barrettes, which made her look girlish. I sat on her old couch, which she had covered with a crocheted blanket to hide the wear.

"I'm sorry I haven't kept in better touch with you girls. Or your moms. I'm not much of a letter writer. Or the computer." She flicked her hand at a desk in the corner of the room, which held a chunky, outdated laptop under a pile of papers and bills. "My nephew fixed it up for me. Saves me a trip to the library to do email if there's weather. I know there's a way to pay your bills on it instead of sending in a check. Just haven't set it up yet."

Luce took a sip of tea from her mug. She uncrossed and recrossed her legs. "I heard about your mom," she said. "You can always come here, Hope. I'm always glad to see you."

"Thanks," I said. When I started driving to Boone, I didn't give a thought to whether Luce would want to see me or not. I assumed she would. I felt the same with Suriya. I viewed them as extensions of my dad, and therefore I felt proprietary about them and felt I could crash with them, unannounced, at any time. But Luce seemed to be telling me otherwise. That I had misunderstood something about our relationship. That my arrival, my trespassing, was forgiven.

Luce had gotten older. There were lines around her lips and the natural dark circles under her eyes now wilted toward her cheeks. She fidgeted in her seat, uncomfortable, maybe uncomfortable with me, since she seemed to be looking in all corners of the room rather than in my direction.

"I'm sorry," Luce said. "About what happened."

"There was nothing anyone could do," I said, "once it got to her lungs."

"No," Luce said. "Not about your mom." She had crossed one leg far over the other and was sitting sideways in her armchair, practically in profile. "When you were kids. I shouldn't have left when I did. It was" — she pursed her lips, searching for the correct word — "inconsiderate of me." She took a careful breath. I could feel the reflex in me to brush it off, to say "It's okay" or otherwise absolve her, but I didn't. I never thought about why Luce decided to break up with my dad when she did. I suppose it should have affected me more at the time, but it was right after Larry. It was when Eden left for boarding school. It was when I stopped going out to regularly visit my dad. I just lumped it in with everything else.

"I never had children," Luce said. "I'd never been a parent other than with you girls. I never wanted to be, really. I had a younger brother I had to babysit all the time as a kid. I didn't particularly enjoy it. It always felt like a hindrance to me, or to what I wanted to do. It wasn't a conscious decision. There are women like that. They make a conscious decision not to have children and are very clear about it. And around that time, my era, there was a big push not to have children. To liberate ourselves from our biology. Because we saw our mothers so defined by it. So thwarted by it. Maybe on some level I related to that. I suppose there was no way I couldn't."

My mom once said something like this too. One time, maybe I was eleven or twelve, I playfully asked her, "Didn't you always want a daughter?" And instead of giving a playful response, my mother gave an honest one.

Luce uncrossed her legs. She planted both feet on the floor and leaned forward with her mug between her hands, hunched over her knees. I couldn't see her mouth, just the deep lines of the furrow of her brow.

"It wasn't about you girls. That wasn't the reason. It was that I couldn't be there for your dad." She shifted her mug to one hand and gestured with the other. "You know, your father's a needy person. And he just needed too much. Whatever it was, I couldn't give it to him. His needs perfectly matched my incapacities. And. That was it."

Luce sat back in her chair again. The emotional part was over. For her, at least. She leaned her head against the seat back and glanced up at the ceiling. "I don't know how to say this. There's no way to say it that will sound right. But in a way, what happened to you girls was good for me. Can you understand that? What I mean by that? I'm not happy about what happened to you. And I wish it had never happened. But I wasn't in control of that. And if I were in control of it, by some supernatural power, of course it wouldn't have happened. I'm sorry it happened to you. You know that."

Luce looked over at me then, for the first time since we sat down. She looked serious. I bowed my head slightly, my eyes closing a little when I did, as if to release her of any remote culpability. Luce gazed toward the upper corners of the room. She favored one corner in particular, then abruptly switched and tilted her head to the opposite side. "What I mean is, it helped me. I realized something about myself much sooner than I would have if that had never happened to you. Maybe I never would have realized it."

"Maybe you didn't want to be around us," I said. I was sort of startled that I said that. I instantly wished I hadn't. But I felt it wasn't fair that Luce was doling this stuff out and I was expected to sit here and listen to it. And chime in at some point with something like "At least some good came out of it." The thought of that being the polite thing to do suddenly made me nauseous.

Luce closed her eyes. The muscles between her brows twitched and then relaxed. She breathed through her nose. She did this for several rounds of air. "Things are more complex than that," she said with her eyes still closed. Then she took a deep inhale, opened her eyes, and stood up. "Let's go outside," she said.

At the kitchen door, Luce kicked off her clogs and stepped into dark green rubber boots that looked too big for her. She reached for the doorknob while still bent over from tugging on the second boot, as if the fresh air would make things easier for her and she wanted to get outside as soon as possible.

We walked through the backyard. It had started to cloud up and the cold air had a mist to it. It felt like it was about to rain. Luce didn't notice. She curled around the house, fingering tall dead plants, letting them bend with her stride and crushing dead flower heads that broke off in her hand when she let them go. The backyard had a couple of Adirondack chairs and a circle of rocks with powdery remnants of a fire.

Luce headed into the woods. She ducked under a low-leaning branch, walking quickly, distancing herself from her house, and maybe civilization, and maybe me. She stopped when she reached a small creek carved into the ground. She watched the thin current of water percolate over stones and transport a wayward leaf, as if its movement possessed the potential to soothe her. "I own the ground, but not the water," she said. "Isn't that something?"

A bird cawed from somewhere in the trees. Luce took this as her cue to move along. Her boots slapped into the mucky dead leaves and pine needles along the creek bed. She grabbed on to a spindly tree sapling on the opposite shore and took a large step over the water.

On the other side, the woods sloped sharply uphill. Luce took long strides, leaning over occasionally and pressing her hands into the tops of her knees for support.

The ground leveled off in a grove of maples. Luce stood upright and breathed through her mouth. She wiped away a little moisture running from her nose. Spigots were drilled into a few trees and some of them had wooden buckets hanging off of them. Luce gave them a pat as she skated past.

"You know, Suriya stayed with me for a while last year," she said out of the blue. "In the winter before she went to India. She helped me with the Christmas markets. I do a lot of that in November, December."

We stopped near the top of the hill at a boulder. "Here," Luce said. "It's easy to climb." There were natural indentations for footholds and the top of the boulder was flat. We climbed to the top and had a view of the woods below, and because there were no leaves on the trees, we could make out the farms in the valley.

"I feel safer in the woods," Luce said. "Sometimes I think I'd like to sleep out here on this rock, but it's always too cold." She paused. "It gets windy up here. You're not protected." She raised her cheeks in a reluctant smile, realizing her contradiction—she felt safe, yet wasn't protected. "Huh," she said.

The wind picked up. It blew Luce's hair in strands across her face. She combed them back with her hands and reclipped one of her barrettes, but the wind freed them again. Luce gathered her hair together, twisted it, and stuffed it under the collar of her sweater. She drew her knees up and wrapped her arms around them, hugging them toward her chest. She reached down and peeled wet leaves off her boots.

"When I was born," Luce said, "I didn't meet my father for days. Not because it was a different era and they wouldn't allow fathers in the maternity ward. They told him I was born and he disappeared. No one knew where he was. No one could find him. Though I'm not sure if anyone really tried. Maybe they sent one of my uncles out to look for him. He didn't come home for a week. I used to think my mother exaggerated that story; she was in a postpartum haze and simply didn't remember him being there. Or my grandmother kept him out of the room. Or she confused it with being in the hospital and coming home. But it wasn't that. He just disappeared. 'Hi, your daughter's been born,' and poof, you take off. Maybe he was drinking, I don't know. I don't think so. Maybe he started by drinking in celebration. He wasn't a

drunk. He didn't go on benders, much less for days. I think
he just couldn't handle it. All that responsibility. Being completely responsible for another person's life. Completely responsible for the fact that they exist. And for whatever happens to them. And for whatever they do. Whatever they
inflict upon the world."

Luce rocked in place, flexing her heels deep in her rubber
boots. She looked down between her knees and closed her
eyes. Her rocking stopped and she was still. In the distance
someone was hammering something, chopping wood, or doing some kind of work on a house. A distant tapping would
start and stop.

Luce opened her eyes and looked up. Her hands slipped up
her legs, over her knees, and disappeared into pockets.

"We're alike, you and I, Hope," she said. "I see a lot of myself in you. But you're stronger than me. Maybe that's another part of what I couldn't handle. A part of what you said
was right. Not so much that I didn't want to be around you.
But I didn't want to be around evidence of my own weak-
ness."

Luce slid off the rock until her toes touched the ground,
then hopped the rest of the way down. I scrambled forward,
but realized it was too difficult to get down that way from
my position. I crawled over to the footholds and awkwardly
climbed down. We started to walk back a different way.

Luce drove her hands into the pockets of her vest. She
looked at the ground. The ground that she owned. Maybe it
gave her solace. Maybe it comforted her. Maybe it confirmed
her. It must feel good to own land. It must give you a foundation. I had lived in rented apartments all of my adult life,

most of them as someone's roommate, lover, or illegal sub-tenant. The only time I had my name on a lease was when Noreen and I lived together.

"I couldn't have survived what happened to you," Luce said without looking up. "Maybe only you could. You were the only one who was strong enough. I don't think Eden was."

I stopped walking and watched Luce keep moving through the woods. Her boots trudged through dead leaves and twigs. Her pace was interrupted when she had to step over a log. My breath made small clouds that obscured my view of her before they quickly vanished.

In a few moments I caught up with her. A path materialized and we followed it to a clearing. In the middle was a sandy canvas tent, the kind you see in movies when people go on safari in Africa. Inside, it was empty except for a round cushion, a roll of white paper, a pot of black ink, and a paintbrush resting in a tin coffee can. It was barely big enough for two people. Luce explained that this was her meditation space. "There are monks in Asia who practice drawing the perfect circle, which is, of course, impossible. But you try. I do one a day," Luce said. "Then I burn it. It's a practice in detachment. To not get used to things. And to not hold on to things. To let things go."

Down at the house, Luce pulled off her boots and stepped back into her clogs. She started washing vegetables in the sink and asked if I was staying over. I was planning on it, but I lied and said I was staying with some friends who lived forty minutes away. "I went to college with them," I said. "They just had a baby." Luce continued scrubbing carrots with a brush. I had no friends forty minutes away. I sort of knew someone in Asheville, but I hadn't spoken to her in years. I didn't want to stay over at Luce's and wake up with Luce still here. I felt I was disturbing her and that I had disturbed her ever since I was fourteen. She had an ongoing meditation that I had interrupted at the age I began menstruating. I wondered if it was my femaleness that disturbed Luce. Not that I was that traditionally feminine, or traditionally gender-conforming; I sometimes forgot about my female body. Whatever it was, to her I was the person who represented pain and discomfort and underlined all of her limitations and weaknesses. I reminded her that she never had children. That for whatever reason, whether she wanted to or not, she was psychically incapable of it.

I asked Luce if she had any idea where I could find Eden. If she kept in touch with her. "I see Suriya now and then," she said. "Eden I haven't seen since you were kids. I think your mother gave me an address for her when she was living on a farm. I sent a few cards, boxes, but never heard anything. Suriya doesn't know where she is?" I shook my head.

"Good luck," Luce said.

13

When Eden and I woke up it was still dark out. I didn't remember going to sleep. I vaguely remembered someone giving us a blanket in the back seat of The Camper. But we weren't in The Camper, we were in a truck. The back of a truck. Someone gave us a blanket in the back of the truck because it was cold or in case it was cold. I remembered thinking that it smelled gross or it was dirty. I remembered I tried to say thanks and put it under my butt because I was uncomfortable and there was nothing to sit on and my butt had gotten cold. Someone pulled it out from under my butt and put it over my head.

I didn't know where we were. For a second I thought we were camping. Maybe it was one of those times when you are very sleepy and you can't really remember what had happened late at night or at the end of the TV movie and you were half dreaming and it was all mixed up. I had gone to

my first high school party not too long before and had gotten pretty drunk. My friend Dena's mom was out of town,
so Dena had a party. It was only going to be a few of her
friends, but then everyone found out about it and everyone
came over. I was drinking rum and Coke because it was one
of the few drinks I had heard of. That, and gin and tonic.
Wine and beer were boring and I didn't like the taste. I
drank rum and Cokes until I couldn't taste the rum in it anymore. I started kissing a guy named Jonah, who had never
shown any interest in me before. I also kissed three other
guys. Maybe more. I kissed a guy named Kyle, who tasted
like the sour-cream-and-onion potato chips he was still
chewing in his mouth. Somehow I wound up with Jonah in
another room. He turned out the lights and we lay down on
the floor behind a couch so that if someone walked in the
room they wouldn't see us. That must have been his strat-
egy, because I don't remember it being mine. He rolled on
top of me, writhing through his clothes. Then he moved
off to one side and tried to slide his hand down the front of
my pants. I was wearing a belt of my mother's that was too
big for me. I had wrapped the excess tongue around itself
so it wouldn't flop all over the place. Jonah couldn't figure it
out. I pulled at it and freed it. Then someone walked in and
turned on the lights and Jonah sat up like nothing was going on. I fixed my belt. Then I sat up and the guy who had
walked in on us said something. Or whistled. Or made some
joke. Maybe I had kissed him, too. I didn't like Jonah in that
way. He thought he was smarter than he was. He boasted
that he knew what his IQ was and that it was 144, which, according to him, was borderline genius. At some point Layla
picked up my hand and led me away from Jonah. The two

of us sat in the backyard in plastic lounge chairs, the kind that look like they are made out of giant rubber bands and leave marks on the backs of your thighs in summer. I don't remember what we talked about, but Layla kept holding my hand and it felt good. She got up and brought me a big glass of water and I didn't know I was so thirsty. She dragged her chair right next to mine, the way some people try to make a double bed by putting two twin beds together but there is always a crack. It was kind of awkward because the armrests of our chairs clacked against each other and it felt like they were in the way of us sitting together. Layla tried to make them fit, sliding one armrest in front of the other, but it didn't really work and she gave up and crawled into my chair instead and kicked her chair away with her foot. We had to hug in order to fit. Layla was shorter than me and she put her head on my chest and I could feel her breath on my skin and she slipped her leg between my legs and I reached my top leg over her so we were very close and tangled up. Some guy came out at some point and said, "A couple of lesbians out here," and Layla said, "Shut the fuck up," but she didn't move and the guy didn't say anything and Layla said, "Fuck off," to make sure he would go. We heard the screen door to the kitchen slam so we knew he was gone. And I don't know how it happened but Layla and I started kissing and she slipped her knee up and pressed it against my crotch and everything felt good. Like it wasn't a dare. Like I wasn't trying to prove anything.

At some point Layla got up and said she had to go to the bathroom and never came back. Most of the people had left. I fell asleep outside in the lounge chair. When I woke up it was really early. Someone had thrown a beach towel over me and it was damp from dew.

Later in the morning a bunch of us made scrambled eggs and we rolled some hash into a cigarette and smoked it. Layla had brought the hash. She and her boyfriend had slept in Dena's mom's bed. Layla said, "Don't worry, we didn't mess up the sheets." Her boyfriend was older. He was old enough to be in college but he wasn't in college and no one knew what he did or where he came from. I had forgotten Layla had this weird boyfriend. I had forgotten that she had taken free condoms from the guidance counselor's office. I guessed our kissing didn't mean anything to her. But kissing all those guys didn't mean anything to me. I wondered if it was the same thing.

Now I was in the woods somewhere. And it slowly came back to me that I wasn't sleeping outside at a party. We weren't camping with my dad. My dad hadn't come to pick us up. He sent a friend of his that I didn't know but Eden did. I was cold and I would've taken a gross blanket now. Or a damp beach towel that had been left out all night. And thankfully someone helped me up and I felt like a little kid who had fallen asleep on the car ride home and it always felt good to be lifted out of the car by your dad when you were half asleep and carried inside and carefully put to bed. Carry me, I always wished as a little kid. I felt a little like I was drunk.

I would've preferred being in a tent if we were camping, which we were not. We weren't camping. But we were outside. I curled up over my knees and wrapped my arms around them and tried to rest my head. My nose was cold. But I wasn't supposed to be in this position. I was supposed to sit up. Someone sat me up and leaned me back against a tree. And someone moved one of my arms around the tree. I think that's when I knew for sure it was a tree. I tried to bend my elbow and reclaim my arm but someone straightened it out again. I wiggled my shoulder to slip my arm out of my jacket sleeve but someone wound a piece of rope around my wrist, keeping me inside. That's when I tried to stand up. I pressed my free hand into my knees and straightened my legs. I was wobbly and the tree helped me stand. I circled around to my tied-up hand and hazily pawed at it. I mumbled, "Stop it." I shoved whoever it was aside. I said, "Let me do it," because I was good at undoing knots. I was good at detangling necklaces. I was good at combing out ratted, snarly hair without causing pain. I could do it. Someone pushed me and I took a few steps backwards and bumped into the tree. Maybe I was drunk, but I don't remember drinking. Maybe I was too drunk. I should go. Someone should give me a ride home. Someone who hadn't been drinking like that girl Cathy who was a Mormon. The farthest she went was drinking coffee. And I saw her try to take a drag off a cigarette once but she just coughed and said, "Oh my word, no," and waved it away. Or there was that guy Shiva who didn't drink most of the time either. He would only drink when his parents were in India over Christmas so there could be no way they would ever know. I needed one of those people. I didn't know either of them very well. I would have to get their phone number from someone. I felt better about calling Cathy. Maybe because she was a girl.

I looked around. It was dark. There were trees. I didn't see any houses or lights. The moon was the only light. Where

was Eden? "Eden?" I called out. I think I said it. My mouth felt
like at the dentist's. Pasty. Cotton. My cheeks felt funny. I had
to think. I had to think to think. "Eden," I said. I know I said
it out loud. I spiraled around to my tied-up hand. "Don't do
that," I said. I started to pull at the rope to loosen it and work
my hand out. Someone punched me. In the face. I had never
been punched before.

14

I drove The Camper back to my dad's because I was out of ideas. The only idea I had left was to look through boxes of childhood stuff and see if I recognized any of Eden's friends in old photos. Maybe I could call Marshall and see if he remembered them too. Have Zara find their contact info for me by hacking into some database. All shots in the dark that had only minuscule chances of turning anything up. I imagined my dad giving me a pat on the back, telling me I did my due diligence, and probably somewhat relieved that if he couldn't find Eden, I couldn't find her either.

There were no cars parked at my father's house. I thought it was better this way. It's easier if I'm already here. If I pop in on him and Beth having dinner, it's intrusive. Or they'll worry something is wrong. Why am I saying "they"? Who knows how long Beth will stick around? My father drives all women away. That's cruel of me, I know. My father has a big heart and perhaps a greater-than-average capacity for romantic love that I obviously did not inherit. Maybe he just has bad luck or makes bad decisions or loves too many people. Why does love have to be limited to the duality of just two people? I picked up that line as a kid. Some friend of my dad's said it during a dinner party. Of course, they probably came up with it to rationalize their infidelities, or to rationalize that fidelity was an unnatural institution. My friend Jamie briefly dated a shrink who said everyone always says gay men are promiscuous, but all his straight clients ever talk about are their affairs. I actually think my dad is pretty traditional. I think he would've preferred to work it out with Luce. He would've worked it out with my mom, but she wanted to split up. I don't think my dad has ever broken up with anyone. They all leave him. Including Eden. I'm the only one who stayed.

I opened the refrigerator. It felt like a habit. I'm at one of my parents' houses. I'm coming home from school or somewhere. I just got off the bus. I open the refrigerator. I have carte blanche to eat anything that doesn't look like it's part of a planned meal. Or anything except one of Beth's expensive kombucha sodas. I rested my elbow on the door and peered in.

I shut the door.

Something clicked and whirred. My father always kept the ringer on his landline turned off so it didn't disturb him while he was writing. I thought this was ridiculous given the fact that he couldn't possibly be getting that many calls. I picked up the cordless receiver and said "Hello?" but the person had already hung up on the answering machine's outgoing message. I replaced the receiver and pressed STOP. The machine ignored me and automatically began to play messages.

"Shit," I said to myself. There was another hang-up first. I didn't know if the machine erased the messages after playing them or not, it was so ancient. I looked around for a pen and paper. A recorded ad with a friendly female voice teased that they might have won a Caribbean vacation. Then there was someone calling for Beth from a doctor's office. He started to leave a message and then Beth picked up, but the machine kept recording.

"Oh, hi there," Beth said. "Sorry, sorry, sorry, I just walked in the door."

"Is now a good time?"

"This is fine. It's great. Just give me one minute while I find the . . . how to turn the machine off." Beth must have pressed the wrong button because the machine started blaring a beep that would not end. I pressed STOP again, and then STOP and REWIND together. The machine wound itself all the way back to the beginning of the tape and began playing everything it held.

"Fuck," I muttered.

I pressed buttons as a woman from a credit card company mispronounced my dad's name and left a toll-free number for him to call back. The machine kept on going. It must need to play itself out in order to stop. The next caller didn't speak right away. There was dead air before a voice came on.

"Hey, Dad. And Beth, I guess. It's Eden . . . Anyone there? Screening your calls? . . . Hello? Maybe . . ."

"Yeah, hi." My dad had picked up. "Hang on a sec." There was fumbling and clicking and then the tape cut out.

The machine beeped again.

"Hey, guys, it's Brian. Just wondering if you could give me the name and number of your go-to plumber guy again. I know you gave it to me before, but for the life of me I can't find it. Okay, talk to you soon."

The machine babbled on. Hang-ups. Telemarketers. Vacation offers. Insignificances. Beth's doctor and the eardrum-piercing beep again. All of it coming out of this little box. I stared at it. I was afraid of it. I had been looking for Eden this whole time, but this whole time she had been inside this answering machine, this little outdated plastic box attached to this outdated cordless phone. Someone had shrunk her and she lived inside the answering machine and she could only communicate with the outside world by making the phone ring. The answering machine stood undisturbed in its special spot, the top shelf of a low bookcase that wasn't quite level with the windowsill. A modest little plastic house in a neighborhood of books and kitchen appliances. No one seemed at home. It was the middle of the day. On a weekday. Everyone was out or at work. If I knocked on the door, who would answer?

The machine rewound itself back into position. It clicked and silenced itself and the flashing light went dark.

I reached over and rested my finger on the PLAY button. I pressed it timidly, softly, feeling its miniature springs begin to engage. It resisted beneath my finger, demanding more pressure if I really wanted the machine to get up out of its chair and do its job. If I really wanted to hear it. "What do you want?" it asked me. "Do you want to hear the whole thing again? Do you need confirmation? Didn't you believe me the first time?"

I pressed the button and held it down. The anonymous lady singsonged the toll-free number.

"Hey, Dad. And Beth, I guess. It's Eden . . . Anyone there? Screening your calls? . . . Hello? Maybe . . ."

"Yeah, hi. Hang on a sec." Fumble. Click. Beep. And the guy wanting the plumber's number. I fast-forwarded through the other messages since the machine previously ignored my rewind commands. It hit the end of its recordings. Rewind back to the beginning. These are the things a machine could do. The flashing light went dark. The machine was motionless and ready. A trap set, waiting to be sprung. I didn't dare move.

A car turned into the driveway, picking up speed. It knew the way. It knew how to punch the gas on the incline up to the house. Then it sees the hulk of The Camper occupying its preferred parking spot close to the deck. It slows down. Pauses. Assesses the situation. Slowly turns and begrudgingly takes the other parking spot, even though it doesn't like that spot very much. Shuts engine. Opens door. Puts feet on ground. Shuts car door. Walks to house.

Opens door.

"Hey there." Juggles keys and plastic grocery bags. Dumps everything on kitchen table. "Didn't know you were coming. The old warhorse made it, huh?"

Walks a few steps toward me. Puts arm across my shoulders and squeezes. Asks, "Is Beth home?" Doesn't seem to notice that I am frozen and can't move. That I am staring at the answering machine. That I have not looked at him since he came in the door. Since he dropped groceries on the table. Since he realized I was here.

He sorts through some mail. Throws junk mail directly into the paper recycling bin. Turns an envelope over and looks at the back. Tosses it on the table to read later. Grabs plastic grocery bags and transfers them to kitchen counter. Opens refrigerator, transfers items from bag to fridge. Shuts fridge. Opens cabinet and takes out glass. Presses glass into refrigerator nook for automatic ice dispensing. Stops when glass is half full of ice. Shifts to automatic water dispenser. Fills up glass. Lifts glass to mouth. Sips carefully because he has filled the glass too high. Looks at his daughter. Me.

"Hello, Hope? Earth to Hope?" Swallows. His daughter is unable to speak. Her throat has dried up. The muscles of her larynx, no longer functional. The Camper fared better than she did. At least that behemoth managed to start itself up. To bring itself back from the dead.

His daughter looks as if she might pass out. She looks white with pain. All the blood of her body draining to her feet. Her feet swollen. Her head light. "Hope?" he asks again. More concerned. Something could have happened to her. Something horrible. Horrible things do happen. They've happened to her before.

He takes another sip of water. Out of nervous habit. Or his body has taken over and knows what to do with a glass of water in its hands. He doesn't know he's drinking it at all. He knits his eyebrows together. He wonders if he's done something wrong. Something that might warrant this behavior. Or if there is some horrible news she must tell him. He wonders where Beth is. Sometimes she is home before he is, but it's not so late that he would worry that she's late. He spoke to her today already. This morning. She called him again during the day sometime. To tell him how her day was going. To remind him of something. Just to say hello and I love you. He can't remember what he said back.

"Hope? Are you okay?" he asks, wanting the rote answer of "Fine."

My legs move me to the side of him and past him and my hands lead me back to the answering machine. I press buttons. I fast-forward to the second beep.

"Hey, Dad. And Beth, I guess. It's Eden . . . Anyone there? Screening your calls? . . . Hello? Maybe . . ."

"Yeah, hi. Hang on a sec."

Then the guy wanting the plumber. I hold down the FAST FORWARD button. The end. The machine rewinds itself.

My back is to my father. He doesn't say anything. He is waiting for me to turn around, and he knows I will. He needs these few moments to run through all his emotions and excuses. But he doesn't want me to wait too long, because I am scaring him.

He sets his water glass on the kitchen counter.

I turned my head to look at him over my shoulder. I thought this was kind. Or maybe I was scared. He was looking at the floor. He was leaning on the kitchen counter, holding on to his sweaty ice water for support. He looked in pain.

He shook his head a little. He opened his mouth to speak but couldn't find words. He lifted his hand and dropped it. He repeated all of this. He closed his eyes and scrunched them shut. He raised his free hand in defeat.

"She calls sometimes," he said.

I looked at my father's pants. Old jeans that were out of style and too baggy on him. His relatively new sneakers. He only ever wore sneakers. Even though he never jogged or played any sports.

"When?" I asked.

"I don't know. It's random. Whenever. Sometimes . . ."

"Sometimes what?"

"It's not a regular thing. Sometimes a year or so will go by."

"What does she want?"

"I don't know. One time she needed some money and asked me to do one of those . . . what do you call it? Like a telegram thing. Western Union. But that was just once. Years ago. Maybe ten years ago. I think she . . . I don't know . . . I think sometimes she just wants to say hello."

I started crying. It wasn't at my father's deception. It felt strange and unfair to even call it deception, though he let me drive off on a wild goose chase in a rickety camper. But why did Eden call him? Why did she never call me?

"I'm sorry," he said.

I wiped my nose. I tried to catch my breath. "Where is she?" I asked.

"I don't know," he said.

"What number was she calling from?"

"I don't know."

"Why didn't you find out?"

"How could I? You can look at my phone bills. They're all different numbers."

"Yes, I would like to look at them," I said. I was angry now. My father was incompetent. He was only good at letting things be and letting people walk away from him. "Where are they? Get them out."

"You're going to call all the numbers? First you're going to have to figure out which ones they are. How are you going to figure out which ones they are? Are you going to call every-one who happened to call the house in a certain time period? And by the way" — he was angry now too; he had given up on the hangdog routine and was now gesticulating with his hands — "that message was from a long time ago. It didn't get erased. We don't erase it very often because not many people call the landline. Actually, I've been meaning to get rid of it. It's just a waste of money."

"But then how would Eden call you? You've had the same number since we were kids. She knows it by heart. You keep it for her."

My father walked by me and stomped up the stairs.

Get a hold of yourself, I said to myself, or he won't give you anything. He'll repossess The Camper and put you on a bus back to New York.

He came back downstairs, taking the steps quickly like he was late for something. He threw a manila folder full of phone bills at me triumphantly. "I'm pretty sure she's in California," he said. "That should narrow it down for you."

He turned around and began to climb the stairs again. "Did Mom hear from her too?" I asked.

"How the hell should I know?" he answered angrily without turning around. He walked down the upstairs hallway and shut the door to his bedroom.

I flipped through the old bills. My father was right. They were numbers without names. I could pull out all the ones with California area codes, see if there were any repeat calls. I could call all the California numbers and see if I could recognize her voice. Did I recognize it on the answering machine? When she said "Hey," and before she said her name, did I know it was Eden in those few seconds?

I walked upstairs carrying the phone bills and knocked lightly on his bedroom door. "Yeah," he said from inside. I opened the door. He was lying in bed with his clothes on and his shoes dangling off the end of the mattress. The TV was on. I leaned against the dresser and he muted the television with the remote. "I saw her once," he said. "She asked me not to tell you."

"She came here?"

"No. She asked me to meet her."

"Where?"

"Not too far from here. I don't know why she was here. I thought maybe she was in trouble."

"What kind of trouble?"

"I don't know. Maybe nothing. I was trying to put together why she dropped out. I wrote down all the possibilities: drugs, mental illness, post-traumatic stress disorder, religious conversion or cult, involvement in something not entirely legal but politically volatile. Just a theory. Maybe it was something political. I don't know. Eden's not stupid. Eden wanted life to mean something. I mean, I'm really just speculating. She never told me anything one way or another. I tried to communicate that if she was involved with something, I could help her out because I'm a journalist. I said that sometimes raising your profile is good. It builds public support and sentiment. That's what the SDS and the Weathermen did. That's how Bernardine Dohrn and Bill Ayers turned themselves in relatively unscathed and got off easy. Eden could've done the same thing. Could've gotten a book deal. Then you can sell film rights so you can have something to live off of. Or a documentary. That's good for speaking engagements. If she could build herself up into something like that, I think it could protect her. Instead of all of this hiding. But who knows? Maybe that's just my fantasy. Maybe it all goes back to what happened. Now this latest thing bringing it up again. It's not even about anything. It's a cold case. Random. It doesn't mean anything."

"Larry killed a girl," I said.

"Yeah," my father said, "he did." He watched TV for a few moments. His eyes looked barely open. He looked old. He needed the TV so he wouldn't have to look at me.

"We could've been killed," I said.

The downstairs door opened and Beth sang hello in her cheery voice. Beth has doctors' appointments. Beth could be ill. Beth could die. And then what? And then my father could have another tragedy to nurse for years. To blame for his life not going the way he wanted it to. But this is the way he wanted it to go. He likes these things that define him. His damaged daughters. His trail of women who broke his heart. His lackluster career. His stature among his fellow midlist writers as the real deal who never caught a break. The one who always got passed over for something because he had such bad luck. Kids getting kidnapped. Married a lesbian. Divorced twice. Long-term girlfriend left him because he didn't have the balls to follow her. One daughter completely disappeared. The other a failed queer playwright. He likes it this way. He likes that we didn't surpass him. He likes that we survived, barely. If we had died, we would've been better than him.

Beth came up the stairs and knocked on the doorframe to the bedroom. As if this house wasn't hers even though she's been living here and helping to pay the mortgage and taxes. Even though she's planted her herbal tea garden out back. I looked at Beth as she tilted her head to the side, as her hair fell away from her face exposing her dangly earrings, as she

smiled meekly, as her eyes asked if it was okay for her to enter her own bedroom. Beth was pretty. She was girlish. She
had a nice smile. She had nice hair, dark brown with silver
tinsel weaving through it. She was trim and almost a vegetar-
ian. I had been so horrible to her. I could've been nicer. I wish
at times I was a nicer person. But I just couldn't be. It wasn't
in me.

I felt myself choke up. I was going to cry. I closed my eyes
and shook my head, clutching the folder of phone bills to my
chest. I mumbled that I was sorry and pushed my way out
of the room, down the stairs, and out onto the front deck.
I thought I would be able to breathe once I was outside, but
the oxygen was too much. The air overwhelmed me. I pulled
open the door to The Camper and climbed in. Start, I thought.
Please start. Please start right away. I dug the keys out of my
pocket and sifted through them to find the right one. Please
start, I thought as I jammed the key into the ignition. Please
don't embarrass me. Please let me go. Just let me go.

15

I think I slept. Or I was knocked out.

I was so tired, so uncomfortable, so cold. I coughed.

There was snot in my nose. When I breathed in, mucus got caught in my throat and made me cough again.

I felt like I was underwater and was trying to come up to breathe.

Someone was holding me up by the arms and I tried to get my arms back so I could wipe my nose, but I couldn't, so I tried to wipe my nose on my shoulder, but I could barely reach it.

I lifted my head. I looked across at Eden. She was tied to a tree. She was wearing only her underwear and a bra. And her headphones around her neck with the cord dangling down. I was tied to a tree too. I was in my underwear too. Eden was looking at me. She had been awake longer than I had. It was just starting to become light. When I was twelve I went to a lot of slumber parties and the big thing to do was to try and stay up all night until it was light out. When it got light out, then we could go to sleep. It was a test to see if you were cool, although I couldn't remember who started it or who made up the test.

I expected Eden to say something to me, to ask if I was all right. She didn't say anything. I wanted to ask her what was going on, but I got the feeling I shouldn't. I tried to move my arms around. My hands were cold and asleep. I couldn't feel much.

Something moved. I think I made a little noise in my throat because it still wasn't totally light and I was afraid. And then I saw it was Larry, who had fallen asleep in the dirt and he was moving around now and the dirt and leaves were brushing against his clothes and he was sitting up. He cleared his throat and spat to the side.

He sat cross-legged in front of us and started scratching at the dirt. As the light came up I could see that he was digging with a big knife. So big it looked fake.

He walked away into the woods. When he was gone I looked at Eden. Eden looked at me. I tried to say something. I was going to say, Are you okay? Can you get your hands free? Where are we? What's going on? How did we get here? But Eden didn't know the answers to those questions any more than I did.

"Is he going to kill us?" I asked. Eden just looked at me. She was wearing her sea-green bra made of stretchy lace and black cotton underwear. She had bought that bra at the Victoria's Secret store in the Fashion Square Mall. My eighth-grade friend Ellie liked to go to the Victoria's Secret at the Fashion Square Mall, and I would go along with her even though I really wasn't into frilly stuff. But Ellie was, and she would try on stuff and pose for me and ask me what I thought, and I liked that. Ellie spent all of her babysitting money on lingerie stuff. I once bought a white lace bra because I thought Ellie would like it that I bought something with her. But I never wore it because it itched and the seams showed through T-shirts. I usually wore cotton bras and that's what I was wearing now.

I wondered who had taken off my shirt and my jeans. Larry must have done it when he punched me. My head still hurt from that. But before he punched me we were here, but I couldn't remember how we got from Larry's house to here. I wondered what else I couldn't remember. I wondered what else Larry did, but the only thing that hurt was my head. I didn't think he did anything else. I didn't think he raped me. I hadn't ever had sex so I thought I would know if I had.

Eden started rubbing her back against the tree. Maybe she could shred the rope that way. I leaned forward so the rope around my wrists rubbed against the tree. I didn't think it would work. It would only work if he kept us here for a long time and we slowly worked at it like a prisoner who tunnels his way out of jail with just a spoon. It could take months.

Larry came back. He unscrewed the top of a soda bottle and cursed when it exploded over his pants. He held the bottle away from his body until it stopped erupting. He shook off excess soda from his hand, transferred the soda to his free hand, and shook off the other one that had been holding the bottle. He tilted the bottle up to the pink sky and emptied it into his mouth. He tossed the empty plastic to the ground, out of his way. He took out a pack of cigarettes from his pocket. Pulled a cigarette out. Stuck it in his mouth. Lit it with a lighter. Sucked on it. Walked around. Paced. Smoked.

Found the empty bottle on the ground and kicked it. Stuck the cigarette in the corner of his mouth. Turned his back to us. Unzipped his fly. Pissed.

He zipped up and turned back around. He finished his cigarette and flicked the butt away. He brought his hands up to his mouth. Breathed into them. Stuck them under opposite armpits for warmth. Paced. He bent over and picked up a long stick.

I went through all the rape-prevention strategies I knew of. I used to tuck my long hair into my jacket when I was walking home from a friend's house after dark so people wouldn't think I was a girl. No one told me to do that; I came up with it on my own. And no one told me to walk the long way home along the busy street instead of the more direct route. Right now I wished I had my period. That might be a turnoff. He might not want to rape me if he sees I have my period. I wondered if Eden had her period right now. Last summer I got a rash all over my inner thighs and crotch because I had sat around in a wet bathing suit all day after swimming in a lake. It was ugly and red and looked gross. And I was so embarrassed about it I didn't go swimming the rest of the time we were at the lake that summer. I lied and said I had my period and didn't want to go swimming, and Luce took me aside and said if I wanted, she would show me how to use a tampon and I could go swimming. I had only had my period a few times and was still using pads. I shook my head because I didn't want her to know about it and make a big deal about it even though Luce wasn't the type to make a big deal about things. She would've probably given me a tube of some kind of cream and hid it in a towel and said, "Here's the extra towel that I forgot to give you." Luce was good like that. She was good about privacy. I would wish that rash back if it meant Larry wouldn't rape me. But then I remembered my mother saying that rape isn't about sex, it's about power and control and violence and it has nothing to do with the way you look. People who say it has to do with the way you look or what you are wearing are trying to blame the victim and justify violence against women. So I didn't know if any of those things would help me at all. I didn't know if any of them mattered. I really had to pee. I was worried about peeing. I didn't want to tell him I had to go to the bathroom. I tried to hold it in. I was worried about it. I tried not to think about it. I thought eventually I was just going to have to release it and pee. Maybe that would make him so mad he would rape me. Or maybe it would gross him out and make him pick Eden. I wondered if I could get through it if he did decide to rape me. If he just did it and it didn't take long and it didn't hurt and then he would let us go. If I didn't get pregnant and I didn't get a disease, no one would have to know.

It started to rain. A few drops at first. You barely noticed it. Then you saw it on the ground, dappling the brown leaves and dirt. Then it was pouring. My hair was getting wet. My thighs were getting cold. My ears were cold. I moved my head from side to side trying to dislodge the hair tucked behind my ears. I thought even with my hair wet, if it covered my ears they would be warmer. My muscles were tired. It was raining on my face. I wanted to wipe my nose but couldn't. Larry hitched his jacket up over his head and walked back to his truck. I bent my head forward and looked at the ground.

I started to cry.

I thought, No one is going to find us. No one knows where we are. We don't know where we are. It's Saturday now. If

Luce finally picked up my dad from where he got his car towed and then they went to Larry's to pick us up, they wouldn't find us there. Larry's weird cousin doesn't know where we went. He didn't want to hang around us. And maybe my dad didn't know Larry at all. Maybe Larry was a rapist who picked up girls from bus stations with a good story. What happened to Dad? Did Larry kidnap him too? Or did he never show up? If my dad got the weekends mixed up and never came to pick us up, then no one will wonder where we are until Sunday, when my mom goes to the bus station to get us and we're not on the bus. Then she will call my dad and ask if we took a later bus and why didn't he tell her before she left the house so she wouldn't have to go down to the bus station twice. And our dad will say, What are you talking about, it's not my weekend. And my mom will say, Are you kidding me? I put them on the bus Friday afternoon. And then they will think it is our fault. That Eden put me up to it. That we wanted to do something like go hang out at a friend's house all weekend. A friend whose parents were away for the weekend. A place where all teenage kids descend and raid the liquor cabinet. My mom will yell at my dad saying why didn't he check with her about changing weekends. She will say the girls don't get to decide about this. There are other people involved, she will say. They need to learn some consideration and responsibility. She is basically saying that about my dad, even though she is blaming us. My dad will say no one told him about anything. He will say it wasn't his weekend, they were here last week. And my mom will say no they weren't, check your calendar. She will hang up. She will drive home and start to call all our friends, try to figure out where we are. She is not mad that we would change the weekend to go to a friend's, she is mad that we wouldn't consult her. She likes to have dialogues about things. She doesn't like to be cut out of the process. You have to tell me, she would say. And eventually my dad would think to check his calendar. The Save the Wildlife calendar with pictures of different, almost-extinct animals for each month that hangs in the kitchen next to the refrigerator. He knows he is right and my mom is making a big deal out of nothing. He thinks that's what my mom always does. That kids will be kids and we are at that age and you've got to allow them some freedom to explore and make mistakes and figure out who they are. He would say you don't want them to be little automaton versions of you and me. He will be rehearsing a version of this speech in his head for when my mom calls to apologize. And he thinks about how he will get to be the bigger person and say, Don't worry about it.

But then he will glance at the calendar. He'll do it for validation. To feel good about himself. To pat himself on the back for being a good divorced dad. And first he will stare at the calendar. He will wonder what day it is today. What week it is. He will squint at the dates. He will tap at them with his finger. He will run his finger along the weeks. He will be confused. He will check to see if the correct month is displayed. Then he will start to get nervous. His stomach will feel dry. He won't know what to do. His legs will be frozen. Luce might come in and notice him standing there and start talking to him, but then she will say, What's wrong? And my dad will finally snap out of it and grab the phone and desperately dial my mom's number and start talking very fast in circles trying to explain himself, and he might start crying and he'll ask my mom if she's found us yet. And my mom will tell him to call the police where he lives.

But all that won't happen until tomorrow in the afternoon. Today and tomorrow. Almost two whole days. Here in the woods it is only Eden and me. And no one will save us. No one will think we need saving for almost two days. Anything can happen in those almost two days. And Eden is tied up too. And she is scared. She thinks this is her fault because she didn't want to use the phone and she is the one who said we should go with Larry when I didn't want to go. And she's the one who wanted to hang out with him and smoke pot and drink beer. And somewhere in the back of her head she feels bad about that. But right now she is afraid.

Eden can't save me, I thought, and that thought made me cry. My big sister can't help me she can't save me she can't get me out of here. She is here, but I am alone.

16

W hat play?" Noreen asked.

I was at my desk in the railroad apartment Noreen and I had moved into together. My desk was in the windowless middle room that also served as a closet for our closetless bedroom. I was reading an email from my old professor Cortland with the subject line "Good News." Right when I graduated from college, I had written a play called *Bind Me*. Cortland had nominated it for an award for new playwrights and it won. I was twenty-two at the time, and I used the money to go to Greece to participate in a production directed by Nico Kis, an aging star of European experimental theater who had once worked with Fassbinder, then spent a decade kicking heroin. He taught a workshop my last semester in college. Nico walked in the first day of class, a scrawny queen dressed in an oversized 1940s-vintage men's suit, his hair dyed an aggressive cherry red. He looked not unlike a smaller, more ferocious David Byrne. He said, in his gravelly, sort of French, sort of Hungarian accent, "I apologize, but I must smoke in class." And so we all smoked in class except for one girl who complained, and then we couldn't smoke in class and Nico was forced to gnaw on licorice-flavored twigs from the health food store, which made him look feral. We loved Nico. When I acted, he would stare at me and breathe heavily through his nose. "I love what you're doing, but the audience won't. You're too internal. The audience is too stupid. I hate the audience, but without them we're nothing." It was Nico who told me to give up acting and become a playwright. "Fassbinder is dead," Nico said. "There are no more good roles for faggots like us."

All of my friends were going to Nico's in Greece. Jamie was going. But I didn't have the money, since none of my parents were the type to give me cash as a graduation present. Then suddenly, when I got that award, I had the money to go. But when we all arrived in Greece we found out the production had fallen through. The theater said it had been canceled weeks before. Nico was in Budapest and he wasn't coming. He left no apologetic note for us. We were a small group of poor American theater students, which didn't make sense to the theater people in Greece, who assumed we were all rich. They didn't give us the free hotel rooms they'd promised, the youth hostel was full up with Swedish tourists and had no beds for us, so we slept on the beach. We made friends on the beach with the girls who worked in the kitchen at the youth hostel, and they let us sneak in to take showers in the morning and told us to blend in with the Swedes to get free breakfast. Jamie got the idea that we should reenact the theater department's production of Shakespeare's *The Tempest* that we did last year. After all, we were shipwrecked on an island. We performed it one night on the beach and someone passed the hat and we made enough money to all go out to dinner. One of the waitresses at the restaurant started drinking with us and later took me downstairs to the basement where there was a break room with a couch, and we fucked on the ratty couch. After that, Jamie and I got free lunch at that restaurant, and Jamie said, "Finally you're beginning to understand how to get ahead in the world." One night the police gave us a ticket for having a campfire on the beach, but we couldn't read it, so we threw it in the trash.

Cortland said that a theater festival in London wanted to produce all of the plays that had won the same playwrights' award over the past ten years. He said Nico wanted to direct my play. The festival couldn't offer me much money, but it would put me up in a hotel when I got there and feed me. I would be a part of the rehearsals. I would have to pay my own way there, but my small fee would cover the cost of the ticket. *Let me know as soon as possible if you can confirm,* Cortland wrote. *I think this would be a good opportunity for the London scene to get to know you.*

"You're basically going to London for three weeks and not getting paid," Noreen said. I said this was a great opportunity. "I don't see the 'great' part," Noreen said. I said no one was getting paid, and Noreen said, "I'll bet Cortland is getting paid." I didn't have anything to say to that, because he probably was getting paid, since he would be there longer than me, seemed to be organizing the whole thing, and was on the nominating committee for the award. I said he probably gets paid by the university from some sort of fund. "You never stand up for yourself," Noreen muttered as she walked out of the room.

I excitedly called Jamie. "This. Is. Really. Fantastic," he said slowly. He asked if Nico was using the same staging as in the original production. Jamie had choreographed the play when we did it at a storefront theater in New York, right after Greece. I said I didn't think so. I didn't know what Nico was planning. "But the direction, how it was choreographed, that's what *made* your play. I mean, Hope, I think I should be a part of this. I should be there with you and Nico." It was true that Jamie contributed a lot to the play, and he figured out how to do the complicated physical things in the script. I told him I would talk to Cortland about it but doubted I had any say in the matter. "You're the playwright," Jamie said. "Of course you have say in the matter."

I avoided asking Cortland because I knew the answer would be no. Jamie pestered me about it, and I said I hadn't heard anything. I said Cortland was writing in a cabin somewhere in Iceland, near a volcano, and he wasn't checking email very often. I said he was waiting to hear from Nico and the people in London. I said it might be a problem because of visas or unions or something. I wrote emails to Cortland but didn't send them. I mentioned it to Noreen. "Why do you feel hesitant about asking him? Don't you want Jamie to help you with the play?" I said I wasn't sure. Noreen asked, "Which play is this? Have I read it?"

Noreen hadn't read it, so I gave her a copy of the script.

In the play, two girls are tied together back to back, naked. Someone has dragged them into the woods and left them there. The stage is littered with dead leaves that Jamie and I raked up from Tompkins Square Park. The girls can't remember anything. They can't remember if something has happened to them or if something is about to happen to them. Slowly, still tied up, they manage to wiggle around and face each other, embraced and entwined, and they begin to have thrashing sex. They thrash around the floor so furiously that the ropes unravel and unwind. When they finally stand up, the lights swirl and a loud sound score comes on. The girls look out at the audience, then up, and the lights dazzle as if a UFO is about to land. Then the theater goes completely black. When the lights come back up, only one girl is there, naked and alone. The other girl doesn't come back for the curtain call. Only one girl takes a bow. And then leaves the stage.

"This is a very weird play," Noreen said when she finished reading it.

"I was young," I said.

"What's it supposed to be about?"

I hated talking about my work. I recited the description I used for writing grants. "It's about two people who are connected and then ripped apart." Noreen looked more confused by my generic sentence. I said, "Critics thought it was a statement about queer love. This struggle, this self-definition, this defiant physical sex that leads to their freedom, but then they are literally struck down by external forces, and in the end, we're all alone." Noreen was still looking at me strangely. "People really connected to the ending," I said. "They said that after watching this long struggle where the characters try to get out of the ropes, and then this really long sex scene, that when they finally get rid of the ropes and stand up, the actors are so physically exhausted, and then one of them vanishes and doesn't come back. The audience really feels alone. They feel the loss," I said. "They said it felt universal."

Noreen looked down at the script in her lap. She fingered one of the brass binder studs holding the three-hole-punched paper together. It was a short script mostly full of physical directions. I spent hours at a Kinko's copying photos from the production and putting them in the script so readers would have an idea what it looked like.

"But why did you write it?" Noreen asked.

17

When I left my dad's, I thought I would drive The Camper all the way back to New York, but it started raining and I was immobile on the Beltway for almost an hour, until I followed an aggressive driver who bluntly cut across three lanes and drove on the shoulder to the nearest exit. I followed him and someone else followed me and my passenger-side wiper decided to quit and half my view was severed, so I pulled into the parking lot of the first restaurant I saw.

I hopped from The Camper through vertical sheets of icy rain to the entrance and was sopping wet when I pulled open the door. It was an upscale Mexican restaurant with sculpted terra-cotta-colored walls that made the place look like a cave. Electric candles flickered in nooks. The carefully designed glow would have felt cozy and warm, but it was too early for dinner and the only person there was sitting at the bar.

I sat down at a table and took off my soaked jacket. I wiped my face and arms dry with two cloth napkins and then piled them in a damp heap on the edge of the table where a waitress could easily take the hint to get rid of them. I sniffed and wiped my nose. I was cold. I ordered a hot tea just to hold something warm. The waitress placed it in front of me and I hovered over the steam, pressing my hands around the mug.

"Hey, over there."

The bartender and her customer were chatting. Snickering about something. They were the only other people in the restaurant, but I assumed they weren't talking to me.

"Hey there, lonely girl," the bartender called out. I looked over. She was smiling. The guy sitting at the bar was looking over his shoulder at me. "Don't make me ask if I can copy your chemistry homework," she said. I didn't get the joke, if she was making one. "Hope," she said, "you can sit over there and we can ignore you, or you can join us and I can make your hour a happy one."

I stood up and walked over, slightly dazed, taking my tea with me, my shoes squeaking wet. The bartender gestured to her chest with both hands. "Layla," she said. And then, not believing my confusion, "From high school. Or have you blocked all of that out?"

"Oh, hey," I said, smiling awkwardly at the weirdness of it all. Of running into a friend from high school at a suburban Mexican restaurant nowhere near where we went to school. Of not recognizing Layla, although she looked the same, just harsher, her hair dyed dark, her eyeliner still thick. She wore a black T-shirt that had a quote in Spanish swirling in white ribbony script that I couldn't quite read. I sat down at the bar, leaving a stool between me and Layla's friend. "Sorry," I said. Layla reached across the bar and hugged me with one arm.

"Yikes, you're soaked." She refilled my mug with hot water and added a healthy shot of whiskey, then disappeared into the kitchen and returned with a gray hooded sweatshirt. "It's clean," she said, "but put it on even if it isn't, so you don't get pneumonia." Her friend laughed. His name was Sam. He had tattoos creeping up from the collar of his shirt and a stud piercing below his bottom lip.

Layla passed me the sweatshirt. I didn't like to borrow clothes from my friends. I never wore Noreen's clothes even though most of them would have fit me. But I was freezing, so I put it on, threading my arms into the sleeves. Layla reached over and pulled the hood up over my head and pressed the sides of my skull, blotting out the water from my hair. Then she pushed the hood back down and mussed my bangs.

Layla's friend Sam asked where I was from, and I said New York. He said, "You don't sound like you're from New York," and I said I wasn't. "So you're from New York and you're not from New York." "I live in New York," I said, "but I grew up not too far from here." Layla was shoveling ice in a bin under the bar and heard only half the conversation. "She's from Charlottesville, like me," she said. I said, "Yeah, and my dad lived up near here." Sam said, "That makes sense, you don't seem like you're from here either." "She left a long time ago," Layla said, "and she never came back to visit. She figured out early on that it was a shithole." I said, "It's not a shithole." And Layla said, "History likes to rewrite itself."

"Whether it's a shithole or not," Sam said, "it's probably not the same place it was when you grew up. Everything's constantly changing. The place where you're from no longer exists." He took a sip of his beer. Layla cleared away my

empty mug and replaced it with a pint of beer. "Good rid-
dance," she said.

"So," Sam said, "you're from New York now. And someday
you won't be. Just like you're no longer from here. Life is a se-
ries of orphanages. Sad but true."

"My Daddy Warbucks is going to show up someday," Layla
said.

"Never happens," Sam said. "We're all waiting around for
it to happen. Never does."

"Isn't he a ray of sunshine?" Layla asked. I smiled. Sam slid
off of his barstool and went to take a piss.

Layla asked me what I was doing here, and I said I was
looking for my sister. That I hadn't seen her in years and
needed to get in touch with her, but she was sort of off the
grid and that made it hard to find her. Layla said, "I don't remember your sister. Was she older or younger than us?" "She
was older," I said. "Was she in school with us?" Layla asked.
"Yes," I said, "but she went to a different school after."

"After what?" Layla asked.

I downed the rest of my beer. I was drinking faster than I
usually did. Layla replaced it, filling it to the brim and carefully setting it in front of me. I leaned over it and sipped it
down. I said, "That thing that happened to us freshman year."
Layla nodded blankly and I wasn't sure she understood what I
was talking about. Or if she was confusing it with something
else. "You know," I said, "when we were kidnapped." Layla
looked at me askance, like I was any other customer telling
a tall tale at the bar, but Sam had come back and caught part
of our conversation and said, "Who was kidnapped?" I said,
"I was. Me and my sister." It was sort of weird that I was say-

ing it, because I never talked about it, never told anyone, but I thought Layla knew. I thought everyone I went to high school with knew. I was the girl who was kidnapped freshman year. "Was it like a custody thing?" Sam asked. I said, "No, it was a regular, dark alley, bus stop, stranger-danger type of thing. It was in all the papers." "Wow," Sam said.

I suddenly felt nervous and had a cold sweat. I put my forehead in the crook of my elbow and wiped my brow with my newly acquired sweatshirt sleeve. Maybe I shouldn't have said anything. I always talk too little or too much, always end up feeling awkward about what I reveal about myself. "You could share more," Noreen would often say to me after a dinner party where I barely participated in the conversation.

"So what happened? I guess you're okay," Sam said.

Layla poured us shots. "L'chaim," she said, clinking my glass, and drank it down. I drank mine too. I didn't feel cold anymore. "Yes," I said. "I'm fine."

Sam leaned against the bar between two stools. He looked at Layla lovingly and I guessed they were a couple and he was waiting for her to get off work. Hanging out here, getting a free drink, waiting for her. It was a ritual. Another bartender came out of the kitchen and Layla tossed her towel away and walked around to our side. She asked me what I was up to now, and I said, "Nothing." "You're not waiting for someone?" she asked. "No," I said. "My car was being funny and I didn't feel like driving." I was worried they were leaving and I didn't want to be alone. She asked me if I wanted to hang out. They were going to her apartment. Maybe smoke some grass and chill out. I said, "Sure." I didn't want to go back to my dad's and I didn't want to go back to New York and Suriya's camp was way too far to drive with one windshield wiper out of commission. Maybe I could stay on Layla's couch, or maybe she had an extra room. Sam said we could take his car, and I thought that was a good idea since I was already somewhat drunk. If I crashed The Camper I'd never hear the end of it.

I couldn't tell how long we drove. I might have fallen asleep. We arrived at an apartment building that looked like an office park. There were clusters of parking spaces around entrances. There were entrances on all sides. Layla used a card to get in, like a hotel.

The apartment was a one-room studio with a kitchenette on one side and a mattress shoved into a corner on the other. There was something temporary about it. Like she had lived there awhile but never expected to stay long. Layla tossed her purse on the kitchen counter. The floor was parquet squares, and a lot of them were loose and they shifted and clacked as she walked around. "There was a game like that," I said. "A wooden game." Layla rubbed the top of my head, messing up my hair, as she passed me.

I collapsed in an armchair. I pulled my feet up under me, curling into it. I hadn't eaten much of anything all day. I was sort of dizzy and wanted to stabilize myself in the chair. I thought if I was completely surrounded by something, encased in something, that would help. It did, sort of. I said, "Hey, do you have anything to eat?"

Layla moaned that I should've mentioned that before we left the restaurant. She could've gotten us whatever we wanted. She surveyed the messy room. Piles of books and magazines. Piles of clothes. There was a lot of makeup stuff on top of a dresser. Lots of tiny free samples you get from a department store or a hotel. Somewhere in the debris Layla found a bag of Cheetos and dropped it in my lap. I usually didn't eat Cheetos, but I was hungry. Starving, in fact. I ate handfuls and licked the orange powder from my fingers. Layla poured us bourbons and sat down on the floor with her back against the mattress. Sam had taken off his shoes and propped himself up on one elbow. He nudged his stocking foot against Layla's neck. "So I guess you had to escape to New York after the kidnapping," Sam said. "And start over."

I took a small sip of bourbon. "I went to college there," I said. Then I felt bad about it. I wasn't sure if Layla had gone to college or not. I didn't keep in touch with anyone from high school. When I moved to New York, I felt that was my real life and I lost interest in my past. I didn't want to have a past. I only wanted to be who I was when I arrived. I only wanted to be who I became.

Layla squinted at me. "Do you want some dry clothes?" she asked. I said, "No, I'm okay." Layla put her bourbon glass down on the floor and reached for my hand. She gently pulled me out of the armchair and walked me over to the dresser. She rummaged through some drawers and found a pair of jeans and a long-sleeved T-shirt. She pressed them into my hands and said, "The bathroom's over there." I stumbled toward it. I didn't know if I wanted the clothes or not. The bathroom was small, with a matted maroon bath rug. I hate the color maroon. I might have said that out loud. The bathtub had sliding glass doors. They looked frosted, but they might have been covered in soap scum. I called out, "I'm going to take a shower," and I heard a distant "Okay" yelled back.

I stuffed the dry clothes into the wedge of space between the towel rack and the wall and lifted the sweatshirt off over my head and skinned off my clammy clothes. The tub was kind of gross. Someone had tried to clean off the layers of grime and then given up, and you could see the whisker marks left behind by the scrub brush. I stood under the hot water and it felt good. I leaned my head back and let the water run through my hair. Then I leaned my head forward and let it massage my neck. I felt dizzy in the steam so I squatted down in the tub. It was cooler there. I didn't feel well. Maybe I was coming down with something. I thought I might throw up.

When I stepped out of the shower everything in the bathroom was wet. My borrowed, clean, dry clothes were wet. My old clothes were wet. The ugly maroon bathmat was wet. Maybe I hadn't closed the shower doors correctly and the water had sprayed out. And now I was dripping on everything as well.

I wrapped a towel around my torso and wandered back out to the living room. Layla and Sam were sitting on the bed. I said something was wrong with the shower. The doors didn't close. They leaked. Water got all over the floor and everything. I said I was sorry. I said, "Maybe you have a dryer? Or there's a laundry room?" I asked Layla if she had something else I could wear. Layla stared at me. Her eyes were glassy. I think they were smoking something because the room smelled smoky and there was a draft like someone had opened a window. Layla got up and walked over to me. She smiled and cupped her hands around my cheeks and kissed me. And it felt warm. I felt warm. I was turned on. But also woozy. Like I might fall over. But I kissed her back and pressed the towel between us.

When Layla came up for air she let go of my face and

went to get me new clothes. I looked over at Sam on the bed. He was rolling another joint, licking the paper. He smiled a glassy-eyed smile. "What do you do in New York, Hope?" he asked. Layla gave me some more clothes. I said I was a writer. "I told you she was smart," Layla said, taking a puff of Sam's joint. She passed it to me. I took a puff but didn't hold it in too long. I took another. I passed it back to Layla.

I went to the bathroom and put on the clothes: green cargo pants and an oatmeal-colored hoodie that zipped up the front. Layla didn't give me a T-shirt or anything to wear underneath and she didn't give me any underwear. I didn't want to put on my wet underwear so I didn't wear any. I gathered all the wet clothes into a ball and went back to the living room.

The armchair where I had been sitting was wet. The faux leather glistened where my ass had been. I dumped the wet clothes on the chair. Layla had poured me some more bourbon and I drank it down and felt warm again. I crawled onto the bed since it was the only cushioned and dry place to sit. I leaned my head back against the wall. "Could I stay here?" I asked. "If you want," Layla said. "Just for tonight," I said. "If it's too weird I can sleep in my van." "Were you planning on sleeping in your van?" Layla asked. "Umm . . ." I said. I didn't know the answer to that. "I don't know," I said.

"What are you doing here again?" Sam asked. "You had to find someone?"

I drank a large gulp of bourbon and let it burn my throat. "I'm using the van to find my sister."

"Is she missing?" Sam asked.

"Yeah," I said. "No one's heard from her in years."

"How come you waited so long to look for her?"

"It's complicated," I said.

"That means it's interesting."

"No," I said. "Not really." I yawned.

"Was it the kind of thing where you lived with your mom but she lived with your dad?" Layla asked. I looked at Layla. Maybe she didn't remember. Maybe she thought I was making up the kidnapping story. Maybe she thought I was crazy. "No," I said, "we both lived with my mom and then she went to a boarding school for a little while." "Boarding school or rehab?" Layla asked. "Boarding school," I said. "So it's not that kind of complicated," she said. I closed my eyes, rested the bourbon glass in my lap. "Don't you remember?" I said and yawned again. "Everyone knew."

I think I fell asleep.

It always felt like Eden and I were a unit when we were kids. The way all our parents referred to us as "the girls." I always wanted one best friend whom I could tell everything to, more than I wanted a big group of friends. I really was a loner. I isolated myself, as Noreen said. In New York, lots of people became friends doing plays together and kept up those friendships and called each other, but I never did. I always felt so alone after a production closed. Like the cast and crew all went into the forest together, but we each came out separately.

My eyes drifted open. I looked across the disheveled room with its mounds of dirty laundry. The room Eden and I stayed in at our dad's was never messy because we didn't keep much stuff there. We always dutifully brought our clothes and our toothbrushes every other weekend. But we had a room there. And a cheap stereo in our room because my dad hated the music Eden listened to and he didn't want her to play it in the living room.

I sat up in bed. The apartment was empty.

I wondered if I had slept through the night, but when I looked at my phone and saw that it had only been an hour, I walked to the bathroom and knocked softly on the door. "Layla?" I called. I opened the door slowly. No one was in there, just the soggy maroon bathmat still on the floor. I lifted it up and hung it over the edge of the tub so it would dry more quickly. I went back into the main room and poured myself another glass of bourbon. Maybe they ran out somewhere. Maybe they went to pick up food. I drank some more bourbon. I picked up the Cheetos bag but I had already emptied it. I wandered over to the kitchen counter to look for a note. Layla's apartment was such a mess, as if she never cleaned, as if she did laundry once a year, as if she hated being here and came home only when she had to. I wondered what had happened to Layla. She was always so smart, so tough. I always thought she could walk right out into the world and do whatever she wanted. But maybe she didn't want anything. Maybe she wanted nothing and to be nowhere.

I looked out the window and the view was of the parking lot.

I thought, This place is so depressing, I could never live here. But then, I'm not really living anywhere right now.

I sat down on the bed. I leaned over my knees, my face in my hands. I felt shaky. I suddenly felt so alone. My mother had died. Eden was gone. I had just ripped a huge hole between me and my dad, or he ripped it. Suriya and Luce each went on their merry or not-so-merry ways. I slid my fingers over my forehead and into my hair, which was still damp from the shower. I had nothing.

I started to cry but shook it off. I thought about taking

another shower. I thought about drinking more, though I was already drunk. I could drink until I fell asleep again. Or I could leave.

I needed to leave.

I found my shoes. I didn't know whether to change back into my own clothes. They were still wet. They would feel horrible. I decided not to. I balled up my jeans and my jacket and held them under my arm. I walked to the door. Layla and Sam hadn't locked it. The knob turned easily in my hand as if it had been waiting for me all along.

I walked out to the parking lot and found my way to the main road. A car blew by, honking at me. I didn't see any signs of civilization so I picked a direction and started walking.

It was cold. It was late. A random cab slowed beside me and the driver lowered his window and asked if I wanted a ride. Maybe it was a cab or maybe it was just a car. I didn't answer. The driver asked if I wanted a lift to a Metro station. He asked if I wanted to go somewhere else. If I wanted a free ride. I didn't answer. I didn't get in. I walked a long time. Ignore it, I said to myself. Ignore the cab. Ignore the empty street. Ignore the night. Ignore the fact that you are lost. You can walk anywhere. You can be from anywhere. You can be anyone. You can be no one at all.

18

I woke up in the woods. I didn't know if it was the same day or the next day. It was light out, a cloudy gray day. I wondered if Eden was awake. I was scared about calling her name or making any noise. I wanted Larry to forget about us and drive away.

I tried to move my hands. There was a piece of bark stuck between my wrist and the rope. I twisted my hand and tried to break it off. It was soft and it crumbled away. After it did, the rope was looser. I narrowed my fingers together like a te-pee and was able to slip one hand out.

Eden was still asleep. I was pretty sure she was. Her head drooped toward her knees and she wasn't moving. I looked around but I couldn't see where Larry was or if he was coming back. I lowered my hand to the ground and shook it out, trying to get some feeling back into it. My whole arm felt numb. I had to consciously think to flex my elbow, to make it move. It flooded with sensation rushing back in, and all at once it felt like it was being stabbed with a thousand tiny needles. I tried to shrug it off. The prickly feeling stopped and it felt numb again, but not so much as before. I slowly twisted my body around to my other hand and tried to undo the knot. But then I heard footsteps against dead leaves. I didn't want Larry to see because he might tie me up again tighter and then I would never get out. I wrapped my free arm back around the tree the way it had been. I held on to the rope in the back.

Larry went over to Eden and untied her. Eden was skinny and she was always cold. She was the kid at the pool whose lips turned blue and who shivered under a massive beach towel when she got out of the water. When Larry untied her she could barely stand up. He put his arm around her and rubbed her shoulder like they were old friends and pulled her deeper into the woods. She could barely walk. She kept tripping and falling to her knees and Larry had to pull her up. And Eden sort of gave up and collapsed and Larry had to drag her along.

I dropped the rope and reached around to try and undo my other hand. My fingers were still numb and my joints didn't work right and it was taking so long to loosen anything. I heard someone coming and straightened up. I put my free hand behind the tree like it was still tied up.

But it wasn't Larry and Eden. It was a group of boys, younger than me. They had big nets and backpacks and handmade walking sticks. One of them had a canteen hanging off his belt. They were just boys out in the woods playing camp or war or doing their own version of Boy Scouting. They stared at me. I stared back at them. I didn't know what to say. I was wearing only underwear and a bra. They were younger and had probably never seen a live teenage girl in her underwear before. I thought I might pee in my pants. One of them coughed and laughed and then his friend hit him in the arm and whispered, "Stop." "You stop," the laugher said and pushed him back. The friend tried to push the laugher's arm out of the way and then the two of them jumbled themselves in a shoving match. "Cut it out," another boy said.

Finally, I said, "Help me," in a low voice and went back to trying to untie my hand. I looked at them over my shoulder. "Help me," I said again because they hadn't moved. "A man kidnapped me and tied me up here." Something about the word "kidnapped" snapped them out of their play. It was a word their mothers had drummed into them. It was what happened to the kids who had their pictures on milk cartons and *Have You Seen Me?* posters at bus stops. They dropped their camping things and came over to help me.

One of them had a pocketknife and he started sawing at the rope. He said he was worried about cutting my hand so he sawed a foot over. When he had finally cut all the way through the rope, he had to untangle it before I was free.

I stumbled a few steps away from the trunk that had supported me for almost two days. I turned around and looked at it. It looked like a person. Like someone who was sad to see me go. But even trees could be evil. Nothing could be trusted. Not these boys. Not this tree.

The boys picked up their gear and started walking into the woods, away from the clearing. "It's this way," one of them said. "This is the way out."

I followed behind the boys. My legs were bare and I didn't have any shoes. I let them stomp down a path ahead of me.

I was a good head taller than all of them. The laugher boy used his walking stick as a machete, hacking leafless saplings out of the way. I let the boys' calm manner take over the situation. There was nothing unusual about it to them. They had gone hiking in the woods one day and freed a girl who had been kidnapped. And now it was time to go home for a snack. I didn't encourage them to run. I didn't explain anything. I went along with their game, not to keep them from being frightened, but because I preferred their game. Because at the end of their game was a peanut butter sandwich and a cup of juice. There was no man pulling off your pants and tying you to a tree. Their game had none of that. It had an ending that was happy and familiar.

When we heard Larry's voice in the distance it didn't bother them at first. It was just someone else in the woods. Maybe a hunter or a hiker. They looked in the direction the voice came from but didn't stop walking. I tried to keep up with them. I tried not to hear anything. But eventually I couldn't walk anymore.

The boys noticed and turned around and stared at me. "What's wrong?" one of them asked at a normal volume.

"That's the guy," I said in a whisper. "The guy who kidnapped me."

They stared at me. And the realization washed over them that I wasn't playing a game. That it wasn't a bunch of bullies who tied me up as a joke. They noticed that my bra was wet and dirty and that I wasn't wearing shoes and that I was shaking.

Larry shouted something. I turned in the direction of his voice and saw him in the distance, his jacket flickering through the tree trunks as he ran up a dry creek.

The boys dropped their stuff and ran.

And there I was. I thought I would follow the boys back to their house, their house that couldn't be that far away. They had walked here. They could run home. And I could have followed them. We all could have made it. Larry wouldn't have caught us all. We had a good start. He was a safe distance away. It would've been hard for him to catch up to us. But I couldn't run.

I couldn't stand still either. I ran back into the woods. Circling away from Larry, who was coming up the creek. Away from the boys running toward home. Back into the woods. Toward the way I had come. Back to the tree that held me. To Eden.

19

had to tell Noreen what the play was really about.

Noreen knew that I hadn't seen or spoken to Eden since I left for college, but I never told her about Larry. I think, in her social-worker head, she had decided that Eden was probably mentally ill. She brought it up and I didn't correct her. She once said, "That, or there's something she absolutely will not forgive your parents for." Since I didn't talk about Eden, Noreen rarely mentioned her. But suddenly she was intrigued by this play. She asked to see the video of the old production. I stayed in the bedroom working on my laptop with my headphones on while she watched it. When it ended she came and stood in the bedroom doorway. "That was kind of violent," she said. "It was pretty disturbing."

She rambled on about why she thought it got positive reviews. Sure, people held it up as a kind of feminist manifesto, but they were reacting to the sexual violence. She felt I was playing into their porn fantasies of watching two women go at it. It was both a cat fight and two girls fucking. She said it played right into straight-male fantasies about lesbians. "And then of course one basically dies in the end, and the other is made to suffer—the textbook cliché in mainstream media where you have to be punished for being gay, either by death or desexualization."

Noreen paused and looked down at her feet. I was trying to swallow and lubricate my throat so I could say something in my defense.

"But then," Noreen said, "I have to admit, it was compelling. It was sort of riveting. It was so violent, and yet it was a turn-on, and I wondered why I was getting turned on by these two people tied up together and trying to bite through the ropes or bite through each other. It was disturbing but I wanted to know what was going to happen. It kind of hooks you. And I feel disturbed that it hooked me."

Noreen was still standing in the doorway. "I guess I was surprised you wrote it," she said. "It's nothing like your other plays."

I hadn't said anything in a long time, so I cleared my throat and said, "Yeah, I guess not."

Noreen came over and sat down next to me on the bed. I pushed my laptop aside. Noreen looked down at her hands and picked at her nails. "But how did you come up with that? What made you write it?" She peered up at me with a look on her face that I knew meant she loved me, that she wanted to know more about me, she wanted to excavate me so she could love me more. "Was it something to do with Eden?"

It was then that I told Noreen what happened.

Noreen fluctuated between shock, being upset with me

for never telling her, and putting on her professional social-worker hat and trying to control her reaction. But she
couldn't keep it together. She started crying hysterically. I put
my arms around her and stroked her back. I tried to calm
her. I so wanted her to stop crying that I sort of brushed it
all off like the kidnapping wasn't that serious a thing. She became confused and pushed me away. "Oh my god," she said.
"Are you fucking kidding me? Are you making this all up?" It
was an accusation and a plea. I almost wanted to lie to her.
But I said it was all true. I said she could call my parents and
confirm it with them. That made her cry more. Noreen had
met my parents, had gone down to visit them with me, had
looked through old photo albums of me and Eden as kids,
and no one had ever mentioned it. "You are all so incredibly
fucked up!" she said.

When we went to sleep that night, Noreen turned to me
and said, "I'm so sorry that happened to you." I didn't know
what to say in response. I glanced down at the sheets. "Do
you feel safe with me?" she asked. I said I did. Of course I did.
"But why did you never tell me about it?" I said I never talked
to anyone about it, and Noreen said, "But I'm not just anyone."

Noreen insisted I see a therapist. I tried to say I really
couldn't afford it, but Noreen called around and got me a re-
ferral to someone who would let me slide to the bottom end
of the sliding scale and so I had no excuse not to go.

The therapist's name was Janet. She had an office on the Upper West Side that was a hellishly long subway ride from our
apartment. I was buzzed into a waiting room that whirred
with white-noise machines. Inside her office, Janet sat in a

knockoff Eames chair and I sat opposite her. Between us was the ottoman that matched her chair, and after she sat down she slipped off her shoes and propped up her stocking feet. Janet was probably sixty. She had short sensible hair and glasses. She asked me how I knew Noreen, and I laughed and said, "She's my girlfriend." Janet chuckled a bit and said, "Good thing I don't know her very well."

A silence settled in, and after I missed my chance to bring things up on my own, Janet asked me why I was here.

"It was actually Noreen's idea," I said.

"Why did she want you to come?"

I never told many people about what happened because I never knew where to start. The bus station? My dad forgetting to pick us up? Eden? I'd have to explain my whole family situation. I'd have to draw out the family tree and explain the intricacies of everyone's relationships. It was too much to talk about, which is why I wrote a play with hardly any words in it. I thought it was clear. It felt clear to me. It was only Noreen who was confused and wanted it explained and spelled out. I wasn't sure what to make of her critique before I told her. It seemed she didn't want to like the play but did so only begrudgingly, and if someone else had written it, she wouldn't have liked it at all. She would have preferred I write a different play about what happened. And this was the play she wanted me to write: a two-character drama with a therapist in which I explain myself, recount my experiences, sob or punch a pillow, and somehow, through this exposition, then expulsion, I find relief and let go and everything is all right in the end. I hated that kind of resolution. Everything is not all right in the end. In the end, your bruises become scars and they make you who you are. This kind of erasure of the past as therapy disturbed me. It angered me. My trauma was my trauma. Larry was mine. He was mine and Eden's. I did not see the purpose of performing him to Noreen's standards, of processing him the way she thought I should.

I said something like that to Janet. She said, "You sound angry."

"Why can't I be angry?"

"You can be angry," Janet said.

We didn't say anything for a moment. I wondered how much time was left, but the clock was positioned so that only Janet could see it.

"Survival can be hard for other people to understand," Janet said. "Often people don't understand that it's an ongoing process. They think it begins and ends with the trauma." Janet sat up in her chair and pulled her feet off the ottoman and placed them on the floor. She leaned forward and rested her elbows on her knees. "People automatically put themselves in your position and wonder what they would have done. If they would've gotten into the truck. If they would've used the pay phone."

"I know we should've called!" I snapped at her. I wasn't sobbing. I wouldn't sob. I wouldn't play this game. This was not my play. "I know we shouldn't have gotten in the truck. But we got out of there. And we were fine."

20

ran back. I found the trees. Eden wasn't there.

I turned around in place. In all directions the woods looked the same.

I knew I shouldn't stay in the same place too long. I knew I shouldn't yell for Eden. I didn't know which way Larry would come from. I didn't know these woods. I didn't know any woods except the shortcut through the trees behind my dad's house to the swimming pool at The Pines.

I saw the glint of Larry's truck and ran over to it. I crouched down when I got close, in case he was there. He wasn't there. But he was close. And he would be here soon.

Eden was lying down in the back of the truck. She looked asleep. For a second I froze, thinking she could be dead. He could have killed her and then gone back for me.

I reached for her foot. I touched it, then wrapped my hand around her ankle. She felt cold, but we were cold because we had been in the woods for almost two days. I squeezed her ankle. "Eden," I said quietly, "wake up."

I pulled on her leg. Larry hadn't tied her up. Maybe he could see that Eden was tired and weak. Maybe he made something up and told Eden he was taking us home, but she should know not to believe him. "Eden," I said. I grabbed both her ankles and pulled, dragging her out of the truck. I got her to the edge of the truck bed and then pulled her arms to make her sit up. I put my arm around her and put her feet on the ground. She tripped and stumbled to her hands and knees. I helped her get back up. I said, "Come on." I took her hand. I didn't know which way to go at first. I thought about finding our pants and putting them on. At least our shoes. I wondered where our backpacks were, if they were still in the back of Larry's truck and I didn't think to grab them and I wondered if the school would charge us for losing our textbooks. Maybe we could try to drive the truck since Eden knew how to drive. She could drive if she would only snap out of her zombie thing. I looked in the driver's window to see if the key was inside, but I couldn't quite tell. I ran around to the other side and looked in. I don't know why I didn't think to open the door but I didn't. I didn't see the key. My heart was pounding in my chest. It was so loud and so strong I thought it must be pushing through my ribs. I picked up Eden's hand again. We ran. We ran through the woods. Branches scratched our skin. I thought we could run faster if we didn't hold hands, but when I let go, Eden grabbed my wrist and she wouldn't let go, so we ran awkwardly and not very fast. And everything hurt under our bare feet. I didn't know where to go or how far. I told myself, Just keep going.

I didn't know where Larry had taken us. He could have

taken us to a state park and we could be running in these woods forever, until dark, when we would have to stop and we couldn't make a campfire out of two rocks or two sticks because then he could find us. At one point Eden stepped on something and yelled out in pain and I told her to shut up and pulled on her arm so hard she yelled again, but then she shut up and we kept running.

Abruptly the woods ended and we were on a lawn. The woods had spit us out somewhere. Vomited us up. The trees had said, Enough of you. Go back somewhere. Go somewhere else. Eden and I slowed down out of shock. Shock at the manicured lawn that was a neighbor to the woods. We stopped. But only for a second. We were too easily seen here. We stuck out. No one was around. Larry could be right behind us and drag us back into the woods and we would be swallowed alive and never get out. We ran.

There was a building on the far side of the lawn. I didn't know what it was. An office park. A private school. A small shopping mall. The parking lot was full of cars but they all looked dead. People had parked their cars here and then vanished. Got on a spaceship and blasted off to a new colony. It felt like there were no people left in the world. Like the entire world had been wiped out by a plague while we were in the woods.

I didn't know if anyone was in the building because its windows were all tinted like sunglasses. I thought, At least it will be warm inside. At least the floor will be smooth. At least there will be a bathroom and a phone. The doors are glass so if they are locked we can break them. And who cares if it sets off an alarm because then the police will come. Larry won't come inside if the alarm is going off.

The door drifted open in my hand. Easily. Without any weight to it. Without requiring any heft from me. There were people inside milling around. It was like an ant farm. A bunch of bugs exposed going about their lives under a rock. A pretty receptionist in pristine clothes picked up a phone to call security to get us out of there. Two wet, dirty, scratched-up, muddy, bloody girls in their bras and underwear. Me with my face beat up. Eden with her headphones still around her neck. By then Eden has begun to shake uncontrollably. And to gasp. And to not really breathe well. They probably think she is epileptic. Or has some kind of disability. Or is on drugs. We are both out of breath. I pull Eden over to the receptionist's desk. I put my hand on the counter. My hand that still doesn't feel right. And I start screaming something.

I think I just scream.

21

I woke up in a Metro station. I had fallen asleep again. My mouth tasted horrible. I was still clutching my wet clothes, still wearing the clothes Layla had given me at her apartment. I wormed my arms into my musty jacket and left my folded wet jeans on the bench. I studied the map. A cleaning person came by. I asked him what train line I was on.

Noreen's address was in my phone. I figured out the station nearest to it. Her apartment building was much nicer than any of our old ones; it had a wide front stoop and her last name was etched into a tiny gold plaque over the doorbell. I pressed the bell with my thumb.

It was still dark out. I slid down to my ass in the corner of her front door. I think I fell asleep there. I remember someone giving me a pillow.

———

I had slept on a couch in a living room. My neck hurt. Soft noises drifted from the other side of the coffee table. A gentle tapping. I pressed my hands into the couch cushions and pushed myself up to sit. A baby was playing on the floor with plastic bricks. I think she was a girl. She paused and looked at me, determining if I was a friend. She held up a blue brick and passed it to me. I took it and rested it on the couch. She smiled and went back to her sorting. She banged two bricks together, enjoying their sound, the simple pleasure from action and result. She looked over her shoulder at me. I offered her the blue brick. She laughed and gurgled. She scooted closer to me and gladly took it back. I wondered where I was.

"Okay, sweetie," someone sang. Noreen's wife walked into the room. I had met her only once before. She had changed her hair. When I'd first met her she had given me the cold cursory survey one gives a partner's ex. Don't even think of coming back here, the look said. You hurt her enough. I can't believe she ever loved you. But now (Nikki, I think her name was) she swooped in and scooped up her daughter and talked about me in the third person with an air of friendly inclusiveness. "Were you playing bricks with Hope? Is that what you were doing? Were you sharing bricks with your new friend?" Nikki brushed the girl's baby-fine hair off her face. "Bathroom's down the hall if you need it," she said, not looking at me.

I staggered down the hall. I felt like shit.

The bathroom was painted in seascape gray with tiny new hexagonal tiles made to look antique. There was a plastic basket of bath toys shoved against the wall. I sat down on the toilet and peed. A rubber ducky greeted me hello with a garish lipstick smile from a corner of the bathtub. A froggy hooded towel stared at me with bulbous eyes. Why were these things made for children? They were frightening. They looked dead.

I couldn't quite remember what had happened last night, the order of what had happened, or how I got here. I didn't think I smelled like sex. I didn't think I'd had sex with Layla or with Sam. I vaguely recalled being on the bed. I would've remembered if I had had sex with Sam because I hadn't slept with a man for several years, since college, so I couldn't summon up what it would feel like afterward. Would there be fluids if he had used a condom? Would it feel the same inside afterward? Would my cavities feel different? It would feel a little raw, I thought. It would sting when I pissed. But I've had other things inside me. What's the difference? The oozy possibility of life? Of putting something in your body that you can't get out?

I wiped myself with toilet paper. Nothing felt different. Nothing looked different. Nothing had happened. We drank and they left. That was it.

I washed my hands and face. I hesitated, but then thought, Fuck it, and borrowed someone's toothbrush and brushed my teeth. I used some fancy face and hand cream that smelled like lemon cake. I ran my fingers through my hair and slicked it in place with water. I was as presentable as I usually was.

When I came out of the bathroom I heard the front door shut. Noreen was at the end of the hallway. She walked toward me. "I'm sorry," I said. My voice sounded hoarse. She put her hand on my shoulder, looked me straight in the eye, and asked if I was okay. I looked at the floor and Noreen ducked her head under mine to make me look at her. "I'm okay," I said.

She poured me some coffee. She had the most perfect kitchen, with a wooden farmhouse table. There was a perfect bowl of seasonal fruit and shelves of turquoise glass jars filled with different kinds of rice and legumes. There were colorful alphabet magnets on the refrigerator. A vintage chalkboard hung on the wall. Noreen and I had bought it together at a tag sale upstate. I let her keep it when we broke up. It was strange to see it here. In a different place. In a different city.

Noreen sat down across from me. I held on to my coffee mug. My fingers looked bony. "I just got in a little over my head," I said. "Doing what?" she asked. I said, "I'm working on a new play." "About what?" she asked. "I'm not entirely sure yet," I said. "Sort of about me and Eden. Mostly about Eden. Trying to figure out what happened to her and where she is."

My throat clenched up when I said this. My voice felt strained, as if each word was painfully extracted from my neck. I was worried I would cry, and that if I did, it would be mostly out of exhaustion and confusion, but Noreen would read it as something to do with her. Of me wanting something from her. Or being lost without her. Or needing her. And I couldn't say that none of those things were true or not true.

Noreen studied me. "Does anyone else know you're doing this?" "My dad knows," I said. "Not about the play. He loaned me his van." "Is that how you got here?" Noreen asked. "Not exactly," I said.

We didn't say anything for several minutes. I knew Noreen was torn between getting involved and knowing she shouldn't get involved. And knowing she should not want to get involved. That she no longer had to get involved with me and my projects that never pan out. When we were breaking up she said, "I invested too much in you, Hope."

It was paining Noreen to have me here, sitting at her expensive, beautiful kitchen table, invading her perfectly renovated new life. I wondered what she had ever wanted to do with me. I felt so out of place here. It was the type of house I only visited. It was the type of place that hosted parties that were good to crash because there was fancy food that could substitute for dinner. Their cheap party wine bought by the case would be more expensive than I could ever afford by the bottle. I had never lived in a place like this. This nice. I'm not sure if I ever could. I was never good with money and could never hang on to it. One time I was well paid to ghostwrite a lawyer's horrible screenplay, but I used the money to self-produce one of my plays. I didn't have anything left over in the end. It was the same with Noreen. I let her have everything. All I owned now were a few boxes stored in Zara's studio.

She could never know me, I thought. I felt my throat tighten again. I stared into my mug, at the creamy surface of my half-drunk coffee, the little muddy skating pond that only I could see.

I said I was sorry again. I stood up and said I would go. "Where did you park?" Noreen asked. She looked down at her lap, cursing herself in her head, probably, for asking me that. You don't need to get involved, she was telling herself. "I took the Metro," I said. "From the suburbs somewhere. I'll figure it out." "Just let me drive you," she said as she got up and grabbed her coat and bag. "It's pouring out," I said. "I can go in late," she said.

We drove silently against morning rush-hour traffic. "My office was thinking of relocating out this way," she said. "It would be farther, but it would take the same amount of time as driving downtown and it would save us so much on our annual operating budget, even if we had to rent space in town for events." She ran through the list of my friends in New York and asked how they were. I said Jamie was working on a project with Julianne Moore. "Really?" She was impressed. "That's great," she said. "He needed a break like that." I thought, Maybe I'm getting better at this, this giving-people-what-they-want thing. Telling them what they want to hear.

I saw the Mexican restaurant and Noreen turned into the parking lot. It was closed. The Camper was the only car there. It looked naked sitting in the lot all by itself. Noreen shifted into park. She didn't turn off the engine. The wipers kept working against the windshield. "What are you running from, Hope?" she asked. I didn't answer. I studied the rivulets of rain trying to make their way down the windshield before getting swept up by the wipers. Each of them trying to make it to the bottom where they might have a chance. I didn't answer because Noreen knew I didn't have an answer. I didn't want to say that my entire life had been fucked up by Larry. Maybe I'd be the same fucked-up person I was if nothing like that had ever happened to me. I'll never know. So maybe it's true. Somewhere in my head I thought surviving Larry gave me a certain kind of strength, an invincibility. No one could destroy me. Although, at the moment, I appeared to be doing a good job of destroying myself. What is anyone running from? Where are any of us trying to get to? Couldn't there be things in life that we don't know and we don't get? I couldn't tell you why I first fell for Noreen, I just did. I didn't know why I wanted to find Eden, I just did. I thought about saying those things out loud to Noreen, but my inarticulateness would be too familiar to her. If there was one reason why we broke up, it would be that. I loved Noreen deeply, but I couldn't give her what she wanted. I couldn't give her myself.

"Go back to New York," she said. "Go back to your real life. To your real family. You're chasing old ghosts who only want to hurt you." I couldn't say anything. I just sort of bobbed my head, assenting so I wouldn't have to open my mouth. It would be too much for me to get into a long-drawn-out emotional thing that would surely end with me breaking down and sobbing. I managed to say "Thanks," and Noreen reached over to give me an awkward hug, restrained by her seat belt.

I had to run when I left her car. By the time I made it to The Camper my borrowed pants from Layla were soaked through and my hair was plastered to my forehead. I could change, but my stuff was in the back and Noreen would wonder what was wrong, why I wasn't leaving. I pulled up the bottom of my shirt to wipe my face. I would've stayed sitting there for a few minutes in the white noise of the pattering rain and tried to think things out, but I had a feeling Noreen was waiting to make sure The Camper started up. In fact, I was positive of it. I started the engine and turned on the lights. And for good measure I backed out of the parking space and turned The Camper toward the exit of the lot. I didn't see Noreen's car. That had been enough to get her going. On her way to work. Back to her regular life. The kind of life she always wanted.

22

Two months before Noreen and I broke up, Jamie called me for a gig.

"Hope, you're broke," Jamie said resolutely. "This is an opportunity for you to earn five hundred dollars in three hours and all you have to do is set your alarm for six a.m. Some people have to do that every day."

"Some people earn a lot more than five hundred dollars every day."

"And do you know what? They get up pretty early to do it."

Someone must have dropped out, because Jamie was still mad at me for not including him in the London play and he rarely called me anymore. I think he was secretly smug that my career didn't magically take off after Nico's production. It got only tepid reviews and no one seemed to take much notice. A French theater producer talked my ear off after the show one night but never returned any of my follow-up emails.

Jamie worked for an agency that contracted dancers to work at corporate parties as low-end celebrity spokespeople who didn't speak. They would dress as sprites and toss giant balloons, dash through the crowd with long ribbon streamers doing jetés or pirouettes or cartwheels. The less desirable gigs were for bar mitzvahs where they encouraged people to get on the dance floor. Jamie had inherited this gig from another dancer, and he held on to it for so long he was now the dance captain, or whatever you wanted to call it.

I did need the money. I always needed the money. And if Noreen had known about it, she would have insisted I go. Noreen thought I never worked hard enough at things that would make money. And it was true, I didn't.

I met Jamie at seven the next morning in the lobby of a midtown office building. The dancers were huddled in a corner, most of them looking disheveled and as unhappy as I was about the time of day. They looked like a group of homeless people or anarchist gutter punks begging you to drop change into their wilted paper cup. Jamie towered over them with his tall thin frame, looking like a court-appointed caseworker in his neat clothes. "We're just waiting for someone from upstairs to sign us in," he said.

I leaned against the glass wall and watched the office workers arrive for the day. They walked with such purpose. They had their ID cards out, ready to swipe through turnstiles, as if taking the time to pull the card out of their pocket would slow them down and somehow jeopardize their careers.

Finally, a perky young woman carrying a bunch of keys came up to us. She led us to the security desk and sweet-talked the guard by explaining that we were "guest dancers and circus performers." The guard didn't want to bother filling out visitor badges for all of us. He buzzed us through, saying to the perky girl, "You're responsible for them," as if we were a group of schoolchildren or pets.

The perky girl's name was Jenna. She was barely five feet tall and wore her hair blown out and long, almost to her waist, as if to make up for her lack of height, although it produced the opposite effect, making her seem even shorter than she was. She wore a nondescript gray suit with pitifully tight-fitting pants and her eyes were unnaturally bright for so early in the morning. I wondered if she was on cocaine or some doctor-prescribed upper to help with her residual childhood whatever. She led us to an elevator, holding down the DOORS OPEN button and flipping her hair over her shoulder. She wedged herself tightly into the corner and said, "I think we can all squish."

We were on an express elevator that bypassed everything below the twentieth floor, headed someplace in the thirties. When we got to wherever it was we were going, Jenna slinked out of the elevator first and led the way down a hall, through double glass doors emblazoned with some corporate inscription I didn't bother to read. Jenna skirted the main cube farm and herded us through a lesser-used part of the office, then down a dead-end hallway where she triumphantly turned around to face us. "So I guess you can change in here," she said, indicating the bathrooms.

Jamie was intolerant of any form of disrespect because he was a dancer. He strode ahead of the group, looked left and right at the gender-binary bathrooms, most likely filled with cramped stalls and urinals, and turned to face our escort. "This is unacceptable, Jenna," he said. "We need a dressing room. We're not preparing in a public toilet." Jamie always made a point of remembering people's names off the bat. And in this situation, using her name made her seem like his student, like she worked for him, as opposed to the other way around.

Jenna's big bright eyes searched the hallway with worry. To her credit, she had led us to rarely used bathrooms and was prepared to stand guard and ward off passersby with a shushed and friendly "There's somebody changing in there!" She was only thinking of us, but she wasn't thinking of us in the way Jamie wanted her to think of us.

Jenna opened her mouth, perhaps to say something in her employer's defense, that these were well-maintained *private* toilets and that she was certain we would find them comfortable and well stocked. Or perhaps to apologize to us, that these toilets were the best she could do. Or to say that her boss was really the one in charge, but she was on maternity leave and Jenna just had so much on her plate these days.

But Jenna didn't do any of those things. She bit her bottom lip and put her thinking cap on. Then she smiled and said, "Okay, follow me." We picked up our bags and threaded through the office warren.

Jenna unlocked a conference room and stood aside to let Jamie assess the new quarters. "This will do," he said, "if you can find us a mirror." Jenna grinned and skipped out. Jamie took charge. "Sorry about that," he said to the group. "Some people have no idea."

We sloughed off our bags and street shoes and each claimed a chair around the conference table as our station. Jamie knelt down and opened the costume suitcase. He passed around unitards. They were orange and blue, which I noticed were the brand colors of this establishment.

We undressed and were pulling on our costumes when Jenna returned with a cheap full-length mirror she had pried off a coat closet to fulfill her duty. "Whoops!" she said when she entered. She tried to back out. "You can come in," Jamie said. "None of us are shy." "Sorry," she said, now not sure of what she was apologizing for, walking in on us or being shy herself.

I had brought the wrong kind of sports bra. The straps didn't line up with the scoop neck of my costume. I decided to go without it, since the unitard was made of a thick spandex and felt more like I was wearing a wet suit. I peeled off my bra over my head and caught Jenna staring at me when I was top-less. She smiled and blushed and tried to cover it up by pulling her hair over one shoulder and obsessively petting it. I smiled back at her. Jamie saw the whole thing and rolled his eyes.

Jenna was now on our side. We were her ticket out of her daily job drudgery. If it weren't for us, she would be stuck be-hind a computer all day doing data entry. Our assignment was to run and flit through the offices and do cartwheels and flips (those of us who could), and there was one dancer who could walk on his hands. We were to toss around inflated silver beach balls and remind people that the company picnic was tomorrow. "Everything should have an exclamation mark to it," Jamie said. We proceeded before our ungrateful audience, Jenna following us with her phone hooked up to a portable speaker. The corporation was spread over three floors, and we started on the top floor and descended with Jenna down the fire stairwell for each new act. As Jamie danced by a desk, the guy sitting there said, "I'm sure your mother is proud."

Jamie batted a silver beach ball over his head and pretended not to hear him.

When we were finished Jenna guided us back to our dressing room. "That was so great," Jenna gushed. "It was like Cirque du Soleil!" Jenna loved us. She said she'd try to get us to come back for other events, definitely for the holiday party. She offered to get us passes to the picnic, which was being held at a private beach club in the Hamptons. "There's a free shuttle bus," she said. "And there'll be lots of free food." Everyone declined politely. "Thanks, but we have a show," everyone said. Even though we didn't.

Jenna's normalcy intrigued me. "Sorry I can't go to the picnic thing," I said as I waited for the elevator. "But maybe we can hang out sometime." It felt terrible. Like a line. It was a line. And Jenna picked up on it and responded with a perky "Sure. That'd be great!"

I invited Jenna to a performance Jamie was dancing in. Jamie gave me two comps. Jenna was impressed, or she acted like it. She glowed with the same sort of excitement you'd have if you were given the best table at a fancy restaurant because you were friends with the chef. Instead, I got her free tickets to a dance concert in a semiconverted warehouse in Bushwick with indoor air polluted with asbestos and other unidentified particulates. She was overdressed in a skirt and high heels and I could see the shimmer of makeup dusted across her cheekbones, designed to catch the light just so. She smelled of designer perfume. She clung to my arm and grinned at the scowling scenesters. The performance was pretty boring and I was glad Jamie had gotten us in for free instead of guilting us into paying. But Jenna said afterward, "I thought it was really interesting. It gave me a lot to think about. And they were *such* good dancers." I scooted her out of there before Jamie emerged from the dressing room, because I hadn't told him about Jenna and didn't want it getting back to Noreen, who was out of town at a conference. Noreen would be instantly suspicious. "Why did you invite her," she would ask, "when you have so many other dancy friends?"

Jenna and I had an affair. Mostly at Jenna's apartment, which she shared with two roommates whom she delighted in shocking with her new lesbian romance. Her bedroom was separated from the living room by flimsy French doors with glass covered by sheer curtains. If a light was on, you could see right through them. So everything Jenna and I did was in the dark.

I wasn't that attracted to Jenna, but it was refreshing to be with someone who knew nothing about me, who wasn't constantly scrutinizing my motives and putting them in a psychotherapeutic context, who thought it was great that I wasn't bogged down with a regular job, and who really wanted to read something I wrote. Everything I did sexually was a thrill for Jenna. That was the part that turned me on.

It was when Jenna said something like "I don't know, maybe you and I could get an apartment together," that I knew it had come to an end. I had to break up with her. Jenna didn't take it well. She demanded to know why. She thought we had a perfect relationship. "But we have so much fun," she said, "and we're so compatible." I said, "Because I already have a girlfriend. I live with her and I've been with her for years. I'm sorry, I should've told you, but I didn't know how." Jenna asked if I was breaking up with my girlfriend. I said, "No, I don't think so." She asked if I was still in love with my girl-friend, and if I was, then why did I sleep with her, and if I wasn't, then why didn't Noreen and I break up. I said it wasn't that simple. And Jenna said, "Yes, it is."

Jenna sobbed for a long time and I held her as we sat on the edge of her bed with her billowy down comforter un-derneath us. She ran out of tissues and I shook a pillowcase off a pillow and passed it to her as a handkerchief. "That's so gross," she said and slapped it away. I eventually got out of there by promising to meet her after work the next day and giving her a long hug and kissing her when I left. But I can-celed on her at the last minute. I texted her and said I couldn't meet. She texted back, *I thought you were different, but I'm not surprised.*

Jenna must have looked up my address on the tax form I had filled out for Jamie's gig, because she sent Noreen a letter detailing our affair. "Wow, she's a kid, Hope," Noreen said. "What's that about? Just easy pickings? Where did you think it was going to go? I hope you got off. I hope she had a nice ass because she doesn't sound terribly smart." Noreen insisted on our staying together. On doing the work. "We've been to-gether for a long time. We both have a lot of trauma from our childhoods. It was bound to happen. People get through this sort of thing. It was something you did without think-ing. I understand." She refused to accept that the affair had any meaning, refused to get angry or feel much of anything, because it wasn't the story she wanted. She would patch it up until she figured out her next move.

Noreen demanded we go to couples counseling. It was ex-pensive. Noreen said, "You always use money as an excuse. I'll fucking pay for it." I relayed that to the shrink and Noreen got upset with me. The shrink asked me what I felt about it. I was quiet for a long time. Noreen said, "It's just how she operates." I screamed at her that she never gave me a choice, that there was never any space for me, that she didn't have a clue how I felt or how I operated. She was quiet for a while after that. She said, "It's so difficult to be with someone who doesn't admit their pain."

I stayed at Zara's, house-sitting for a week while she was in Europe at an art fair. She called me from Switzerland and said that she was petrified to leave her hotel room. Her gallerist had given her a prescription for sedatives. Or something —Zara couldn't read the German printed on the bottle. She was crying so much she sounded like she was drowning. I told her to toss the pills into the toilet. "Do it, Zara," I said sternly, worried that she would try to choke them all down. I heard her drop the phone. "Z?" I asked. I heard the toilet flush. "Yeah, okay," she said. "I need to get out of here." I told her she should go to the airport and fly standby. I had to stay on the phone with her while she rushed through the hotel lobby and into a cab to the airport. I stayed on the phone with her until she went through security.

Noreen called me later that day, the day I was supposed to come home. "If you want to break up, we can," she said. "You can break up with me. It's fine. I can't stop you. I can let you go. You're not really here with me anyway. I'm not sure you ever were."

23

Eden and I sat on connected plastic chairs in the emergency room waiting area. The policeman who had brought us in had given each of us a blanket and sat beside us. We hunkered there under our blankets like we were immigrants who had swum across a river. There was a TV bolted to the ceiling, but it was switched off. There were no other people in the waiting area and I thought it odd that we had to wait at all. But I didn't mind waiting because I didn't want to go around the corner and down the hall and into a space that was separated from someone else's bed by a thin curtain.

A guy and a girl came through the sliding glass entrance door. The girl was clutching her arm to her stomach. She was shaking. The guy talked to the emergency room nurse in the booth and then he and the girl sat down. The girl kept saying, "Oh, it hurts. Oh, it hurts," in a weird voice, like she was coo-

ing, like she was faking it or acting in a play. But she kept doing it, so I thought it must be real.

Eden stared at her. "Somebody fucking help her," she muttered and leaned her head against the wall.

The policeman who was sitting with us had been fiddling
with his pad and pencil. I thought he was making notes because later he would have to write a report about us and hand
it in, but when I looked over at his pad I saw he was doodling,
drawing patterns of interlocking triangles and coloring some
of them in.

The nurse called my name. The policeman got up and I
started to stand, but Eden held the corner of my blanket and
said, "We're not going anywhere until you take care of that
woman." She didn't say it loud enough for the nurse to hear,
so the nurse called my name again. The cop turned to us and
used a sweet and friendly voice and said, "The doctors have a
system." "Obviously their system isn't working," Eden said,
"because that person is screaming in pain and we are not. Or
should I start screaming? Because maybe that's what it takes
to *not* get attention around here."

Our cop went over and talked to the nurse. We couldn't
hear what he said, but the nurse shuffled her clipboards and
walked over to the girl who was clutching her arm and rocking back and forth.

Eden said in a low voice, "They're going to ask us questions." I said, "I know." I said, "I feel bad for Dad. It was his
friend." Eden said, "He's not friends with Dad. He just said
that." I said, "I thought you met him when you were little."
Eden said, "No." She said, "Or if I did, I don't remember. I
don't remember my fourth birthday party, but everyone al-

ways talks about it, about how I cried through the whole thing. I don't know what I remember and what I don't. That's what this is going to be like." "This?" I asked.

Eden didn't say anything for a minute. She looked bad. She looked sick. I probably did too. Eden had scratches on her face from running through the woods. I probably did too. I touched my cheek. The cops had given me an ice pack for my face, for where I got punched, but I didn't want to be cold anymore so I had left it in the police car. I looked down at my feet, which were all cut up. I thought I shouldn't be walking on this floor, barefoot and bleeding, where there were lots of germs. My feet should probably hurt but they didn't. Everything should probably hurt but it didn't. I didn't feel anything except itchy because the blanket the police gave me was wool, and wool always itched me. But I couldn't get rid of the blanket because the only other thing I was wearing was underwear and a bra and they didn't match. I never understood how you were supposed to wear underwear and a bra that matched because that meant you had to have as many bras as you did pairs of underwear and I didn't have that many bras. I didn't know anyone who did, but then maybe people did and I didn't know because I didn't see their bras every day.

"Don't tell them I said I knew him," Eden said. "I won't," I said.

The sliding doors opened and a policewoman came in. Our cop went over to her right away. He looked relieved she was there. They talked for a bit and the policewoman nodded. They walked over to us. "This is my associate, Officer Moore," our cop said. Officer Moore smiled at us. "You girls can call me Jess," she said. She took off her police cap. She had freckles and brown hair pulled back in a French braid.

She was short. She knelt down in front of us and looked up at our cop, who said, "Okay," and wandered off to the other end of the waiting room, near the nurses' station.

"We're going to get you a doctor right away," she said. "We're going to get you a woman doctor or specialty nurse, okay?"

Eden didn't say anything so I didn't say anything either. "I'm going to stay with you," Jess said. "I'm here for you." Eden leaned her head back against the wall. She rolled her eyes toward the dead TV.

"Have your parents been contacted yet?" Jess asked. Eden didn't look at her. I wasn't sure what to say so I didn't say anything. Jess looked at each of us, inviting us to speak. She said, "I need to check on something. I'll be right over there." She went over to the other cop and started talking to him. She sounded angry. "Where are the parents?" I heard her ask him. I couldn't hear what the other cop said back. He said something into his walkie-talkie. Jess came back to us, quickly, like she was marching. She stopped halfway across the room, closed her eyes, and took a deep breath. When she got to us she said, "We're not sure if they've gotten in touch with your parents yet. Let's try calling them again from here. They're probably worried about you."

I turned to Eden. I said, "Should we try Mom or Dad?" Jess said, "We can call them both. And if they're not at home, we can call anyone who might know where they are." I looked at Eden but she wasn't paying attention. She was watching an imaginary television show on the black screen. She was trying to turn the TV on with her mind. I knew that when Eden did this, when she did her I'm-not-talking-to-you-anymore routine, she was pretty good at it. I said, "We live with my mom, but our dad lives closer." I recited our dad's number. Jess wrote it down on her pad. "Hey, Bill," she said over her shoulder. She ripped off the paper and handed it to the other cop.

The nurse came out again. We were the only ones in the waiting area so she walked over to us. Jess was in front of us. She put one hand on my shoulder and one hand on Eden's shoulder, like we were in a three-person hug. She helped us to our feet. We were in a huddle. I closed my eyes. I started crying. Jess wrapped us closer, held us tight. She put her head against ours. "You will get through this," Jess said.

24

didn't drive far. I was still hungover and tired. I took the exit to Ocean City in Maryland. My aunt used to have a condo there when she was alive. We used to visit her every summer when my parents were married. Mostly Eden and I would play by ourselves because we didn't relate to our sporty cousins, who were teenage boys when we were kids and they weren't interested in us anyway. My aunt's condo building had gray wood siding and looked like it had been built in the seventies. If you lived there you could park in the front, and if you were a guest you had to park in the back. She had a balcony, and our cousins would stand out there and spit down on us when Eden and I got back from the beach, so we always made a point of leaving the beach before they did. Also, if one of us took a shower, the other one had to guard the door because it didn't lock and the cousins knew it but pretended they didn't and never knocked. My aunt got divorced right after my parents got divorced and she sold the condo. It was a relief that we didn't have to go there anymore.

I had no idea where to find the old condo building. I pulled into the parking lot of an apartment complex called The Easy Breezy. The lot was almost empty since it was off-season. I turned off the engine, closed up all the curtains, and anesthetized myself by staring at bullshit on my phone until it ran out of juice. I slept the rest of the day and most of the night. I woke up the next morning and peed into a paper Starbucks cup and poured it out the window.

I walked to a coffee shop by the beach so I could charge my phone. I ordered a large coffee and a blueberry muffin, which tasted like cake and I couldn't eat it. I went back to the counter and paid a dollar for a banana that was still a little green, then took a seat by the window and stared across the boardwalk and out to the cold gray sea. It was windy. I couldn't tell if I saw snow flurries or just sand kicking up from the beach.

When my phone came back to life, I had an email from my dad. *Hope. I'm sorry. I don't know where she is. I'm not keeping anything from you. Just wanted you to know that. Let me know if you find anything. Love, Dad.*

I walked back along the boardwalk. Most places had their metal shutters down. The wooden walkway had drifts of sand and debris blown over it. It felt deserted, as if the denizens let nature take over for the winter and do whatever it wanted.

I climbed into the way-back of The Camper and under the sleeping bag for warmth. I wondered if this was how people slowly became homeless. First they live in their car, then under increasingly squalid conditions, and then their friends and family just let them disappear.

I have friends, I thought.

I called Zara. She didn't answer. I called Jamie.

"What car?" he asked. "You have a car now?" I said it wasn't a car, it was a van, a camper, and I had borrowed it from my dad, sort of on perma-loan for the foreseeable future. "So you've inherited it? Are you bringing it back to New York?"

"I don't know," I said. "At the moment I'm kind of living in it."

"Zara said you lost your apartment, and I meant to call you about it. I worry about you, Hope. But maybe this van could be a good investment. Maybe you could live in it and shower at the gym. I had a friend who did that." Jamie asked if he could borrow The Camper for a future project. "If I go on tour," he said. "You know, Merce Cunningham and John Cage went on tour in a bus like that. Cage would drive the bus and forage for mushrooms and wild herbs, and that's what the dancers would eat when they camped for the night. Maybe they even roasted a squirrel or two. But what is this vision quest all about, Hope? Is this for a play? I really hope so, because you haven't produced anything for so long."

"Sort of," I said. I wondered if he had talked to Noreen, if she had called him after she found me drunk on her doorstep. "I'm doing research for something."

"Oh, that's good," Jamie said. "Just don't get trapped by it," he said. "Sometimes you can do so much research it becomes about that and you forget why you set out on the road in the first place."

"Right," I said. It started to rain and drops pattered the roof of The Camper. I slunk down deeper into my sleeping bag. My phone was under the covers and the edge of the sleeping bag brushed my face. I inhaled, wondering if the odor would remind me of being a kid, but it just smelled musty.

"Did I tell you I was in a film?" Jamie asked. "A feature. It was an ensemble piece, but I was one of the main characters. It's already been accepted at Sundance. It's an independent film and they're hoping it gets picked up for distribution, which it will. They have an agent already. I'm heading out there next week to do talk-backs, parties, that sort of thing. I've got to pay my own way and the hotel, but it's worth it. I should definitely go. It's important to invest in yourself. It's just the money. I'm getting too old to grab a quick go-go job. Or even a cheap trick. I'm sort of out of that business, if you know what I mean."

I started to laugh and then stopped myself. Jamie said, "It's okay. It was a joke.

"I'm really happy," he said. "Things could finally be turning around for me. I've lived the whore's life for so long, I forget that people actually do have breakthroughs. Things can change. And not slip back. Look at us, for instance," he said. "We haven't really changed since we were in college. And how long ago is that now? I sometimes get really depressed and feel that this hard-luck life is all there is. This is how it is and how it's going to be. And that only one person, once in a blue moon, gets a big boost, and it's totally random and it's not a meritocracy. The rest of us suffer and toil away. Looking for something beautiful. Never finding it for more than a second. But I guess we choose that. We set ourselves up for it. And if we had known that all these years later it would be like this, would we have still chosen to be artists?"

I pulled the sleeping bag away from my face. My breath made little clouds when I exhaled. "Who knows?" I said.

"I think we would have," he said. "You would have, for sure. You're the real thing. I'm just stuck here now. What else can I do, really? At this point in my life, what else is there for me?" He sighed grandly. "And don't tell me to become a Pilates teacher or a massage therapist. As if that is remotely related to dance. Oh, because it uses the body. Is that all I have, really? This mortal corporeal coil?" Jamie sighed again. "Shit," he said. "Fuck, I've got to take this call. I'll talk to you later, Hope."

I couldn't think of any reason to protest ending our conversation. Jamie hung up.

I sat up and peeked through the rear window curtains. It was still raining and cold. I couldn't see much out the window. I thought about putting the key in the ignition and turning on the wipers. I thought the rhythmic wiping would calm me. But I knew it would be a drain on the battery, which undoubtedly had little life left. I rewrapped myself in the sleeping bag and looked at the beads of rain. They were mixed with tiny snowflakes that melted as soon as they hit the window.

I called Zara again. She picked up right away.

"I'm at an impasse," I said. "What if being a disgusting artist gets you nowhere? What if your savage use of raw material doesn't amount to anything? What if cannibalizing your childhood trauma just causes more trauma?"

"Art is like a bad lover who doesn't reciprocate," Zara said. "Yet we stay in the relationship and we jerk off when no one is looking so we can at least get through the day."

"But what's the goal?" I asked. "What are we in it for?"

"I'm not sure," Zara said. "I think we're in it because we don't know why we are in it." Zara paused. "That's kind of a dodge, I admit it," she said.

"So we're in it because we're lost?" I asked.

"It's as good a reason as any. It's not like you're in it for the money, although you can be. But I don't know," Zara said. "If you think too much about why you're doing it, you'll start to be really disgusted with yourself and talk yourself out of it all. It's like sex. It's walking a fine line between repulsion and love."

"I've spent the last day living in my dad's van and peeing in an old Starbucks cup," I said.

"See, that's gross, but I love you for peeing in an old Starbucks cup. I think it makes you lovable."

"I'm such a fucking failure," I said.

"I'm a fucking failure too. We're all failures."

I heard footsteps and panicked that someone was going to tap on The Camper door, ask me for my parking permit, and tell me to move along when I failed to produce it. But whoever it was hurried by and faded away.

"Can you look something up for me?" I asked Zara to look up Eric and see if she could find a phone number or an email or something. She asked who it was, and I said it was Eden's teacher whom I think she had an affair with or was involved with. It didn't take Zara long to find me some numbers. "It's interesting," she said. "You asked me to look up the boyfriend, but not Eden. You always approach things indirectly. You never knock on the front door." I told Zara that there was a certain thing called anxiety, and she said, "Yeah, I know."

Zara told me she had checked around for Eden anyway, in case I wanted information later, and couldn't find anything. "You could pay for a background check but it will probably only give you her birthday," Zara said. "On that note, I don't think she's dead."

We said goodbye. I called one of the numbers Zara found.

"Hel-lo!" I was startled by the massive cheeriness with which the person answered, as if he were the last person in the world who actually enjoyed talking on the phone. I was a little dumbfounded and unsure of what to say. I felt like the inexperienced telemarketer I had been for one particularly dreadful week at a temp job. "Hi," I stumbled. I cleared my throat. "I'm looking for someone named Eric."

"I happen to be someone named Eric."

His merry charm relaxed me a bit.

"Did you used to teach at a boarding school in Pennsylvania?"

"In the very distant dream of decades past, I did indeed teach at a school in Pennsylvania. Did I just win a sweepstakes? Or are you checking things off a list in order to steal my identity? Do you also know my favorite color and the name of my childhood pet?"

"No."

"Are you a former student? If so, I'm afraid that take-home exam is long overdue."

"No, but my sister was."

"Oh! Who was your sister?"

"Her name is Eden. I'm trying to get in touch with her."

"Oh," he said. "Uh . . . hang on one sec." I heard footsteps, as though he was walking away from something or someone, or changing rooms. Retreating somewhere. He spoke more quietly and asked how I got his number. I said I found it online and took a chance. "Huh," he said. I said I would've emailed but I didn't have his email address. He said he didn't email all that much. He was pretty private with technology. He wasn't terribly interested in the Internet. "It had a lot of potential in the beginning," he said, trying to pick up his

perkiness again, "but it turned into the wrong kind of potential." He chuckled nervously. "Sounds like a lot of paranoid anarchistic jargon, I suppose." I heard him take a slurp
of something. "But I'm rather glad, for instance, that I am
not a teacher now, with all these consumer reviews posted in
public. Back at that school . . . let's just say they fired me, although I don't recall there being anything felonious that pre-
cipitated it. I didn't think I was doing anything dramatic, but
I guess somebody did. If that happened today, I would be in
a virtual stockade, which wouldn't be all that virtual because
it would render my reality, my nonvirtual reality, quite impo-
tent and infirm," he said. "Ha."

There was a pause.

I said, "Then you lived with Eden, right?"

"Yes," he said. "After that imbroglio at the school, I had
a group of very dedicated students who elected to keep me
in their lives. We outgrew what I could provide as accom-
modations, so we all moved down to that rotted farm in Virginia. I can't remember whose idea that was. Maybe Eden's.
You know, we were just sweet young people who thought we
could outcalculate society in our search for . . . I'm not entirely sure what it was we were searching for. I think it was au-
thenticity. It had nothing to do with politics. Hmm, I take that
back. It *was* political. Our existence is always political, and we
are always at the hands of capitalistic creeps bigger and better resourced than ourselves. But it's a lovely dream, isn't it?
Trying to form a more perfect union. A vegan, environmen-
talist union of equals dedicated to liberal, freewheeling in-
tellectual pursuits. I mean, who wouldn't want to do that? I
think we were lucky to have had it for the little time we did.
Now? Jeez. We live in a world with such narrow, unisystemic

thinking. Such corporate, monopolistic ideology. Those were some good times, though. Some galactic fantastic times. It's such a blur now. Youth is like that. And then suddenly, bing, it's over and everything scatters."

He paused his babble-a-thon. "So, you're Eden's sister?"

"Yes," I said. "I'm trying to find her. We sort of lost touch."

"Right. So you must be Hope."

My throat tightened. I felt sweaty and pushed the sleeping bag off of me. They could still be together after all these years. Eden could be there with him, wherever he was, right now.

"You're Hope," he said. "The little sister. The playwright in New York. And you were also a witness to my boxing demise at the hands of your father."

"Yes," I said, suddenly confused, perhaps confused about who I really was. As though the situation were reversed and he had called me.

Eric took a deep breath and let it out. "I can't exactly go on without knowing specifically what you want. The great story swivels on the pin of my personal compass of ethics."

"Okay," I said. There was an awkward silence while I waited for him to ask me questions, but that wasn't what he wanted. He wanted elocution. "I need to find her," I said. "My mom died and I need to get in touch with her. It's actually about a legal matter. Not about my mom, about something else." I was stammering. He said, "Hmm." Maybe he didn't believe me, or maybe he did and was trying to decide if this was a good enough reason to give me what I wanted.

"Do you know where she is?"

He slurped on whatever it was he was drinking. He swallowed. "Eden is a tricky character. Angry, intelligent, mes-

merizing, beautiful, that's how she walked into my classroom. She had the gravity of a war veteran and she was only
a teenager."

"Were you and Eden lovers?"

"We were. But then, like most romantic partnerships, we
plateaued. Her interest in me waned. I still loved her when
we were on the fritz. You know, the usual. I thought we could
patch things up. I thought we still loved each other."

"So she broke up with you and left? And moved out? Do
you know where she went?"

"Okay," Eric said. "This is a lot for me to process." He
took a deep breath. "I admit I'm not prepared. And I feel like
I'm winging this. I'll tell you the whole kit and caboodle, although I'm not sure if I should. Partly from my own feelings
of loyalty and guilt, and partly out of consideration for you
and your feelings, neither of which I know very well, or at
all." He took another good breath.

"I know everything that happened to you," he said. "Eden
told me. At first she just told me the journalistic facts. Then,
when we left the farm and it was just the two of us trying
to figure out our lives, that's when things imploded. There
was a certain barrier, a certain boundary between us, keeping us apart, or keeping her apart from me. I craved a close-
ness she didn't want to have. And part of that had to do with
you, Hope."

"What do you mean?"

"You know, I didn't have a great relationship with my parents. And I regretted my lack of interest in my own family.
But your family seemed eclectic and interesting and kind of
cool, even your dad, who I'm going to assume doesn't punch
everyone he happens to be introduced to. I didn't know why

Eden had cut you all off. I couldn't fathom the reason. I finally comprehended it on the last day we were together, the day our interpersonal morass turned into an all-night, heartbreaking, breakup conversation that left us both strung out from tears shed. I was trying to rescue Eden with my antiquated, patriarchal, paternalistic I-don't-know-what. And Eden couldn't stand being rescued. She didn't need my rescuing. But she needed yours that day in the woods. And she couldn't live with that."

Even if I wanted to answer him, even if I wanted to say something, I couldn't. I never told Noreen that detail. I hadn't told Janet the therapist. I didn't remember if it was in the police file the DA had given me. I might not have ever told anyone. I was pretty sure I hadn't.

Eric took a big breath.

"You went back for her. You found her and pulled her out of the truck and got her out of there. Without you, she would have probably ended up a bunch of body parts in a ditch somewhere, decomposing in a creek."

Eric stopped talking. He was finally quiet. And I knew he would be until I said something. Until I relieved him of this burden of knowing. Eden had told him everything. He knew everything about me. More than Noreen ever knew. More than my parents.

"Hello?" Eric asked softly to make sure I was still there.

"Yeah," I said.

"Eden's in Santa Cruz," he said. "She's been out there a while. She used to work at the university out there. I don't know if she still does. That's about all I know. I'm sorry."

I sat up and pressed my forehead against the rear window. It was cool and damp.

"Why are you talking to me?" I asked.

He coughed, and something about his cough was tender. I thought he might cry. "I guess I still want her to love me. Call me a sap." He coughed at his sentimentality and tried to rake it away. "I understand the desire to find your sister. I don't have a sister, but if one came looking for me, I would want her to find me. I don't know if that's true for Eden. I don't know what answers are out there for you. But maybe that's not important. Maybe it's not about the answer, or even the question. Maybe for you it's about the journey." He coughed again and I thought he was trying to keep himself from choking up. As if my journey reminded him of what he did not have, of what he'd lost, of all the people in his life that he could no longer hold or even talk to on the phone. "I don't know what you hope to find, Hope. I don't know if Eden will talk to you. And if she does, it'll probably be what you already know. Her road is nothing you couldn't imagine yourself."

My phone beeped, and when I pulled it away from my ear to look at it, he had hung up.

25

The Camper made it as far as Arizona. I was in a youth hostel campground when it passed away during the night. The next morning it refused to start. I turned the key in the ignition and nothing happened.

I went into the clubhouse building where the free breakfast was already aflutter. Everyone looked to be college students or twenty-somethings. I was the oldest one there except for an Australian family of four. The father had taken his daughters out of school to see the world. "We are going once around the globe," he said. "Horizontally. Then we'll go home for a few years, get a job again, make some money, put some away, and next time we'll do it vertically. That'll be a mind-opener. Because we always think of 'cross.' Cross-country. Across the sea. We never think of up and down. Above and below. Pole to pole. North to south. Winter to summer. Think about it," he said. His daughters looked miserable. They just wanted to go home.

I poked my head into the kitchen and said my car was dead. I asked if I could leave it for a week. I said I had to get to California but would come back for it. "It probably needs a new starter," I said. "And it's so old the part will probably have to be ordered." They said sure. The head kitchen girl walked out with me and announced to the dining room, "Hey, can some people with upper-body strength help her roll her van to the back lot?" The Aussie dad and a couple of guys helped me out. "Don't make them like this anymore, do they?" the Aussie said.

Back inside, I drank coffee and made peanut butter sandwiches to take with me. Everyone did this. They unfolded and peeled open napkins and wrapped up the food. One guy fished a plastic bread bag out of the garbage and reused that.

I asked one of the guys who'd helped me move The Camper if he knew where the nearest bus station was. He said he didn't. He asked where I was headed, and I said Santa Cruz. He said he was heading to Baja, but "those two girls are headed to San Francisco and they could maybe drop you. They have a driveaway."

My travel companions were a young queer couple, one femme and one maybe trans. They took one look at me and said, "Sure, climb aboard." One of them was short and punky and from Switzerland and could speak six languages, but "none of them with good fluency." The Swiss one used to be addicted to heroin and came here to get away from it all. "Switz is small. You run into the same people all over again, just in circles. I needed to be far from that. I needed to break from it." The girlfriend was pale with long, raggedy blonde

hair. "She's from Seattle. She's very West Coast," the Swiss
one said. "Very interested in astrology. She can tell fortunes."

The Seattle blonde turned around in her seat and smiled
dreamily at me. "Tell me your birthday," she said. "And the
time you were born. And where." When I told her, she leafed
through her dog-eared paperback ephemeris to find my
chart. "You're a little older than us," she said, "so your outer
planets are different. The outer planets move slowly; they are
more generational. You have Jupiter in your first house. People think you are lucky, and you *are* lucky. You're a risk taker.
Sometimes you feel unsettled. You have a great sense of self,
even if sometimes you forget your own power. But you have
the ruby slippers. Just gotta look down at your own feet." I
smiled at her, and she smiled back from behind windblown
pieces of her pale, stringy, half-dreadlocked hair. I was unsure
if I believed any of it. Suriya was into astrology and auras and
spiritual vibrations. I asked the blonde if there was any way to
change your sign or your astrology. I said, "I can't believe that
who I am is set in stone based on the day and time and place
I was born." "But isn't it anyway?" she asked.

We made it past Los Angeles and spent the night sleeping
on the floor of a yoga studio outside of San Luis Obispo, the
deal being we had to wake up early and mop the floor with
essential oils before the first yogis arrived in the morning. We
continued up the coast and my companions dropped me off
in Santa Cruz, near the ocean. It seemed to be the main drag
in town. "There's a bus stop across the street," the blonde
pointed out. I hugged them both and thanked them. "This is
great," they said. "Now we'll go up Highway 1. It'll be pretty."

I watched them drive off. They were so young. Driving
a car that wasn't theirs, that they got to use for free. The

blonde smiled and stretched her torso out of the window to wildly wave goodbye. Then she sat back down and put her bare feet up on the dashboard. Taking off with her European girlfriend/boyfriend with the mischievous grin, whose short spiky hair looked magically great though neither of them had showered for days. They had only two backpacks, a purse, a little money, a little weed, and vegan sandwich wraps pilfered from the yoga studio. They were young and together and didn't know each other very well, but were sure they were very much in love. They cared only about getting to the next place they wanted to go.

I watched their car disappear, heading north.

I thought, I'm not young anymore.

I walked to the bus stop and studied the schedule and the route map. I noticed the area code of the bus company's phone number. I opened my bag and pulled out my dad's phone bills. I found one with the same area code and dialed. "UC Santa Cruz," a friendly lady answered. I was caught off guard. I asked to speak to Eden. "I'm sorry, there's no one by that name in this office." I said I was sorry to bother her and hung up. The bus came and I took it uphill to the university.

I hiked through the campus. Paths wove into stands of redwood trees and then unfurled into parking lots. The buildings were constructed so as to seem to grow out of the earth. The air was cool and sunlight splintered through the dark green trees. Everything felt pure.

I found my way to the library and sat on a cement bench. There was a café on the ground floor and steel boxes with slots to feed in your books for a quick return. An endless stream of students flowed out of the woods. I unzipped my backpack and took out the phone bills again. I dialed a num-

ber with the same area code and got someone's voicemail. I
tried another, but it was no longer in service. Another was a
main department line. It listed its faculty and staff members,
none of whom were Eden. She could have changed her name
a long time ago. I realized I should have figured all this out
before I left the East Coast. I came all this way on one person's word.

I dialed again. I've got nothing else to do, I told myself.

"Hello?" The voice sounded familiar, but different. A voice
I hadn't heard since I was a senior in high school. Since I was
seventeen or eighteen years old.

"Eden?"

"Who's calling?"

"It's Hope."

Pause.

"I'm in Santa Cruz," I said.

"Oh, that's great," she said in a way that made me think
she was not alone.

"I'm outside the library."

"Oh, okay. I'll come down."

I said I was on the side with the café, outside near the path
that goes into the woods. "Well, you probably know better
than I do," I said. "I'll find you," she said.

I waited, wondering if I should change the bench I was
on. If I should sit in profile because I wasn't sure which direction she would come from. I put my bag next to me on the
bench to save a seat for her. I looked over my shoulder at the
path from the woods. A footbridge was suspended between
two redwoods, traversing a ravine. I suddenly felt cold. It was
cold in this stone plaza, a sort of way station, a chilly oasis. I
was shivering. But also sweating. I was so jittery. I scanned the

students casually loping along their way, locomoting without any urgency or cares.

"Hey."

I turned around and stood up. It was Eden. Older. But her. "Still got your short hair," she said. Hers was long, cut to make it look messier and curlier than it was. It was streaked with lighter shades that might have been from the sun or might have been dyed. She was shorter than I remembered. She was wearing a dress that was kind of loose and flowy.

"What are you doing here?" she asked.

I stared at her.

"I wanted to see you," I said.

She laughed. "That took long enough."

Eden's response was so familiar. Her sharp adolescent cut-down. It stung like I was still thirteen years old. It was what I knew, but it wasn't what I expected. I expected her to be moved that I wanted to find her. But Eden was turning this all around. She seemed mad at me. I should have tried to find her long ago. I should've moved in with her at the commune instead of going to college. I should've accidentally picked up the phone at Dad's when she called. As if this was all part of a game. Or a dare.

"Yeah, okay," I said. "I have a reason." I unzipped my backpack and rooted around inside. I pulled out her copy of the letter from the DA. "I thought you might want to read this." She looked at the envelope that was crumpled from having been at the bottom of my pack for so long. Its corners were gray and feathered with lint. I held it out to her, waited for her to take it. She angled her head to read the return address, partially obscured by my thumb. "No," she said. "I don't. You can burn it. It never got to me."

I put the letter on the bench between us. "Do you want me to tell you what it says?" I asked.

"You can tell me whatever you want." She reached up to her hair, pulled her sunglasses down over her eyes, and leaned back on her hands.

I'm not sure what I expected from Eden. Part of me wanted to cry and hug her and have her be so, so happy to see me. I wanted her to tell me that she missed me. That she thought about me all the time. That she loved me. I wanted her to be my big sister and take care of me. I wanted her to put her arms around me. I wanted to rest my head on her chest. I wanted to curl up into her. I wanted her to take me home and make up the sofa bed for me and heat up leftover dinner for me and lend me money to take a plane home. I wondered how long she had been living out here. I wondered if she was married, if she had kids.

The envelope lay between us, not touching Eden. I didn't want to play all my cards right away, but I knew she could outlast me in the silence game. Eden would have never come looking for me. I was the one who had caved. It was like she had expected me all along. She knew that one day I would show up.

"It's about Larry," I said. "He's up for parole." Eden didn't show any reaction. She lifted her cheeks in something resembling a smile but more designed to cover up any other kind of emotional response. Maybe that wasn't what she was expecting, though she seemed to know the script to this scene we were playing out, whereas I was unprepared and forced to improvise. I said, "They want to talk to you, to see if there's any more evidence you could give. They're trying to convict him of murdering a teenage girl. From around the same time."

Eden made her mild smile and didn't move. She lifted her face and basked in a sliver of sun that glimmered through the trees. Her long shaggy hair falling down her back toward the bench. Her cotton tights disappearing into cowboy boots. She looked like she had been born in California and had never left.

"I'm sorry about that," she said.

"Do you want me to tell you more about it?"

"No. Not really."

"You would let him get out of jail?"

"I don't know what you're getting out of this or why you want to hang on to it. Or why you want to hang on to me."

"You're my sister."

Eden pulled up one leg and rested her heel on the bench. "We're not kids. We're grown up. We can choose to be who we want."

"You really think that's true?"

"Maybe you like being this way. Maybe you like who you are and where you came from. But what has it done for you? I don't know, Hope. If you're free, why do you want to tie yourself up again?"

I thought, I had come all this way for Eden to tell me that coming all this way was a sign of my inferiority.

"That's a weird, kind of perverted, semi-Buddhist yoga thing to say. I didn't know that was your thing now," I said.

"There are a lot of things about me you don't know."

"Maybe I would know more about you if you hadn't dropped off the face of the planet."

"You could've come anytime."

"How?" I was unsure whether I was going to laugh incredulously or cough out tears. "Nobody knew where you were. You cut everyone off. You just left."

Eden shrugged and the neck of her dress slipped down her shoulder, exposing a bra strap. "Why would I have stayed?" she asked.

"Maybe for the parents? Maybe for me?" My throat tightened. I felt bad about my last line. Like I was guilting her. "I'm sorry," I said, not entirely sure what I was apologizing for. "I'm here now."

"You only want to have something to do with me if it has something to do with our past. You don't care about me or my life now. You're not really interested in me or in helping some lawyer, you're only interested in how this whole situation can help you. You're like Dad that way."

"Mom died," I said. I don't know why I said it; it just spilled out of me. "Cancer. She had cancer." Eden looked at me queerly. Why did I say that? What did I want from her? What good would it do to have her put her arms around me and say, Oh, I'm so sorry. I didn't know.

Now I was doing my best not to cry. I felt my bottom lip quiver like a little kid's. And then I did start to weep.

I bent forward and covered my face with my hands. I sobbed into my fingers. I breathed erratically. I couldn't stop. I was shaking, and snot and tears pooled into my cupped palms and dripped onto my pants, my borrowed pants from Layla, clothes that weren't even mine. It was so unlike me to cry in public. It was something Noreen held against me. That I couldn't express myself. That normal emotional reactions were foreign to me. I felt Eden put her hand on my back. I thought, Eden never even met Noreen.

I wiped my nose with the back of my fingers and sat up. I looked at Eden, who was still wearing her dark sunglasses. Like she was wearing a mask. It was so strange to be looking at her. Here is someone who was so much a part of me. Here is someone I used to look at every day, but haven't laid eyes on in years.

Eden pushed her sunglasses up on top of her head. The sun had moved behind a hill on its way down to the ocean and the glare was gone. Eden had dark circles under her eyes and lines running across her forehead. There was a small strip of gray on her hairline and sprouts on her temples.

"Don't tell Dad where I am," she said.

Eden got up and walked away from me. She blended into the current of students, all going along their way. I sat there in the same position, unable to move. I didn't want to leave this place where there could still be some connection to her. I put my hand on the spot on the bench where she had been sitting, feeling for her leftover warmth. After a while I stood up, picked up the letter, and dropped it into the trash can stuffed with garbage from the café. A student came up to me and asked for directions. I said I didn't know where that building was. "I'm not from around here," I said. "No one is," the student said.

26

I wandered through the campus, unable to figure out where to go. I circled around buildings with bike racks shaped like triangular clothes hangers. I wanted to go inside and rest on one of the couches in the student lounge, but I couldn't bring myself to enter any building. I walked slowly, following paths lined with wild grasses. There was a constant movement of people funneling calmly around me, disappearing through glass doors or turning off into the woods. I let them pass me by.

The sky was a clear, relentless blue. The parking lots had long-reaching vistas, and in the distance everything merged in a haze down by the sea with only a pale strip separating atmosphere from water. I didn't know how far it was to walk, but I thought that if I headed downhill, I would eventually wind up back in town.

Most of my walk was in the sun, and it felt warm and good.

I followed a narrow bike path through a scrubby meadow. I was alone in the field except for the one biker, who whizzed by calling out, "On your left!" and making me hop onto the grass. I played the conversation with Eden over in my head. Water would well up in my eyes but I could inhale and blink it away, and if anything escaped, the sun dried it up quickly. There was no cover on the meadow path and I felt damp patches forming where my backpack rested against my lower spine and where the straps pressed on my shoulders. A film of sweat covered my forehead. I was thirsty and licked my upper lip and tasted the salt.

The bike path deposited me onto a street. A sidewalk appeared. I took comfort in the methodical rhythmic tromping of my feet, heavy, keeping me from tumbling downhill all at once, head over heels. While I waited at a stoplight, I wondered if I was in Eden's neighborhood. If she had a little house near here with a hedged-in front yard, with a lemon or an avocado tree, or something else that grows all year round out here. I wondered if people around here knew her. I thought about what Eric had confessed to me when he said, "I guess I still want her to love me," and I guessed I felt the same way. I wanted her to love me. But Eden was Eden. I couldn't say if she still loved me or not. She loved me how she loved me, if she did at all. Or she hated me for reminding her of what happened with Larry, or she hated herself. Because we wouldn't have gotten in the truck if she hadn't insisted. If we had used the phone at the bus station or called collect from a pay phone. None of it would have happened and we would be someplace else. We might be totally different people. And yet, I didn't want to be anyone different. I wanted to be us. Who we were. I wished I had said something like that. But even if I did, Eden would probably have responded the same way. And if she did love me, there didn't seem to be a dial or a switch to turn her love up or turn it off, or adjust it somehow. It was just there, how it was. How it had always been.

When I made it into town, I started thinking about where I was going to stay. I had a friend who lived in Oakland, but I didn't know how to get there, and I didn't tell him I was coming. I thought about calling Zara and asking if she would buy me a plane ticket home and I would pay her back in a month or so, or six, and if I could live at her loft while I got back on my feet. Zara would probably buy me a ticket with frequent flier points that she never used. I wondered how much a motel would cost. I wondered how much money I had available on my almost maxed-out credit card. Now I wished I had The Camper with me. But The Camper was in Arizona, and somehow I would have to figure out how to get back there and get it fixed, if it could be fixed.

"Fuck." I sat down on a curb and took out my phone. I called my dad.

"I was actually going to call you," my dad said as soon as he answered, "but you know, I wanted to give you your space. So look, I wrote a letter and sent it to that county DA and the parole board and I heard back that parole was denied. Then I talked to a lawyer friend of mine who said they usually shoot them down the first time but it will come up in the future. But my lawyer friend also said that even if he did get out, he wouldn't be allowed to leave the state. Plus, he's old now and probably in poor health since he's been in prison for so long, so you know, even if it did happen, I don't think he would be any kind of threat. I think we would be okay. But we don't have to worry about any of it for at least another year."

I honestly didn't know what to say. I felt relieved. A lightness. And slightly nervous, like I hadn't eaten and suddenly realized I was ravenous. And strangely, Larry felt small and insignificant and far away.

My dad said, "The letter I wrote, it was a damn good letter. I might try and publish it as an op-ed, although, if you're not on staff, they always take the teeth out of it. I have to see if I still have any contacts in the editorial department. Probably everyone's retired. But maybe someone can put in a word."

"Dad," I said. "The Camper broke down."

"Where? Where are you?"

"It broke down at this place where I was staying in Arizona, but then I had to get to California so I left it there, but I can go back and get it."

My dad was quiet. I heard him breathing, with several elongated exhales. Then he said, "Just leave it there."

I was startled. "You're sure?" I asked.

"Yeah," he said. "Let it go."

I was about to thank him, but he cut me off and said, "I'll talk to you soon, okay?" and he hung up.

A city bus pulled up and opened its doors for me but I waved it away. An older woman clipping her hedges asked if I was lost. "Not exactly," I said. She smiled. She said there was a youth hostel a few blocks away and it was pretty nice. I stood up and she pointed me in the right direction.

The youth hostel was a large Victorian house with several guest bungalows in its picket-fenced compound. I unlatched the gate and wandered through the garden looking for the office. All the lights were off and no one seemed at home. I found two young straight guys playing Ping-Pong on the covered back porch. "They kick us out during the day," one of them said. "Come back after six p.m." I asked if it was full up for the night. "I wouldn't say it's high season," he said as he sent the white ball bouncing off the table, "but it is taco night."

They asked me if I wanted to play, but I said no. I sat in a lounge chair listening to the tick-tock of their game. I wondered if Eden was right, if I was hanging on to what happened to us because for some reason it made me feel less alone, because somewhere I always had Eden. I thought about Suriya trying to free herself of people who could claim her, and how during this whole bizarre road trip I was maybe doing the opposite. My accumulated menagerie of people was supposed to put things back together for me, tell me which way to go. And now I've wound up here, at the end of something, at the end of the road. An ending. And I suddenly missed my mother. I could find Eden and see Eden again, but I would never see my mother again. And I should've made more of an effort to see her, but my mother would've probably brushed me off and told me to get on with my life.

I got up and walked to the garden gate. The Ping-Pong ball had popped off the porch and I picked it up and threw it back to the guys and told them I would be back later.

I followed the sidewalk that ran along the top of the cliff at the beach. I passed an old hippie guy who had a VW camper like my dad's, only a different color. He opened a can of beer and poured it into an empty sports drink bottle. He coaxed his dog out of the camper and hauled the sliding door closed. I followed him down the cliff steps to the beach, where he drank his beer and played fetch with his dog. His ruddy skin melted into the landscape. The dog's paws made a pleasant sound as they patted the flat wet sand.

I climbed back up the steps to the top of the cliff and wandered along the scenic walkway. I stopped at a cove and leaned against the railing at the top of a lookout. The sun was setting into the ocean. The sky was pinking up. People were getting out of school or work and filtering down to the sea. They stretched on wet suits and pulled surfboards from the roofs of their cars. They wound their long hair into ponytails. They laughed. They made their way to a staircase carved into the stony cliff beneath me and stepped down until their legs were submerged in the water that slapped against the walls of the cove.

I watched a young teenage boy pull on his suit and work his fingers into neoprene gloves. He was with his family. He seemed to be doing this for the first time. Maybe he was traveling with his family and checking out colleges. He seemed to be sixteen or seventeen. He grabbed his board and headed for the stairs going into the water. His dad called out to him. The kid turned around halfway down the stairs. His dad shouted something. The kid shook his head and smiled. He said, "I can't hear you!" He gestured that the waves were loud and the tide was coming in. The sounds of the ocean were overtaking the sounds of the street. His dad said something again and the kid laughed. "Can't hear you, Dad! I'm going down," and he turned, knowing that his dad couldn't say anything to stop him. He got in the water and paddled out.

The surfers floated in bands outside the cove's border. They bobbed over waves that weren't big enough. The more experienced ones pushed their way past the break and waited for something to happen. The others tried to get out as far as they could without being shoved back to shore or speared by one of the lucky ones who caught a wave.

The teenage boy had problems joining them. He didn't quite have the hang of it. He lay on his stomach and paddled out but the surf kept lobbing him back in, upending his board, crashing over him awkwardly. His older sister stood with his dad on the cliff. "Keep your board down! Board down! Nose down!" she yelled. "Nose down! Get out there! You have to go through it!"

I watched him try and make it back out to the other surfers. I thought, Will I always be that kid on a rented surfboard? Not used to the water. Wading out to where I'm not wanted. Never quite escaping what I try to leave behind. Not recognizing a break until it was already on top of me.

I thought about what Zara said to me before I left. About how I was addicted to continuing. So was Zara, in a way. So was Jamie, relentlessly so. It was what we did. It was how we lived. Make one decision and then another. Make one mark, then another. Write one word. Write another.

I took my notebook out of my backpack, felt around for a pen. I opened to a blank page and wrote: a play where the entire room is white, filled with light, completely open, with a single painted line—a thin stripe in blue painted along the upstage wall, representing the horizon, representing possibility.

I wrote, filling page after page, as the sun disappeared, ending the day, and the surfers paddled back in. When I closed my notebook, the sky had dimmed.

It was becoming night.

The streetlights came on.

In this play there is only one character. A woman crawls silently through the audience. She reaches the stage and pulls herself ashore. She is soaking wet. She is surprised she is alive. Undestroyed. Her body movable. She stands up. And begins to speak.

Acknowledgments

Thank you
   Betsy Lerner
   Bobby Previte
   Helen Atsma
   The Hermitage Artist Retreat
   The MacDowell Colony
   Montalvo Arts Center, Lucas Artists Residency Program

About the Author

Andrea Kleine is the author of the novel *Calf,* which was named one of the best books of 2015 by *Publishers Weekly.* She is a five-time MacDowell Colony fellow and the recipient of a New York Foundation for the Arts fellowship. A performance artist, essayist, and novelist, she lives in New York City.